Prologue

Friday, 10:00 p.m. Ryan's apartment.

"I just heard your message. So that's it? She's in the...TRT game?" Thea's voice on the other end of the line was dripping with excitement. Sighing, I reached for Sierra's waist, lifted her body from mine, and sat up. Switching the cell from my right ear to the other, I inwardly cursed Thea's timing.

"Thea, if I said she's in the game, she's in the game." I moved from the bed and bent down to grab my boxer briefs along with my jeans off the carpet floor.

"Wait a minute..." Thea's tone shifted from excitement to suspicion. Knowing where she was going with it, I rolled my eyes and let her finish her thought, which was out a few seconds later. "You have that I-just-had-sex voice. Who's the slut? Still in bed with you?"

I pulled my underwear and jeans on, then walked toward the door. A mutter came from Sierra's direction. I paused and glanced back. She was lying sideways on the bed, facing me. Her long, bright brown hair was messy, her naked body covered with sweat. Did she say something? I decided it wasn't important and left the room. A wave of fresh air touched my face as I closed the guest bedroom door behind me and headed for the living room.

I returned my attention back to Thea. "Why? Have a sudden urge to send her your sincere apology for the interruption?" I asked.

"Interrupting? So you two were going for another round? My, my, should I be jealous?"

"If I didn't know better, I would almost think you already are." But I did know better. While Thea still had feelings for me, she had never acted as a jealous ex-girlfriend—one of the reasons she'd remained on my contact list.

She chuckled. "Babe, my lack of jealousy for your temporary sluts doesn't mean that I don't miss you. New York is not the same without you. Since you went away, everything here has been so freaking boring. I can't even begin to tell you how much I need this game." I leaned a shoulder against the wall of windows and looked out at the pitch-black sky. "Have you already prepared a plan for the game?"

"Not yet." I still didn't feel like starting a new game.

"What? Are you shitting me? You said in your message that you spoke with her. Wait. You did speak with her, right?"

"Yeah, and she confirmed that the girl who's going to work on the website is the same Emma. The game is on, so don't you worry your pretty little head."

"Can you blame me? It's been like ages since our last game. Why do you want to wait anyway?"

"I just do," I replied.

"Babe, if you're not up to it, I'll just ask Tristan to plan and lead the game, but it would be a shame. Wasn't it you who promised her to destroy this Emma?" Thea's manipulative tone reminded me that when she wanted something, no one stood in her way. Well, almost no one. That was why her attempt to manipulate me by coupling one idea she thought would bruise my ego to another one she knew would get my attention amused me. The corners of my lips pulled up slightly.

"Manipulation, Thea? On me? I mean, don't get me wrong. I do think you're good, but still..."

"Of course I'm good. I had an excellent teacher." The pride in her voice drew a full grin from me. Only Thea could see my calculating nature as a positive trait.

"Who you assumed you can outdo?"

"A girl can always try."

I could feel her smile through the phone. "And I admire this...effort. I really do, but next time try harder and be careful not to break too much of a sweat. We don't want you to ruin your lovely appearance by getting all stinky and messy, now, do we?"

From the corner of my eye, I saw Sierra approaching. I turned to look at her. A short, silk robe wrapped her. "Hey," she whispered, trying not to disturb. I glanced down at my watch. It was getting late, and I still had a lot to do tonight.

"Gotta go, Thea. We'll talk tomorrow." I hung up after the sound of Thea's kiss and a "think of me on your next round" remark. I put my cell on the coffee table and sank down on the couch.

Sierra perched next to me on it. "Who was she?"

"A friend."

"You mean another girl you screw around with." Her eyes flashed with accusation, and it was too bad because up until this moment, I considered her my favorite girl to hook up with.

"Actually *screwed* around with. Anyway, need a ride?"

"Shit, that came out all wrong. I didn't mean to—"

"Sierra, do you need me to take you home or not?"

"Are we still on for tomorrow night?" she asked, ignoring my question.

I wanted to say yes, but with her new attitude, the only answer I gave her was a simple no. Then I took my laptop off the coffee table.

"Why? And please don't give me some crappy lame excuse. I'm a big girl. Just don't lie to me." I debated with myself if I should enlighten her to the fact that people only lie when they care enough to go to the trouble. I watched her. Sierra was smart. She already knew I would tell her the truth.

"Because I'll probably be with another girl and you, my dear, don't strike me as a three-way type of girl." I draped my legs over the coffee table, crossed my ankles, and opened my laptop on my lap.

"Okay, fair enough...I don't need a ride. I'll just take a quick shower before I leave."

Her voice had anger mixed with hurt in it. She stood and strutted toward the bathroom. I turned my attention back to the laptop monitor, ready to reply to a few emails from the interior designer about the martial arts studio.

It took about thirty minutes for Sierra to come back fully dressed and showered. In the same black skinny jeans, high heels, and pink blouse she'd worn a few hours ago, she looked hot. She took a strand of her wet hair and brought it to her nose. She inhaled its scent and closed her eyes. When she opened them, sadness filled her face. She let the strand fall from her fingers. "I've always loved the smell of your shampoo," she said softly. Whatever she was about to say next compelled her to take a deep breath before letting the words out. "Ryan...is this the last time I'm gonna see you?" She bit down on her lip.

"Yes."

Five months or so had passed since I'd used the number from the piece of napkin she'd slid into my jeans pocket that night at the bar. She wasn't the only girl I'd spent my time with during the last five months, but she was definitely my favorite: great sex, great sense of humor, great company. So by now, I should at least feel a bit guilty or maybe even care about that small tear that had escaped her eye and rolled down her cheek. But I felt nothing.

"I know we—" She stopped herself to wipe away another tear. "I know you said you don't want more than what we've had, but if you gave us a chance...we're good together." She walked up to me and dipped forward to caress my bicep with her fingers. When they began to trail toward my bare chest, I captured her hand, stopping her palm's movement. It was time for her to go. Reading my thoughts, she pulled her hand from mine and bent her head to my lips. Her mouth lightly touched them, a goodbye kiss. "Don't lose my number, in case you change your mind," she said before straightening and heading to the front door. After she left, I dragged in a lungful of breath. The smell of lavender and coconut from her body lotion lingered in the air. I tipped my head back, resting it against the couch. As I stared at the ceiling, I let my thoughts drift until the name Emma Winstead surfaced.

I'd seen her twice before today. She was an average-looking girl with zero sexiness and below-zero confidence—completely afraid of her own shadow. The kind of girl I'd usually forget immediately, but for some reason, destiny had decided to fuck with me. Now, this weird creature, who apparently had a thing for walking around with ketchup stains on her shirt, turned out to be the girl I had promised to destroy. I sighed. It was just too bad for her that after I was done with her, she'd end up soulless. Like me.

Chapter 1

Four days earlier.

"And it's due next week," Professor Leigh said before dismissing us and leaving the classroom. Not too happy with the idea that I had to write a paper only one week after the semester had started, I let out a displeased sigh and started to organize my notes in my laptop. Noises of students gathering their stuff and in the process of leaving the classroom filled the space, but it was a specific, feminine voice that caught my attention. From the top row, I gazed at the source of the voice. A brunette with a bob haircut was standing before the front row and talking to two girls who were still sitting as they stuffed their things into their backpacks, listening to her.

"I did say it would work." A cocky smile on the brunette's face completed her statement.

"Wait, he really told you he'd come? Here?" One of the girls asked, sounding like she believed there was a bigger chance that Santa Claus would appear in the doorway than the guy they were talking about.

"Of course. I mean, look at me, why wouldn't he?" The conceited smile remained on her face as she waved her hands over her body. "He's on his way here as we speak."

"Now? Here?" The other girl squealed and stood up, pulling her backpack over her shoulders. The brunette nodded.

I glanced around the room. Only a few students were left in the classroom, doing what I was supposed to be doing— organizing notes. I returned my gaze and attention back to my screen and, with the touchpad on my laptop, dragged a Word document named *Professor Leigh, lecture number two,* along with extra files relevant to this class, into the right folder. A progress bar popped up. Guessing it would take at least a few minutes until the bar line would be completely blue, I lifted my head back to the brunette. The corners of her lips went up while she watched the doorway. I followed her stare, and the moment my eyes landed on the tall guy entering the classroom, something weird happened to me. What exactly? I wished I had a reasonable answer that could explain my behavior, like why my upper body acted on its own accord and leaned a bit forward to get a better look at that guy.

Bib. What was that sound? I ignored the question, straining to get an even better look at the guy. My elbows came in contact with something that had a different texture than the table.

Bibbbbbbbb. That was a different sound; it was an angry sound. What could it—oh! I jerked my elbows from the keyboard of the laptop, and the error sound coming from the computer stopped. At that moment, I realized the first *Bib* had been an audible notification that all the files were now in the right folder. *Shouldn't I take my eyes off him and move them to the laptop monitor?* My brain pushed that thought aside and sent me an overwhelming feeling of awe, then searched for flaws in him.

The guy's spiky, dark brown hair blended perfectly with his ice blue eyes, and the unique, bright color only enhanced his symmetrical face and his strong jawline. The body was flawless, too. Over six feet tall, wearing a fitted, long-sleeved black T-shirt and faded blue jeans, he had an athletic frame— a superb athletic frame. I spent another minute trying to find even the smallest imperfection, and then gave up.

"Here," he said, tossing a jacket onto the table near the brunette. "Next time try not to be so obvious." He was halfway out the door when she grasped his shoulder.

"Ryan, wait," she said, her eyes full of hope. "There will be a next time between us?"

He stopped and turned sharply. The move tore her hand from his shoulder. Free of her touch, he threw her a glacial look, which made hers disappear in a flash.

"There is no *us*. There was never any *us*."

"It's the jacket, right? Seriously, Ryan, I didn't leave it at your place on purpose."

"I'm sorry, but you must be confusing me with someone who gives a shit. If you left it on purpose or not, believe me, I couldn't care less. However, how to make you understand the meaning of the words *not interested*, now that, yeah, that totally interests me." He glanced over at her friends who, like me, stared at him shamelessly. "And any advice would be more than welcome"—he faced the brunette again—"about how to get it through your head. I wasn't interested when you first asked me out, and I'm not interested now. Stop calling me and coming uninvited to my place." This time, his words seemed to hit something deep inside her, if the desperate, longing look she gave to his back as he stepped out of the classroom was any indication. My heart went out to her. Humiliation sometimes hurts more than a physical blow.

She smiled awkwardly as she walked out the door with her friends, who looked embarrassed for her. I related to what she must be feeling: the pain, the humiliation, the need for the ground to open and swallow you up. After years of bullying, I'd developed an imaginary shield, deflecting most of the insults. And what can't touch you can't hurt you, right? But things had changed since I started college. Everything here was different from high school: the people, the environment, the teachers, they were all better. College was like heaven to me. I'd gone from being the most popular target for bullying in high school to being invisible. Okay, maybe I wasn't entirely invisible. You can't be unseen in a tiny coed dorm of seventy-five residents. They knew I existed but, aside from Mia, my mean neighbor across the hall, not one of them paid any attention to me—no insults, no curses, no hellos.

The ring of my cell phone pulled me out of my thoughts and back to an empty classroom. "Hey," I answered Hannah, who was another reason why I wasn't entirely invisible.

"We're eating lunch in the student union. Wanna come?" We? Great. That meant Jenna might be there. Next to Mia, Jenna was the Devil himself. In a contest of who would make me squirm more in my chair—my dentist during a root canal treatment or simply being in her presence—she'd win without breaking a sweat.

Apparently my stomach didn't share my hesitation, because it sent a clear protest in the form of an angry growl and threatened to keep it up unless I replied to Hannah with, "Yes, I'll be there in five minutes." So I did just that.

On my way to the student union, I prayed that Jenna wouldn't be there, but it didn't do me any good. As if a few prayers would scare the Devil...I reached the food court in the student union building and recognized Jenna's straight, cherry-red hair. She sat across from Hannah at a table near one of the square columns in the middle of the room. Hannah spied me and waved. I waved back, bought a takeout box of rice and a can of apple juice, and readied my imaginary shield.

"Ugh," was the first thing Jenna said when I set my tray on the table next to my friend, who shot her a warning look.

"Hey." Hannah looked at me, and the scorn lines on her forehead smoothed out. I smiled at her, and my gaze drifted down to my tray.

"What?" Jenna complained. "It's not my fault she's such a weirdo. Look at her and her clothes. God, who wears—"

"Jenna!" Hannah's fork hit her plate with a loud clink. "Stop being such an abrasive bitch."

I mopped a few spots of red pasta sauce from the back of my hand with a napkin.

"You know what? Don't come crying to me when you become a social *pariah* because of her."

"I swear to God, if you weren't my roommate—"

"Oh, give me a break. You know I'm right. She's a pathetic excuse for a human being. Doesn't it seem strange to you that you and Kayla are the only people who actually speak to her?"

A hand grabbed the chair beside Jenna and dragged it backward. Then a tray with a long sandwich on it landed on the table. "You guys won't believe who's teaching me chemistry this semester." Sitting across from me, Kayla's excited voice eased the tension in the air. Listening to her talk about her crush on Professor Horn, I dug my fork into the rice and started to eat. To my relief, Jenna forgot about me and dove into her crush on a guy named James. According to her, he was the president of Beta Kappa.

"Beta Kappa guys are so hot," Kayla said.

"And assholes," Hannah added. "Remember Tommy? The asshole I dated last summer? He's a Beta Kappa. And you know Donna from the second floor in our dorm? She said a Beta Kappa, Matt, I think his name was, took pictures of her naked and posted them online."

"No way. Matt would never do that, but if he did, she totally deserved it, that skank," Jenna said, and a mental image of her in a medieval torture chair, screaming in agony and covered with blood, sweat, and dirt popped into my mind. I stuffed another forkful of rice into my mouth and almost choked when I heard Justin's voice.

"Here you are. Kay, do you check your texts from time to time?" Justin asked Kayla.

"What are you complaining about? I just wrote you three texts. You're the one who doesn't check them. And one of them, by the way, is about you not answering me whether I should wear the black dress or the pink for the party this F—"

"The party!" Jenna said. "I forgot about it. I don't know what to wear, either."

Red! Anything that had red in it, and if the dress came with horns and a pitchfork—the better.

Justin ignored Jenna's dismay and addressed Kayla's attempt to turn him into her personal stylist. After assuring her that the only thing he knew about girls' clothes was how to take them off, he finished with, "So ask Hannah or Jenna. And, Kay, if you're not getting back to your dorm with Hannah, don't walk by yourself. I got an email from the university today about recent robberies around campus."

A surreptitious glance at him told me he was standing next to Kayla's chair. My heart began to beat faster and the song *Damn, I Wish I Was Your Lover* by Sophie B. Hawkins started to play in my head. With dark, brown hair and brown eyes, he was perfect, at least to me. Hannah and Kayla saw him more as a brother. The three of them had grown up together in a nice neighborhood in Boston.

"Don't worry. I won't stay there till the morning like the last time, so we'll go back to the dorm together," Hannah said to Justin and to me, "Emma, you remember you're helping me with algebra tomorrow, right?"

I nodded to her and got up, taking the tray with me. "Yes, I remember." I smiled at her. She tucked her hair behind her ear and grinned back. Gazing at her, I could see why everyone thought she looked so much like the actress Rachel Bilson. Hannah had wavy chocolate-brown hair that reached her middle back and brown eyes. She was beautiful, outside and inside. We'd met freshmen year, my first day on campus. I was completely lost, and when I finally found the courage to ask people for help in finding the Science building, they ignored me.

"How the hell do they expect us to understand these damn map sketches? It's like reading Chinese." I moved my eyes from the campus map in my hands to the person who said that to see if she'd been talking to me. She was. "We totally need to find some sophomore who can help us out, and I think we just found him." She looked over my shoulder. "Hey, you. Yeah, you. Could you be a sweetheart and help us out?" I turned my head. A guy with gold hair and a flirtatious smile approached us.

"For you, anything," he said to the nice girl next to me and glanced down at the campus map in her palms. "What building are you looking for?"

"We're both looking for the Science building." After getting a full detailed explanation of where it was, he asked her for her phone number. "I'm sorry. I've got a boyfriend, but me and my friend thank you." Linking her hand with mine, she pulled me in the direction of our desired destination. "Science building, here we come." She sounded cheerful. Her gaze turned to me. "By the way, I'm Hannah, you?"

"Um." I cleared my throat. "I'm Emma."

"Emma, I've got a feeling we're gonna be great friends." And since then, we had been. No matter how difficult it was for me to open up to her, she never gave up.

I shook myself out of the memory, said goodbye, and walked away. I stopped next to the trashcan to throw away the box of rice and the can of apple juice, then looked back at Justin. He'd taken my empty chair. I couldn't help but wish that maybe, just maybe, someday I would be among the people he noticed. I didn't live in a fantasy world; I knew he only saw me as the weird friend Hannah had adopted, but I still wished because without hope, there is bitterness, and I'd never be bitter or soulless.

Chapter 2

The next day, after a quick breakfast, I went to class. True to form, I was early, so I switched on my laptop and went over the class syllabus and writing assignments. When I was done, I brought up my email. Nervousness started to build in me. At the end of my last job interview, Mr. Reed, my interviewer, had informed me that if I got the job, he'd notify me by email in a week. Today had been exactly a week. I really hoped I got the job. Coding a website for a martial arts studio was the perfect opportunity for a computer science major to gain some real-world experience, not to mention the high pay the five-week long project offered.

I looked at the screen and gasped, then clicked on the new message from Mr. Reed. The email contained everything he had already mentioned, like the rate of pay, the duration of the project, and the general location of the job. There was also some new information, like the name of my boss, Ryan Damon, details of the martial arts studio website, and the exact address of my new workplace, in Mr. Damon's apartment, a luxury building downtown. It went on to elaborate on my boss's expectations of me and the work schedule. I'd be working four days a week, four hours each day, and I was required to print a report of the progress I'd made each day. I was scheduled to begin the project on Friday at three p.m.

I typed out a quick acceptance, sent it off, and it was a done deal. I had a part-time job. Feeling optimistic for the first time in a while, I smiled to myself. That was the last bit of good news I got that day. After my last class, I had a spate of misfortunate accidents and bad luck. It began with me crashing into someone and finding out that his hamburger sandwich left a nice souvenir on my shirt—a ketchup stain. Then, the coffee machine in the Science building decided to be out of order today, so I had to go all the way to the student union and wait in the interminable line for a mere cup of coffee. When I got it, though, the rich, sweet aroma lightened my sour mood.

Facing the pick-up counter, I took a sip and then pivoted. As I stepped forward, I slammed into someone. Several hot drops of coffee flew at my shirt and soaked through it, burning my skin. God, did I really bump into another person in the same day? Whoever I hit fired a couple of curses into the air, his voice deep and annoyed.

"I'm so sorry." I apologized for the second time today, my eyes on his blue, coffee-soaked shirt. "I'm r-really sorry. A-a-re you okay?" *Calm down. Your clumsiness didn't manage to kill him. Not yet, anyway.* Well, maybe he wouldn't die from the hot liquid, but unquestionably, it must have hurt.

"I'm fine. Where are the goddamn napkins in this place?" he asked, more to himself.

I rushed to a small stand for napkins and spices tucked away in the corner. When I turned around, I almost plowed into him again. I reared back and met his eyes for the first time. It was him—Ryan, the guy who had given the brunette her jacket back. Up close, I could see more clearly the color of his eyes. What I'd thought to be solely ice blue was actually blue with light turquoise, which mixed naturally with the bright, dominant color and was around the pupil. Stunning, utterly stunning. As a matter of fact, his entire symmetrical face was stunning and...and...mesmerizing. I was—

"Given that I'm the one soaked in coffee, I'll throw a wild guess and say that those are for me." Shaking me out of my stasis, he indicated the napkins I was holding.

"Oh, yes, of course, here." I handed them to him, and his eyes flicked to my shirt. He probably didn't miss the huge red mark on it. "It's a ketchup stain." Why on earth did I provide him with this redundant information? Did I really think he might believe I had just murdered someone?

"Right," he said, a note of indifference in his tone. I fought the urge to smack my forehead with my hand. What had gotten into me? Uttering stupid things to strangers and staring at people was atypical behavior for me, to say the least.

People might regard my tendency to avoid looking at their faces as odd, but having Heterochromia, a rare condition causing two different eye colors, had taught me that most people didn't take kindly to my deformity. But if I had an extraordinary, unique eye color like this guy, whose eyes were...on the left pocket of my jeans?

His voice was annoyed when he addressed me. "My hands are a bit busy here taking care of this mess. What's your excuse?" Huh? What was he talking abo—oh! My phone! It was ringing, and so was the front of his jeans pocket.

I pulled my cell out and looked at the display. I'd missed a call from Hannah.

I turned to leave and then paused. Maybe he needed more napkins. "Um..."

He lifted his head and, guessing what I was about to say, he said with asperity, "I'm fine. You can go."

"Again, I'm really sorry." The apology seemed to grate on him, so I left and went to Hannah's dorm, sliding into my jacket to conceal the direct consequences of my clumsiness.

"You're never late. What happened?" Hannah, looking concerned, asked after opening the door to her dorm room. She turned and stepped in as I entered, closing the door behind me. Luckily, it was only me and Hannah here. Jenna was probably busy tormenting some poor frat guy at the Beta Kappa House.

"Nothing," was my reply. She crossed her arms and raised an eyebrow at me, and I released a breath. "The coffee machine in the Science building broke down, so I had to go to the student union and wait in line forever." *There. Now, please let's not discuss about how I bumped into someone? Twice.*

"You bumped into someone, didn't you?" She fell on her bed, and I dropped into the desk chair across from her.

"You did say you want my help, right?"

She looked at me through slitted eyes and then said, "Screw math. You're so evading my question, which means something interesting happened. I want to hear the whole enchilada. C'mon, spill it."

"This happened." I waved the empty cup at her and bent down to toss it into the trash can under the desk.

Her eyes widened. "Oh my gosh. You thought the guy you splattered was hot! Yayyyy." She clapped her hands with enthusiasm.

"What? No! I mean, how did you—what makes you think it was a guy?"

A grin curled her mouth. "It's all over your face, and it's about time you drool over a guy who isn't Justin." She crossed her legs into a lotus position. "So, who is he?"

"I have no idea. Now, let's concentrate on the reason I'm here—math."

"Hellooo, you're blushing. Who cares about math? I want all the deets: what he looks like, how he—wait." Her smile slid away. "Please tell me you talked to him."

"Other than apologizing, no, I didn't talk to him, and I probably won't ever see him again. So can we move on to another subject, like something that has math in it?" I grabbed a heavy textbook from the desk and waved it at her. "Hey, look, here's something with math in it."

She sighed heavily. "Look, sweetie, you've got to forget about Justin and start going out, meeting new guys. You're in college, for God's sake. If not now, then when?" What I felt about Justin wasn't a secret to her, and guessing that he didn't share these feelings, she kept telling me to stop wasting my time on him. "Okay, it's final. You're going out with me and Kayla on Saturday to this new club everybody's talking about, and this time—no excuses."

To end this conversation and to start helping her with math, I agreed to tag along. I stood and sat next to her on the bed, algebra textbook on my lap. Her eyes went to the book, and suddenly my smile was the only one in the room.

Chapter 3

The sound of Justin's voice always made my heart beat faster, even when his mouth was full of food. "Nao, tho homburgers in hore"—he paused to swallow—"are way better than the cafeteria in the Art & Architecture building."

"No, they're not. The tomatoes are always rotten. In the Art & Architecture building, you get fresh vegetables," Hannah argued, filling her spoon with carrot soup. "Oh, and, Justin? Vegetables are not your enemy. You should try them sometime."

"Sorry, H," Kayla piped up, "I'm with Justin on this one. Look around. The room is full because everybody knows they have the best hamburgers here." As if to make her point, she sank her teeth hungrily into her bun. Justin smiled in triumph.

The cafeteria buzzed with noise and activity, but students crammed into it because it was lunchtime, not because this place served the most delicious hamburgers.

Justin drummed his hands on the table. "Ladies and gentlemen, we've got ourselves a winner. And the best—"

"Oh my God, who is he, and why is he not in my life? He's gorgeous." Kayla stared over Hannah's shoulder, a hypnotized look spreading across her face. Hannah, sitting next to me, twisted in her seat to see who had caused Kayla's jaw to drop. I snuck a peek too, and surprise washed over me. The guy I was sure I wouldn't see again pulled up a chair at the table behind us and sat, facing our table. Two of the three other guys with him wore Beta Kappa tees. Ashley, who kissed and nibbled his neck while caressing her hand down his arm, sat next to him.

"Kay, don't bother. He's a dick," Justin said.

"You know him?" Kayla shot her gaze to him, a thrill in her voice.

"What?" Hannah's brows lifted. "You seriously don't recognize him?"

Kayla's eyes went back to where Ryan was. "Right now, all I recognize is Ashley's hands all over him. What's up with that? Is she like dating him or something?"

"Nah, she's just passing her time until she moves to the real thing." Justin pointed at himself.

"Hmmm, let's see. You constantly remind her of your name, and she constantly keeps forgetting it. What does that tell you, huh? Justin, she's not into you."

I couldn't agree more with Hannah. He and I resided in the same dorm. My single room was on the third floor while his, on the second floor, was two doors down from Ashley's sister. Whenever she swung by to visit her, he went out of his way to charm Ashley, which didn't do him much good, though. She'd never had a look of reverence on her face like she had at this moment. Hannah's gaze moved from Justin to Kayla. "And, you, don't even go there. He's bad news."

"If bad news looks like that, hell, I'm all for taking my chances," Kayla responded, ogling Ryan. "Is he a senior?"

"Yeah, he is. You honestly don't recognize him, do you?" Justin said.

"Kayla, it's—"

"No, wait," he cut Hannah off. "Don't tell her yet. I want to see how clueless she is. We're gonna play a little game called 'guess the celeb'."A mischievous smile curled over his lips as he put his food down on his tray.

I glanced at the time on my cell phone lying beside my plate. My next class was in ten minutes. I took the last bite of my sandwich and got up. "I gotta go," I said to Hannah, while Justin was messing around with Kayla.

"Okay, see you later. And you're a real lifesaver. Thanks for the help yesterday."

"No problem." I smiled at her and headed for the door. Hoots of laughter from Ryan's table attracted my attention, but he wasn't among those who guffawed. He and Ashley were chatting with another guy sitting beside them. As if

Ryan felt my stare, he glanced my way before returning to the conversation. Relieved that my mere presence didn't cause him to panic due to the hot coffee accident, I left.

Later, after class, I headed into the library. It was a massive structure, five stories tall, with a row of four arches on columns at the entrance. Every time I walked by this building, I admired its impressive architecture anew. I'd always loved libraries; they were my sanctuary. In them, everyone expected everyone to mind their own business. It was heaven. And as I opened the door and walked into the domed foyer, I was doing just that. My eyes were down, focused on the pen I was playing with, and I slammed into what felt like a brick wall. Not again, I thought briefly before a sharp pain exploded in my nose.

"Jesus," a male voice burst out. Then it asked, "You okay?"

I blinked the tears from my eyes and lifted my head. Him? Again? Oh, boy.

"Yes, I...I..." A warm liquid inside my nose traveled down slowly.

"You're bleeding." Another male voice. I shifted my stare to Ryan's right side. It was one of his friends from the cafeteria. The one he was talking to when I left. He had short, light blond hair and warm, brown eyes. His face was handsome, and he was almost as tall as Ryan. I gently touched beneath my nose and looked down at my bloody fingers.

Angling my head back, I replied, "Yes, but I'm fine."

"Doesn't look fine to me," the blond guy contradicted while reaching into his backpack. "Hold on. I think I got something for that." He pulled out a blue pack of pocket tissue and offered it to me. "Here."

"Thank you." I drew two tissues out.

"You should put ice on it, too," he advised. "It'll kill the pain."

I was amazed at how kind he was. I smiled at him, sticking the tissues to my bleeding nose and picking up my pen from the floor. I looked at Ryan. "I'm really sorry."

He stared at me, eyes narrowing with suspicion. Then, he said, "Oh, it's you." An irritated expression covered his chiseled features. "You think you can manage to get to your destination without killing anyone around you?" The anger in his tone was barely contained.

"Whoa, ease up, man. It's that hot stalker of yours you're pissed off about, not her," his friend said. Sighing heavily, Ryan rubbed a hand over his face, like he needed it to clear his mind, and the tension seemed to ease off him.

He dropped his hands down and gazed at me. "Just watch your steps and try not to injure yourself or others on your way, okay?" His voice was softer.

I nodded and continued walking. Fortunately, the rest of the day went smoothly, and by eleven p.m., I was already in bed, asleep.

In the morning, the alarm went off, shouting at me to wake up. I reached out, pounded the snooze button, and closed my eyes. Five minutes later, the loud beeping sound filled the room again. I snoozed it for the second time. *Just a few more minutes*, I promised myself and rolled to my stomach. *Ouch!* A stinging pain at the bridge of my nose had me sitting up in an instant. I shot an unsatisfied look at my alarm. "And that's how the job's done," I murmured. The memory of yesterday's collision at the library crept into my mind, and my eyes grew larger. I sprang out of bed and stepped to the mirror. My mouth dropped open in horror. My nose was puffy and a red so bright it could make every tomato in town green with jealousy. "Ugh!" I growled and stomped a foot. Shaking my head, I sighed. There was nothing I could do but make peace with the clown nose on my face and start the day.

After a quick breakfast, I rushed to the Science building. I wasn't late, but it was close. My cell phone started to buzz against my thigh as I slid into my seat. I pulled it out and glanced at the screen. Hannah. I debated answering it, but then Professor Chester strolled into the classroom, and I tucked the phone back into my pocket. Professor Chester was one of those teachers who loved to give assignments during class. An hour into it, I'd already done three of them and was the first to end the third. Waiting for the others to finish, I plugged the cell phone headset in my ears and listened to Hannah's voice mail.

"Hey, just letting you know Kayla and I are going shopping for clothes this Saturday, and you're coming wit—" I crossed my legs, and the phone slipped from my lap. I managed to catch it before it cracked against the ground. "...too. And don't use Justin as an excuse for why you won't meet guys in the club. You don't want to stay a virgin forever, right? Okay, call me back." Every single eye in the small classroom was on me. Well, I did save my precious cell phone from the dangerous floor, but in the process, the headset had been detached from the audio jack, and my fingers had accidentally pressed the microphone button. Everyone—including Professor Chester—heard the last part of what Hannah had said.

Chapter 4

I bit my bottom lip so hard that a metallic taste spread through my mouth. "Ms..." Professor Chester, standing in the aisle at the end of the second row, trailed off as he followed the direction of the students' heads, trying to find the perpetrator. I yanked the headset from my ears. When he reached the top row, he stopped, now standing next to me. With no other choice, I slowly looked up at him. "Ms. Winstead, I—" He broke off, his face knotted with concern. He leaned forward to get a closer look at my nose, gazing at me as if I was a science experiment gone bad. "Is everything all right?" he asked.

Why couldn't the ground just open and swallow me up alive? With no such luck, I nodded.

"Very well then. Ms. Winstead, next time I'd appreciate if you keep your private messages—private."

I bobbed my head once. The tittering coming from my classmates spiked my embarrassment level, and the half hour left of class seemed to last forever. When we were finally let out, I sprinted from there in less than a heartbeat, making a mental note to myself—never listen to voice mails in public again.

Later, after dinner, Hannah came to my room. "What the heck happened to you?" she asked as I let her in. Shock coated her face.

"It's nothing, really. But if you ever see me listening to voice mails in public, kill my phone, no mercy, okay?"

I sat on my bed, and she shut the door. In a perfect reality, she would respond with something like: "If you say it's nothing, then of course it's nothing. I won't bother you about it, and I'm all for speaking about how I won't ever leave these kinds of messages in your cell phone again." But I was stuck in this imperfect reality, and what she really said was, "My ass nothing. Have you looked at yourself in the mirror? That is not even close to nothing." Her eyes tapered to slits. "Do I need to go beat the crap out of Mia?"

"What? Oh! No, no beating, please. And it wasn't Mia. It was the guy I plowed into the other day," I corrected.

Her eyes widened and her lips formed a perfect O. "He punched you? Over some spilled coffee? What's wrong with him? Is he some sort of psychopath? How did he even find you? Knocked on every door on campus, demanding revenge for his ruined shirt? You know what? No, I'm sorry, my mistake. What I really meant to ask was how *I* can find him, because when I'm through with him, he'll think twice before raising a hand on a girl."

She paused for a breath, and I rushed out, "Whoa, no, no. You've got it all wrong. He didn't punch me. I plowed into him."

It took several seconds, but then realization dawned on her face. "Again?" she asked, disbelief coloring her tone.

"Yep."

Eyes sparkling with excitement, she came to sit next to me on the bed. "So...twice, huh?" Her mouth pulled into a smile.

"Hannah, please, don't." Exhaling softly, I rolled my eyes.

"And let me guess. You didn't make him ask for your number for the second time." She placed her fists onto her waist, throwing me a look of admonishment.

"Of course not, and I have more important things to occupy my mind with than some stranger. Things like tomorrow, which is going to be my first day at work."

"Oh my gosh, that's right! I'm so glad you found a job."

"Me too, but I have no idea how I'm gonna show up there looking like a freak-show," I said and pointed at my nose. I doubted that my straight, light brown hair and pale skin could ever mix well with the redness in the middle of my face.

"Don't be silly. Your boss won't even notice, not if you wear some makeup and dress—I completely forgot." She lunged to her feet and stepped to my closet and went through my wardrobe. "Gosh, it's worse than I thought. You are so going with us to the mall and pick up some dresses and w—" A muffled ring came from her backpack. She left my clothes to pull her cell phone out of her bag. "Hey, Kayla," she answered. A few seconds later, she said, "Okay okay, settle down. I'm on my way." She hung up and faced me. "I gotta go. Kayla's in some kind of crisis." She tucked the cell phone into her jacket and swung the backpack over her shoulder.

"Is she okay?" I asked.

"Yeah, something about a bicycle and a flat tire."

When she walked out, I carefully touched the bruise on my face. Surprisingly, the pain was almost gone. Would the redness vanish tomorrow? God, I hoped so. I really, really hoped so.

The morning light of the next day flooded my room, setting comfortable conditions for poring over my nose. It went back to its original size, and the redness reduced to a faint red. Things looked promising. "Everything will go as it should today," I announced to my reflection before grabbing my washing bag and exiting the room to the communal showers. Unfortunately, everything hadn't gone as it should have. It was two-thirty. In thirty minutes, I was supposed to be downtown, but after Kayla had accidentally squirted a blob of ketchup on my white shirt, I had to decide: showing up late to my first day at work because I had gone all the way back to my dorm to get changed, or using my jacket to hide the ketchup stain. Last option won.

I swallowed the last bite of my sandwich, got to my feet, and waved Hannah and Kayla, who were still eating, goodbye, then walked out of the food court and the union student building, continuing to the bus stop near the main exit of the university. When I came closer to it, a train of wondering questions about what else could go wrong ran in my head, up until it jerked to a halt as a familiar tall figure stepped past me. Ryan? He stopped. Oh, boy, did I say his name out loud?

His back was no longer in my direction. He looked at me, waiting to hear the reason I called him. He held a black helmet, the same color as his leather jacket. The blue, faded jeans and gray shirt molded perfectly to his sculpted body, and black, heavy boots completed his stunning look.

"Yeah?" he prompted when I stayed quiet.

My face didn't ring any bells to him. No surprise there, yet when his eyes fell on my nose, recognition lit his features. I worried my lower lip, which was already a bit swollen and stung, a result of the debacle that had taken place yesterday in Professor Chester's class, and I tried to think about how to rescue myself from this awkward situation. "I...I..."

"Of course, you again. Lucky me, no coffee or getting smashed today." He was in a better mood than yesterday, his demeanor relaxed, but there was mockery in his tone.

My backpack started to ring, and I took the opportunity to evade his mesmerizing, piercing eyes. I opened my bag and rummaged through it, complaining angrily under my breath, "At least one of us is lucky, considering that I once again have to tolerate your patronizing, pompous attitude." I finally found my phone, but the ringing had already stopped. Glancing at the ID caller, I made a mental note to get back to Hannah later, and then stuffed it back in the bag. I forced myself to meet Ryan's gaze, adjusting my backpack back over my shoulders.

Strangely, a hint of surprise and a smile appeared on his face.

"Um, yes, lucky you," I said, giving him the nice version of my thoughts. I started to walk toward the bus stop, but his next words glued me to my spot.

"You should have added rude, too. It usually goes well with adjectives like patronizing and pompous. Don't you think so?"

Oh God, he'd heard me. I turned around. "I—I didn't mean to...I...your attitude is not...well, it's n-not..."

His eyes drifted to my shirt where, again, a medium red smudge shamelessly posed in the center of it. I zipped up my jacket.

"What is it with you and red stains?" His eyes went to my nose. "Or with the color red in general. Is it some kind of fetish? Not that I'm judging, of course." The mocking in his tone returned, a corner of his mouth curling up a little.

"No. it was an accident. I would've changed, but I was afraid to be..." I trailed off as I watched my bus pull out from the bus stop. "Late." I finished the sentence after a moment, and then I added more to myself, "I just can't believe it."

"Late for what?"

"Unless there is a magical way to get downtown in less than ten minutes, I'm officially late for my first day of work."

"Where are you headed?"

"Main Street."

He stared at me. "3743 Main Street?"

Now it was my turn to stare. "How did you—"

"You're Emma Winstead?" His gaze was filled with dazed incredulity. *"You're* Emma Winstead." He sucked in a deep breath. Then, he said, "You've just got your magical way of reaching downtown in less than ten minutes. It's called a Harley, c'mon." He turned around and stepped toward the parking lot across the bus stop, expecting me to follow him. I didn't move. What was going on? "Emma, we don't have all day. I still have to go through the website details with you before the day ends. So get moving." His voice rose as he walked away.

I felt my brow wrinkle as I stared after him. What was he talking ab—oh, no. Oh, no, no, no, no. He knew my name, the address of my job, and the project details. Ryan. He was that Ryan.

"You're my boss?" Once the question was out, I realized how crazy the idea was. Ryan Damon must be at least in his thirties and definitely wouldn't ever be confused for a gorgeous, male model. Right?

Stopping, he glanced over his shoulder. "I'm the one who's gonna pay you, so yes, I guess that makes me your boss. I'd introduce myself, but it seems you already know my name."

"You're Mr. Damon?" I asked, ignoring his sardonic tone.

"Please, I prefer Ryan. And as I said, we don't have all day."

I forced myself to go after him. God, he was my boss? Could this day get any worse? At the parking lot, he paused beside a shiny, black bike and opened a hard saddlebag on the right side of the motorcycle. He drew out a helmet and handed it to me. He shoved his backpack into the saddlebag, and I put on the helmet. He did the same and mounted the bike. I stood hesitantly next to it. I'd never ridden a motorcycle before.

His head turned to me. "Hop on." His voice was muffled impatience.

I climbed on. Whoa, I was too close to him. Feeling uncomfortable, I placed my palms awkwardly and lightly around his middle. The thick leather of his jacket cooled my fingers.

"Hold tighter," he ordered. I strengthened my hold, and he pushed the kickstand up. The bike roared to life, and all the objects around me began to move, then blur as we hurtled through the light traffic.

He wasn't kidding about getting downtown in less than ten minutes; five, to be exact. We parked inside an underground garage, in a vacant space opposite an elevator. I followed him to it. Inside, he entered a code into a keypad. The doors closed, and we ascended to the penthouse floor. I stepped out into a wide, all-white hallway. Several gold-framed paintings adorned the walls, and the scent of lavender hung in the air. When we reached a white, wooden door, he unlocked and opened it. He motioned for me to enter.

I walked in and studied the room. I was no expert, but even I could tell that a professional interior designer had been here. And by the high quality of the furniture and the room's accent pieces, it was clear his parents weren't just rich, but really rich. The living room was big, or maybe the high ceiling just gave that impression. The white sofa was a half square, accessorized with cushions and surrounding a coffee table. A large, flat-screen TV covered the feature wall facing the sofa. Under the TV, two long shelves supported an expensive sound system and a Bose SoundDock. Behind the sofa, a clean, uncluttered area led to an open kitchen. Floor-to-ceiling windows led to a narrow terrace, which stretched the length of the entire wall from the living room to the open dining room that was next to the kitchen. At the right side of the feature wall in the living room, there was a hallway and a staircase going to the second floor.

He put the strap of his backpack over a chair at the dining table, where he then set his keys, helmet, and leather jacket. He looked over at me. "Okay, let's start," he said, and the project began.

Chapter 5

"Don't bother to text me," he advised after explaining the project. "I never check my texts." This sentence baffled me. Who never checked their texts? "If you need to reach me, call or leave a voice mail."

I nodded, and before he left the room, a home office down the hall, he'd written the security code for the elevator and the intercom of the private entrance to the building on a slip of paper. He'd also given me a duplicate key card to his apartment, in case he wouldn't be home. I placed them all into my backpack and commenced coding.

The next four hours flew by, and I was satisfied with the outcome of the work I'd done. I printed out a report of my progress and headed for the living room, my backpack already on my back. Ryan was seated on the sofa, eyes on the laptop's screen, his cell phone clamped between the ear and shoulder. "...and yesterday she confirmed it was her, so it's on. And, Thea, when you come for a visit this weekend, don't bring Tristan with you. Call when you get this." He hung up, and his eyes lifted to meet mine. I handed him the report. While he skimmed it, the front door opened, and a girl stepped inside.

"Sienna...you're early." He acknowledged her without taking his eyes off the sheet of paper in his hand.

"Yes, I am," she said, smiling and approaching him.

Ryan leaned over to put his laptop and the report onto the coffee table. His gaze went to hers. She sported black skinny jeans and a pink blouse. Her light brown hair was pulled up in a ponytail. I wondered who he was actually dating: Sienna or Ashley. As soon as I decided on Ashley, Sienna bent down to give him a hot, passionate kiss. Categorizing the information about who he was dating as none of my business, I cleared my throat. Sienna stepped back, and Ryan looked at me.

"Um, if you don't have any comments about the report, then I'll be on my way," I said.

"No, I don't," he replied before she put her hand on his jaw and moved his head back to hers. Stealing his mouth again, she climbed into his lap. Without any more delay, I skipped out of there.

Back in my dorm room, I dropped my bag and jacket to the floor, kicked off my shoes, and collapsed onto the bed. At that moment, my cell phone thrilled. Sighing, I swung my feet over the side of the bed and got up, stepping to my backpack and pulling the phone out.

"Soooo, how was it?" Hannah said.

"It went well." Should I mention that Ryan was the one who hired me? From my understanding, she knew him.

"I told you everything would go fine, didn't I? How was your boss?" Yes, I better tell her. I walked back to the bed and sat on it, scooted back and leaned my back against the wall.

"Um...remember the other day at lunch when Kayla gawked at the guy sitting with Ashley?"

There were a few seconds of silence as she tried to bring up the memory. "Oh, yes, why?"

"He's my boss."

She chortled and then chortled some more. When I didn't, her laughter died away. The line was quiet for several seconds. "Wait...you were serious?"

"Yup."

"You're telling me that Ryan Damon, as in the son of Bruce Damon, the late, action-movie star, is your boss?" Her voice's volume elevated.

Wow, I didn't know Hannah had such an active imagination. The idea that my boss was Bruce Damon's son was kind of funny, due to its absurdity, so I laughed and then laughed some more. When she didn't, I realized she was serious.

"You're serious?"

"Yup. Em, you positive it's the same guy? That it's Ryan Damon?" Her tone held disbelief.

"That's his name, yes, and he's the same guy who was behind us the other day. How do you know he's Bruce Damon's son?"

"Who doesn't? Gosh, you and Kayla can be so clueless sometimes."

Was I that clueless? Hmm, now that I thought about it, I didn't even have a clear image of Bruce Damon's son in my head, probably because celebrity gossip and tabloid magazines had never appealed to me.

"Just a sec, I'll look him up." One minute later, with a laptop on my lap, I typed in Ryan's full name. A series of paparazzi photos popped up on the screen, along with articles related to his father. I gasped and stared at the pictures. Even though they didn't do him justice, I could tell that my new boss was Bruce Damon's son. Wow. "You're right. It's him," I admitted.

"I don't get it. Why does he need a website? What kind of website are you working on for him?"

"It's for a new martial arts studio."

"Oh, that makes sense. He recently bought a martial arts studio in New York, but I still can't wrap my mind around it. You working for Ryan Damon..."

"Yes, it's quite unexpected," I said. The stain on my shirt caught my attention. I pulled my top off one-handed and slung it into the laundry hamper near my desk. I needed a shower, so after we said goodbye, I showered, and when I got back to my room, I changed into a clean T-shirt and a pair of pants. I collapsed onto the bed and hauled my computer onto my lap. This time I looked up Ryan's father's name.

He'd started his career as a young, attractive, action-movie actor in the '70s and rapidly rose to A-list status. By the end of the '80s, he was the highest paid actor in Hollywood. His name alone brought a movie to the top of the box office charts. In the '90s, he announced that he was quitting show business and moved with his wife from Los Angeles to New York City. That was when he became a businessman. But his success hadn't stopped with his acting career. On the contrary, he was a brilliant entrepreneur. He made profitable investments that turned him into a self-made billionaire before he turned fifty, and then tragedy hit.

On the rainy night of October 24, a schizophrenic man had managed to steal a gun, and after hearing voices telling him that the Devil had been inside Bruce Damon, he went to the Damons' residency in Manhattan and forced his way into the lobby at gunpoint, and then up to the penthouse floor. There, when the elevator opened straight to the apartment, he shot and killed Bruce Damon, his wife, and their ten-year-old daughter. The whole family, except Ryan, who had been seventeen and in Europe at that time, was murdered. The killer had knelt next to Bruce's body, dipped his fingers into the pool of blood pouring from the corpse's head, and used it to write on the living room wall: *The Devil has died.* After that, he'd committed suicide with the same gun.

My stomach clenched, my breathing accelerated, and sweat started to gather on my forehead at the particulars of the murders displayed on the screen. Why did I read it? Those kinds of things could trigger a panic attack, so I usually tried to steer clear of them. I drew a deep breath in then exhaled slowly, calming myself down. I closed the page and focused on the good part of his life, like a website that presented a photo taken from an interview, where he had a warm smile. I scrolled down and found the video clip. I clicked play and the video started to roll. Bruce Damon was talking about his life and family. At one point, the host asked him what he most wished for his son. The answer? Happiness. My heart melted at the sight of the man looking so proud of his son and wishing the best for him.

Beneath the video clip, there was a blue link leading to another website dedicated to Lily Montgomery, Ryan's mother. Born and raised in a wealthy family in Ann Arbor, Michigan, she'd been a former supermodel, which explained where Ryan got his extraordinary looks. I returned to the results page and looked through Ryan's paparazzi photos. In all of them, annoyance at the attention registered on his face. There was even a picture where he'd flipped the bird at the camera, his profile clearly expressing exasperation.

He hadn't been alone in that photo. Arm linked to him, a girl with long, wavy, brown hair and blue eyes was accompanying him, and, as opposed to Ryan's dislike of the spotlight, she'd loved it, staring right into the camera's eye with a wide grin. There was something disturbing in that smile, something mean. She didn't seem like a good person, and I couldn't put my finger on why exactly I got that vibe from her. According to the website, her name was Thea Vanderbilts, the daughter of billionaire Randolf Vanderbilts. Was she the same Thea he'd left a voice mail for earlier? If so, they had known each other for quite a while. This picture had been taken six years ago.

I clicked on other photos of him, learning that he'd dated the pop star Jessica Ewell a few years ago. They had seemed pretty intimate, especially on a beach in Los Cabos, Mexico, where photos showed them acting like there hadn't been any paparazzi around. Having received enough information about him, I closed my laptop, and my eyes got bigger when they landed on the clock wall. God, how had the time passed so fast? It was late, and I needed my strength for surviving shopping with Hannah and Kayla tomorrow. In ten minutes, I brushed my teeth, combed my hair, and slid into bed. I fell asleep shortly after.

Chapter 6

As much as I hated shopping, I put on a happy face as we bounced from store to store. When it was over, I wound up with three bags of clothes, which was nothing compared to Hannah's and Kayla's hauls.

"Don't forget, eight o'clock in my room," Hannah reminded me as I climbed out of her car.

"Don't worry. I'll be there." I closed the door, waved goodbye, and walked into the dorm. At eight o'clock, as promised, I was outside her room, knocking. She opened it, and there was no sign of Jenna. I smiled. Hannah didn't, though. She stared at my blue navy shirt and black cardigan.

"You do know we're going to a club, not church, right? Why didn't you wear that low-cut, yellow shirt I made you buy because it looked awesome on you?"

"I like this shirt better." I shrugged.

She rolled her eyes, sighing. "You're so hopeless." Her gaze floated down to the tight, black pants she'd also insisted I purchase. "Damn, where did you hide those legs? Okay, from now on, when we go shopping, we're totally gonna concentrate on buying you miniskirts," she said as she turned and stepped deeper into the room.

"Would you stop torturing her? She's blushing." Kayla came to my rescue and appraised my pants as I walked in. "But hey, she's got a point. It's a sin to hide those legs. Why did you wear boots? Why not heels to—" Her face puckered when her eyes reached my top. "Oh, and that shirt..." She shook her head. "No, no, no, it's got to go, along with the cardigan. And why do you always tie up your hair? You need to—"

"Now who is torturing her?" Hannah glanced at Kayla in the mirror, then finished her makeup. Hannah was clad in a coral, short dress and T-strap shoes, looking terrific.

"Sorry." Kayla giggled apologetically. "Sometimes I get carried away." The close-fitting dress she wore reached her knees, and the cone heels added a few inches to her five feet height. She looked nice. "Ugh, I hate this concealer. I can still see my acne scars," she complained while staring at herself in the now available mirror, examining the scattering of acne across her cheekbones.

"Don't touch that zit," Hannah said. "It'll leave another scar."

"Easy for you to say, Ms. Perfect Skin." Kayla glanced at her through the mirror, a slight frown on her face.

"Would you stop? I can hardly see the scars, and you look fine. Now, can we go?"

Hannah asked and slung her handbag's strap over her shoulder. After Kayla piled on the makeup and patted her wayward, pecan brown curls into place, we left.

When we got into the club, after showing fake IDs, which Kayla had arranged for us, we sat at a table with a clear view of the dance floor. This spot came in handy for me; whenever guys hit on Hannah and Kayla, I entertained myself by watching people dance. As the night progressed and the alcohol level in my friends' blood rose, they went from sitting to having fun on the dance floor, and I sipped at my soda through a straw, eyes prowling over the bodies moving to the pop music until Ryan and Ashley, standing out from everybody around them, appeared in the center.

Ryan, in a tight shirt with sleeves rolled back to his elbows, and jeans, held one arm at his side, hand clutching the neck of an open beer. The other palm was on Ashley's perfect frame. Her back was touching his chest, and the way he encouraged her to move against him was rather provocative. I craned my neck to get a better view of her. She was wearing a skirt showing her long legs and a halter top. Her thick, long, blond hair bounced as she danced.

At one point, she turned around and leaned in for a kiss. He deliberately avoided it by turning his head and taking a swig of his beer. When he faced her again, he gave her a half grin. His lips moved, and I was able to read them. "Want a kiss? Work for it," he told her. With an up-to-the-challenge smile, she got even closer to him, teasing him. Then, she offered him her back again, but this time she moved her body with the sole purpose of getting his approval. I never found out if she earned the kiss or not, because Hannah and Kayla came back to the table. I inhaled, but my lungs didn't get fresh oxygen. It was after midnight, and the club was crowded and stifling. I was ready to leave. I paid for my drink and kissed Hannah and Kayla goodbye.

Outside, I filled my lungs with cold air and let my ears get used to the quiet, then headed to my dorm. It was a fifteen-minute walk and normally safe to do alone at one in the morning. But the university had sent an email earlier in the week, warning us, for the second time this semester, of several recent robberies around campus, so I sped up my pace. To my relief, loud students occasionally passed by in groups, but by the time I neared my dorm, I was alone with only the sound of the crickets and the wind for company. I walked faster, pulled my cardigan tight around me, and thrust my hands into the pockets when the wind managed to penetrate my two layers of clothes, touching my skin and chilling me.

The lights from the street lamps allowed me to spot three men stepping up in my direction. Where did they come from? My heart beat quicker. They didn't look like typical students. They looked older, in their thirties, and dressed in all-black. Just when I thought I'd be able to pass them, one of them stepped in front of me, blocking my way. "'Sup, can I borrow your cell? Mine's broken," the one in the middle, most likely their leader, said. He had foul breath. I recoiled in disgust. His lips curled into an eerie smile, and his mouth revealed two front teeth that were cracked and yellow.

Amplifying my terror, his tone proclaimed his intentions. Innocent they were not. He was playing with his prey—me. Run! My mind implored, but rigid with abject fear, I couldn't comply. My heart pounded against my rib cage with the force of a wrecking ball, and my mouth was so dry it took me a few tries before I could answer.

"I-I-I-d-d-on't have—"

A mean laugh cut me off. "What do we have here? A stammer?" Another nasty chuckle came from him.

"Okay, enough with the games," the one on the right said. "Give him your bag, bitch."

It wasn't that I didn't want to do exactly what he'd directed me to do. It's not like I had anything in my bag that was worth my life. But I was immobilized with fear, unable to move.

"You heard him, and don't even think of doing something stupid." The leader's voice went up a couple of notches, and he pulled a knife from his pocket.

"Hey, you over there, what's going on?" a male voice demanded from behind them. Scream! Scream now! My mind urged, yet no sound erupted from me.

"Fuck, man, he's not alone. Grab her bag and let's get the fuck out of here," the third one said. A hand violently tugged at my bag's strap. The force pushed me forward, but my small, fringe tote remained stubbornly over the shoulder.

"Get away from her!" My savior's voice sounded nearer. The three of them looked back and then ran away as a cluster of people approached me. They appeared to be students returning from a party, or going to one.

"You okay?" a guy from the group asked me.

I nodded, incapable of forming actual words.

"I'm calling the police," a girl said, tapping on her cell phone.

Someone near her turned to look at her. "No, it's too late. They're gone."

"Th-th-an-k yo-u," I said at last.

"Don't sweat it," the girl replied.

After I somehow calmed down, I thanked them once more, and they continued on to wherever they had been going. Scared, I ran the rest of the way to the dorm, made it to my room, and fell on the bed, trembling.

I'd experienced panic attacks three times before, all of them in high school, in front of everybody. Now, I was alone in the room. No one would laugh at me. No one would gather around me and keep calling me a freak while I lost control of my body. These thoughts soothed me. My heart rate decelerated, and air started to get in freely.

Fifteen minutes later, the threat of a panic attack was over, and I was finally able to function. I closed my eyes and fell into a memory.

I had been twelve and in Dr. Miller's office. The afternoon sunshine had filtered through the slatted wooden blinds over the windows, creating a pattern of lines on the floor. Dr. Miller, her salt-and-pepper hair twisted up in a clip, had sat in her brown armchair across from me, writing in her notebook. She'd lifted her head and looked at me, her expression filled with sympathy. "Emma, it's okay to be afraid."

Although it hadn't been my first time there, I'd looked around, exploring the room. It was huge, making me feel tiny. The air conditioner sent goosebumps prickling across my skin. I dangled my feet off the leather sofa, ignoring the cold and concentrating on the sound of the big, silver clock on the wall. Tick tack, tick tack, tick tack. It relaxed me.

"Emma? Are you with me?" Dr. Miller asked, and I moved my eyes to her, giving her my attention. "Okay, let's go back to Sadie. You said you dreamed about her last night. Are you still angry at her?" Yes. I was. How could I ever forget what she had done? Two years ago, Sadie had been my best friend. But not anymore. I nodded at her question, and for the next ten minutes, Dr. Miller had been talking about Sadie and why I shouldn't feel anger. Then, Dr. Miller returned to talk about what had happened a month ago, the reason I had been seeing her, and she said, "I want you to tell me how you feel."

"B-b-ba-d a-and g-g-u-ilty." It was tremendously difficult for me to speak normally, like I'd had in the past.

My voice betrayed me! I teetered on the edge of screaming from frustration.

Dr. Miller noticed my state. "Emma, it's normal to stammer after a trauma. Give it some time." If only everyone at school had been so understanding of my stammer, it would have been so much easier, but she'd been right; after high school, the stuttering had ebbed away, coming back only when I was stressed. "And you can't blame yourself. What happened was not your fault. It was not your fault."

But it'd been. If I'd screamed and hadn't frozen, it wouldn't have occurred.

My heartbeat quickened, and I jerked my eyes open. Sweat dripped down my face. Breathing fast, I sat up in bed, mentally exhausted. Only after two hours I was able to fall asleep, leaving the past behind.

Throughout the weekend, I forced myself not to reflect on the attack happening near my dorm. When Hannah called, however, I told her everything, and we were talking about it after she dropped by. I promised her that I wouldn't walk by myself again, not until the police would catch them.

Chapter 7

On Monday afternoon while I waited in the endless line in the student union's coffee shop, someone addressed me. "How's the nose?" He was standing beside me as I fidgeted with my pen. I had no idea what he was talking about or who he was. I hesitantly turned my head to his, not looking directly at him.

"I'm sorry. What?"

"Your nose...you know, it took some heavy blow when you like slammed into my buddy Ryan." Oh, it was the nice guy who had been next to Ryan the other day. A friendly smile tugged on his lips, but I still didn't trust his motives. Was he about to make fun of me? Or was he really just a nice person?

"It's much better. Thank you." I returned his smile and stared at my hands. I was astonished that he remembered me.

"I'm Nate, you?"

"Emma." I twirled the pen nervously between my fingers and scooted forward with the line.

"Nice to meet you, Emma." He sounded sincere.

I slowly returned my gaze to him. My eyes moved up to his. "Nice to meet you, too"

"Listen, I hate to be so forward, but what the heck. I'll just say it. I've got this friend Josh. I think you two could be a great match." Oh boy. This conversation was sinking faster than the Titanic. "Now before you say no, just hear me out, okay? Josh is like a down-to-earth kind of guy. He graduated from BU last year, majored in engineering. C'mon, you've got to at least give it a try."

I leaned to the side to estimate how much time I had left in the line. It was plenty of time for him to try to convince me, so I decided to save him the trouble and say yes. It was one blind date. What was the harm? "Um...okay."

"Really? Sweet." He beamed. I wrote him my phone number, and he went back to his business. Fifteen minutes later, I got my coffee and the energy that came with it, and then I was at work for the next four hours. Ryan wasn't there, not when I came in and not when I left.

Back in my room, I heated dinner in the microwave, and because of the noise in the dorm, I went to the library to do homework and write my English paper. When I glanced at the time after a while, my heart dropped to my knees. It was midnight, and I was still in the library. My dorm was a thirty-minute walk from here. To hike this distance, even late at night, was something I usually did without thinking twice, but after what had happened on Saturday night, I was petrified of doing it alone. I pulled in a deep breath. I could do it. I wouldn't let them terrorize me.

Outside the building, I closed my jacket. It wasn't a cold night, but it was windy. I fished the pepper spray I'd purchase today out of my backpack, and held it tightly in my hand, hustling toward my dorm. Carrying something that could ward off attacks augmented my sense of security, but when I came close to the spot where they had attacked me, dread swarmed through my veins. Walking at a good clip, I put a shaking index finger on the button of the can.

The faint light from the street lamps did nothing to quell my fear, and the chirp of the crickets only bolstered my awareness that I was alone. Just then, two people stepped into view. I stopped, fixed in my spot. My heart began to beat faster. But when they came closer, I felt my stomach unknot. It was just a couple, out for a walk. The guy had his hand in the front pockets of his jeans, and the girl's arm was hooked around his. They neared, and my mouth opened in surprise. Ryan and Ashley?

He stopped in front of me, Ashley too. Suddenly, two shadowy figures appeared from behind them. "Why are we stopping?" Ashley asked, looking up at him. He didn't have the chance to answer.

A menacing voice, which had been embedded in my mind, interrupted. "Your wallets and cell phones. Now."

Ashley flipped around, moving a bit to the side, away from Ryan, and I got a partial view of the men. Two of them, undoubtedly, were the same guys from the other night. Where was the third one? As if hearing my question, he popped out from behind the shrubs to our left and joined his friends.

Ryan rolled his eyes and puffed in annoyance. "I'm so not in the mood for this shit," he mumbled to himself and then turned to face them. That was when I saw the knives in their hands. "Is there any chance that you guys would walk nicely away without me having to lose my precious time over you three dickheads?" What on earth was he doing? They had weapons! I shifted my eyes to Ashley, hoping she would put some sense into him and shush him, but her demeanor was composed, as if Ryan didn't just provoke three armed thugs. Was she as crazy as him?

"You think it's a joke? College boy." One of the robbers waved his knife threateningly.

"Do you see me laughing, asshole? No. That's because I think it's a pain in my ass, not a joke," Ryan responded. Oh God, he was going to get us hurt—or worse.

My grip on the pepper spray tightened, ready to use it. The robber in the middle moved forward to stab Ryan. Anticipating the move, he briskly ducked down and delivered a strong punch to the robber's crotch. Crying out in agony, he dropped the knife and clutched his groin. Ryan stood up. With his foot, he slid away the weapon on the ground. Behind Ryan, the other assailant launched himself at him, attempting to jab him in the back, but he smoothly moved to the left, avoiding the threat, then spun around and threw a fast side-kick to the attacker's chest, throwing him and his knife down to the cement. Blood seeped from his bald head as he howled with pain, coughing and wheezing. The mugger that Ryan had punched in the crotch lurched awkwardly to his feet, standing at his back, preparing to attack again, but

Ryan's body quickly turned almost all of the way to the side as his leg drove back straight into his target's stomach, which sent the attacker down to the sidewalk. Both of the robbers were lying sprawled there, moaning in pain.

I looked for the third one and found him. Fear in his eyes, he was standing near Ashley. His mouth was open in shock, and his wasn't the only one. I closed mine and tried to digest what had just happened as he ran, trying to escape. Before Ryan chased after him, he asked Ashley to call the police. It didn't take him long to catch the third attacker. Five minutes later, he came back, dragging him by his shirt. Once the police arrived, we gave our statements, and they arrested them.

Later that night, as I lay in bed, I replayed the fight in my head. I was amazed by Ryan's strength, speed, coordination, and moves. Only highly proficient fighters could manifest that. Though, I should have guessed that as an owner of a martial arts studio, he would have some kind of a martial arts background. Ashley obviously knew about him knowing how to fight, hence the calmness. Feeling the same as the robbers were not a threat anymore, I was able to fall asleep quickly and soundly.

Chapter 8

The next day, Ryan arrived at his apartment with half an hour left of my shift. "How're things going?" he asked from the doorway of the office room. He wore a tank top with workout pants. A white towel was around his neck, and a thin sheen of sweat covered his skin. Clearly, he just got back from the gym. My eyes went to his right arm, exploring the colorful ink there. It was a snake coiling up his muscular arm from the elbow. The rest of its body and head continued under the shirt. The snake's patterned skin almost looked alive. The artist who had drawn it was really talented. He stepped inside the office, and the room suddenly felt much smaller.

"It's going well," I answered. I had to remind myself to breathe when he bent over my shoulder to look at my work. I jumped nervously when he rested his elbows on the desk. He was too close, so I rolled my chair a bit to the right, away from him.

"Am I making you nervous?" he asked while his eyes scrolled through the coding, his expression cold and sober.

"Y-yes—I-I mean no. I'm fine."

For another two minutes, he looked at the monitor and then straightened. He faced me and propped a hip on the desk.

"So which is it? Yes or no?" His lips curved into a tiny, mean smile as if the sole purpose of this question was to make me feel even more uncomfortable.

"I-I-I...I-I'm o-o..." I took a deep breath, wishing the stammer would stop.

"Oh, for God's sake." He rolled his eyes. "It was a simple question. If you're gonna continue stuttering, do it in your free time. Don't waste mine."

"O-o-o-kay," I said. Figuring that he was done and that he would let me go back to work, I turned to the screen of the computer. He didn't move.

"I believe I haven't gotten my answer yet."

The anger inside me grew to a dangerous size, helping me to move my face up to his without hesitation. "B-b-e-cause I-I-I think it would be unwise of me to insult you."

"To insult me?" He looked puzzled, and then snorted derisively. "You?" he said, voice full of disdain.

The ire I had in me exploded like a volcano and goaded me to continue what I really shouldn't. "Y-yes, b-by answering your question, I assume that you genuinely don't have the obvious answer to this...*simple* question as you put it, and assuming it basically means that I'm calling you—the one who pays me—imbecile.

"But now that I'm saying this word in the same sentence mentioning you, it causes me to think there is a great possibility that I was mistaken. Maybe you do need me to help you out after all. In this case, I'm truly sorry for my bad manners. The answer is yes, you make me nervous."

He opened his mouth and closed it, twice. What in the world did I do? What had come over me? I'd never been in thrall to my anger. I was ready to apologize, but I didn't. His response was what stopped me.

Instead of firing me, the corners of his mouth began to twitch. He was trying to suppress a smile. He failed, and his grin showed immaculate, white teeth before it turned into a soft chuckle. Wow, he had dimples, and they lent softness to the contours of his otherwise stony face.

"I'll admit. I didn't see that coming. Touché. All right then, I'll leave you to finish off." The smile stayed on his face as he departed the room. I stared for a while at the closed door before gaining my senses back. Okay, so he didn't reprimand or fire me. But, to remain unfired, I should go back to coding, with some music. I pulled out my MP3 player from my bag and clamped the headphone over my head.

Half an hour later, I printed out the report. I found Ashley in the living room, but no Ryan. Her back was to me as she looked out the ceiling-to-floor windows. Hearing my footsteps, she turned and faced me.

A blue dress clung to her body. In spite of showing a lot of her long legs and cleavage, the attire didn't seem sleazy on her. Her face was clean of makeup, which made it easy to see its natural features. Her almond-shaped, green eyes, small nose, full lips, and high cheekbones were stunning.

"Hey," she greeted me with a wide, toothy grin, not seeming to recognize me from last night.

"Hi," I returned with a small smile. Her eyes slipped to the report in my hand.

"You're working on that website for his marital arts studio, right?"

"Yes."

"He's taking a shower. He'll be—oh, there you are." Her stare moved left, mine right. Ryan stepped down the stairs leading to the second floor. Being wet, his hair was one shade darker and accentuated his light eyes. He was clad in a black button-up shirt, dark blue jeans, and black leather boots. He was, in a word, breathtaking.

At the bottom of the steps, his gaze raked slowly over her body, lingering on her intimate parts. "You're sexy as hell," he complimented her and didn't even try to hide the offensive way he inspected her, but it didn't seem to bother her. In fact, when he crossed over to her, he was rewarded with a glowing expression. He reached out and curled his arm around her waist, then pulled her up against his chest and kissed her. I cleared my throat, feeling like a third wheel. He lifted his lips from hers and looked at me.

"Um, the report." I held up the two sheets of paper.

"I'll check it out later. Leave it on the coffee table."

I did and got out of the apartment.

At my dorm, exhausted from the day, I tossed my backpack to the floor and trudged to my bed. Right when I flopped onto it, my cell phone vibrated. I sighed and dug it out from my pocket. The display flashed an unidentified number.

"Hello," I answered warily. Who could it be?

"Hi, Emma, I hope I'm not interrupting. Um...I'm Josh. Nate gave me your number." Josh? Oh! God, I'd forgotten all about Nate's friend.

"Hi, how are you?" I asked, kind of embarrassed by the situation.

"Great, thanks. You?" He sounded even more uncomfortable.

"Same here." A few seconds of silence. Then I heard his voice again.

"So, um...I was wondering if you'd like to meet up...say tomorrow?"

As it happened, tomorrow was Wednesday, the day I'd picked as my day off this week. "Yes, tomorrow would be great."

After he said he'd be in touch with me tomorrow, and we hung up, Wesley, the most popular boy in high school, came into my head. He'd been the first guy who ever asked me out. Well, not exactly. It had been in our senior year. The first time he offered to go to a movie with me was when he caught me on my way to the lockers. Doubtful about his sincerity, I refused, yet it didn't dissuade him. He kept asking me out and even protected me from Heather's and Kate's bullying.

In the end, I said yes. Big mistake. He'd thrown his head back and laughed. After he calmed down, he turned his head to Hayden, his on-and-off girlfriend. "I told you I can kick ass in acting. If I was able to convince that miserable thing that I actually wanted to date her, I deserve a freaking Oscar," he bragged. Hayden had snickered and everyone in the hallway around me joined in the humiliation.

I shook my head to shut out the memory. "They are in the past. They can't hurt you again," I said to myself in the empty room.

Wednesday at lunchtime, Josh had called, saying he'd pick me up at six from my dorm. Hannah had demanded the full details as we headed for the Modern Languages building after lunch. She'd clapped and bounced a lot, and then later, as I waited for him, she texted me to have fun, adding a series of smileys at the end.

Precisely at six, my cell phone chimed. He'd just parked. I quickly walked out of my room and down to the parking lot behind the dorm. In jeans and a T-shirt, I scanned the area, searching for someone with the description he'd given me: short blond hair and brown eyes, wearing a black shirt and jeans. Bingo. A handsome, average-height guy matching his description sidled toward me.

"Emma?" he asked shyly when he reached me.

"Yes." I nodded with a soft smile.

"Josh." He offered me his hand. I shook it, and he led me to a little black Mustang.

I thanked him when he opened the door for me and then climbed in. He rounded the car and slipped into the driver's seat. "So, um…where do you want to go?" he asked, eyes on the steering wheel.

"We can go to Anita's. It's downtown," I suggested, feeling surprisingly less nervous than I thought I would. It was like he was tense enough for both of us. I took advantage of the time in the car to break the ice, and it worked. By the end of the ride, he was a little calmer and a bit more talkative. In the restaurant, we sat at the end of the room. A few awkward silences came between our short sentences until the food we'd ordered arrived and the conversation started to flow.

"You and Nate, how do you two know each other?" I asked between bites of corn soup.

"We've known each other since kindergarten." He chuckled, playing anxiously with his fingers.

"Wow, that's a long time."

"Yes, but when we were fourteen, Nate's mom got remarried to some rich dude and moved out to Manhattan. We lost touch after that." He sliced his pizza.

"How did you get back in touch?"

"I got a scholarship to the same private school Nate was going to." He bit into his pizza and then asked, "You originally from here?"

"No. Brooklyn, born and raised." I salted my soup a bit.

"Brooklyn? Nice. And Nate says you're studying here in UM."

"Yes, majoring in computer science." I wondered what Nate could have told him about me, seeing that we'd only traded a few words. "Um, what else did Nate tell you about me?"

Chuckling, he bent his head down and scratched briefly at the nape of his neck. "Not much." He blushed. "He admitted that he doesn't really know you, but he thinks we'll get along great, and given that Nate's never tried to set me up before, I figured it must be worth a shot." Another blush.

"I'm glad he did. I'm having a great time," I said, smiling. "How about you? You graduated from BU last year, right?" I repeated the information Nate had provided me. Our waitress came by our table to make sure everything was fine with the food. We told her it was tasty, and Josh went back to looking at me, chewing a piece of pizza.

"Yes, and now I'm living here. I found a job."

"That was fast. Good for you." I threw him a grin and sipped my water.

"Thanks, Nate mentioned that you just started working for Ryan. As a computer science major, it's a good opportunity for you, gaining experience and all."

"You know Ryan?" My brows jumped up.

"Sort of. We went to the same prep school."

"You all went to the same school?"

"Yes, but Ryan hung out more with, uh...Tristan and Thea, not such a good crowd to hang with."

Thea, that name rang a bell. She'd been the girl with the mean smile in one of the paparazzi photos of Ryan. Intrigued, I asked, "So how well do you know him?" Great. How was I going to erase the look from his face that said, *Congratulations, you just became the millionth girl to ask me about Ryan*? "Oh, no, I'm really not interested in him that way," I said defensively and filled my spoon with soup.

"It's all right. You don't need to explain." He might have an understanding smile on his mouth, but it was obvious that he thought I'd lied. "When he wasn't with Thea and Tristan he was with Nate. I was friends with him, so I know Ryan, but not too well."

My cheeks smoldered, but I couldn't resist asking, "Was Thea his girlfriend?"

"At first they were just friends. Then they became an item for a while, but it didn't last long." He took a swig from his soft drink.

"You said she and someone named Tristan were not such good company. Why?"

His expression turned serious. "Thea practically ran the school, spinning everyone around her little finger. No one dared to mess with her. If she didn't like someone, they were done socially. She could be brutal, just your typical spoiled, rich kid with too much time on her hands. Ryan was one of the guys she considered worthy enough to hang out with her. The second was Tristan. Those three were a pretty tight clique until senior year, when Ryan started to hang out more with us."

I swallowed the corn soup in my mouth and then said, "So he decided to become less of a spoiled, rich kid and spend more time with the good guys, like you and Nate."

He munched a piece of pizza, gulped it down, then corrected me. "No, you got me wrong. Ryan, unlike Tristan and Thea, is far from being a spoiled, rich kid. The dude made two hundred million dollars. And if you add to this sum the heavy amount of money he inherited from his folks...well, he doesn't have to work one day in his entire life. Despite that, he still goes to college, to better himself. I respect that about him.”

I blinked. The spoon containing soup stopped halfway to my mouth. “Did you just say he made two hundred million dollars?” I slid the spoon back into the bowl.

“Yes, didn’t you know about his songs and MyFriends?” What songs? And MyFriends?

My eyebrow drew together, and he elaborated. “Jessica Ewell, you heard of her...right?” He sipped from his drink, and his expression said, *Of course you have.*

The paparazzi photos of her and Ryan making out on a beach in Los Cabos, Mexico flashed in my mind. Josh named five of her major hits. “He wrote those songs for her, and not just for her.” He listed four famous bands and a few of their hits, then added, “He wrote them too.”

I was impressed. All of the songs Josh had named were timeless, touching something deep inside you.

“You seem shocked.”

“I just had no idea he had so much talent.”

His lips tipped up at the corners. “Don’t be fooled by his looks. The man’s a genius, just like his old man was. The big bucks, though, didn’t come from the royalties. It was from the sale of Nate’s cousin’s company.” So that was what he’d meant by MyFriends, the popular social network. It had been bought a few years back for enormous amount of money in a high-profile deal.

“Are you telling me that Nate’s cousin’s company was MyFriends, like the MyFriends website?”

“Yes, and Ryan saw the potential in his startup from the beginning and invested in it. Told you, brilliant like his old man was.” I couldn’t but concur with that. Apparently, Ryan had a good sense for business. Josh looked at my empty bowl. “What do you say about dessert?”

“Sounds great.” And from that point on, we talked about other things, like food, hobbies, and movies. At the end of the night, outside the door to my dorm room, we both agreed that we should do this again.

Chapter 9

"You're like the math whisperer. You can't flunk it." Hannah decided while she walked me to the bus stop. It was Thursday, and today the grades to the linear algebra test I'd taken last week were to be posted near Professor Horn's office door, but I was too afraid to check mine out.

"The test was really hard. It'd be a miracle if I didn't flunk."

"Tell you what. Give me your student number, and I'll go check your grade and text it to you. After you see that you nailed it, you're so gonna say..." She motioned with her hand for me to complete the rest, but rather than doing so, I gave her a questioning look. She gave me a disappointed little frown and finished her own sentence, imitating Justin's voice. "Who's the man? Yes! I am!"

I laughed. "No, I won't. And not just because I'm not, in fact, a man, but also because I don't see how I could have possibly passed this test."

"Oh, come on, you are so the man, lady. I'm telling you, there is no way you didn't ace it." I sighed as we reached the bus stop.

"Thanks for the cheer, Hannah. See you later," I said and got onto the packed bus. The ride to Ryan's apartment was stretched from fifteen minutes to almost an hour because of an accident, and I was late. I entered the living room, closing the door behind me. He wasn't there. I checked the kitchen, but he wasn't there either. Just when I thought he wasn't home, I noticed a door at the end of the hall was cracked open. I headed down the hall, preparing to apologize for my tardy arrival. As I came closer, I heard his low voice. He must have company, so I'd have to make it quick. "I'm sorry to interrupt, but..." I began as I reached the doorway, but the sight before me stole my breath. My mouth dropped open.

A girl who wasn't Ashley or Sienna straddled him on a king-sized bed. She hadn't heard me, and she bent over, kissing him. He wore a sleeveless shirt and jeans. One hand cupped her bottom, while the other stroked her bare back. She was topless but was wearing pants.

"Oh, God, I'm sorry." If there had been a chance for me to slip out without them noticing me, I'd just blown it. Her upper body jolted up, hands flying to her breasts to cover them up. Both of their faces were on me.

"What the hell?" the girl yelled.

"I'm sorry...I...I-I'm sorry." The rational thing to do was to get out of there, but when have I ever done the rational thing? Instead, I was glued to my spot. "I-I didn't mean to interrupt, uh, actually I did. Otherwise I wouldn't have said sorry to interrupt, but I didn't mean to interrupt that kind of...um...that." In the middle of my endless prattle, my eyes landed on her black bra lying next to a closet. Unfortunately, somehow I wasn't in a frozen state anymore. Nothing could prevent my next stupid, idiotic move. I stepped to the closet, bent down, and picked up her bra. "Here...you'll probably...uh...probably feel more comfortable with that instead of your hands over your...your...never mind."

She looked at me like I had escaped from a lunatic asylum and broken into his apartment. Who could blame her? At that moment, I was acting like an insane person.

With revulsion on her features, her gaze locked on the bra. "That's not mine." Oh, boy. Hurt, she turned to Ryan, but the fact that she didn't accuse him of cheating told me it wasn't a secret between them that he had other girls besides her. I noticed that his body quivered, and I moved my stare to his face. He was laughing quietly. Then, sobering, he said, "Kirsten, meet Emma, she's my..." He seemed to be looking for an adequate word to describe me. He found it. "Unusual coder I've hired to write a website for me."

"And I'll get right to it." I looked at Kirsten sheepishly. "I'm really sorry." I set the bra on the dresser and stepped out. In the office, I fell into the chair. What was wrong with me? Elbows on the desk, I hit my forehead against my palm until my phone buzzed with a text alert. I pulled it out of my backpack. Hannah's name popped up on the display, and my heart raced. Had she already checked my linear algebra test grade?

I opened the message, stared down at the screen, and rubbed my eyes. I looked at it again, just to make sure I was seeing correctly.

A minus. I got an A minus. I jumped out of the chair, and like Hannah before me, I imitated Justin's voice. "Who's the man? Yes! I am! I'm the man!" With the cell phone in my hand, I made a silly, joyful dance that was cut short when I spun around and faced the door. The open door. Ryan was leaning against the doorframe and watching me with amusement, hands inside the front pockets of his jeans, one leg crossed over the other. "Um...how...how long h-have you been standing there?"

"Long enough to know who's the man."

I sank into the chair facing him and cleared my throat. "I-I can explain." Where was I going to start? Embarrassed by what he'd witnessed, I looked bashfully down at the cell phone in my hands, searching for an explanation.

"And that should be interesting," I heard him walk into the room, and his black boots came into my line of vision, "but right now, I want you to look up at me." He was standing in front of me. I swallowed and worried my lower lip as I lifted my head up to his flat stomach, hidden under a tight, black, sleeveless shirt. "At my eyes, Emma." It sounded less like a request and more like an order.

"I-I should go back to work."

His knee gently pressed between my legs, slowly separating them. I couldn't resist; I was too overwhelmed by what he was doing. He joined his other knee in, widening the space more, and squatted on his heels. Two, ice blue eyes stared at me. I shrank back. He stayed in place, not closing the gap I'd created. I avoided his gaze, starting to drop mine, but he put two fingers beneath my chin and tipped it up until

I was looking at him. My heart thudded, and his touch sent butterflies fluttering through my stomach. He watched me, and his mood shifted from playful to serious. I waited for a mean joke about the different colors of my eyes. Instead, he withdrew his hand, and then he was back on his feet, heading for the door.

"For future reference, when you're late, don't keep it to yourself. That way I'll know you decided to show up," he said over his shoulder, closing the door, and I immersed myself in work. After I was done with my coding for the day, I found him in the living room. He was on the sofa with his legs crossed at the ankles and resting over the coffee table, typing away on the laptop on his lap.

"Ahem." I sought his attention. His gaze met mine, and I handed him the report.

He skimmed the first page. "You can take a seat, you know." I sat on the far end of the sofa and set my backpack at my feet. His cell phone rang. He settled the laptop and report between us and answered the call. "Yeah?" There was a short silence, and he said, "Yes, she is. Why?" Another pause, and then, "How the hell should I know?" His eyes moved to me. Me. They were talking about me. As I wondered who he could possibly be talking to, Ryan's voice filled the room again. "Or I can just ask her, like normal people do." Phone clamped to his ear, he asked, "How was your date with Josh?" My brows lifted. "Nate couldn't get a hold of him, and he's curious," he added at my expression.

"It was, uh, nice."

"You hear that?" Ryan said into the phone. "Good. Okay, we'll talk later." He ended the call and leaned back into the sofa, pulling his laptop onto his lap. "You should tell Josh you're not interested."

"What? Why?" But even as I said it, I knew he was right. I had a great time with Josh—as a friend.

"Nice is not the way you describe a hot date. You're not into him, and it's fine, but also a shame. Girls like you are perfect for him."

"Girls like me?" My face was drawn with confusion.

"Yeah, all innocent and naive, and virgin." He uttered the word "virgin" like it was a serious illness.

"Virginity is not a disease," I said, my voice exasperated.

He stifled a yawn. "No, but it's boring like hell."

Ugh, he was so arrogant. Suddenly, I found myself smacking his shoulder hard. The anger inside me had turned me into a completely different person. What I did was so uncharacteristic of me. Horrified, I gasped sharply and felt my eyes widen.

"I-I didn't mean to...I'm so sorry."

At first, he seemed confused, then surprised, and finally amused. A laugh sprang to his lips as he closed his laptop and moved it to the coffee table. The laughter slowly subsided, leaving a small smile on his face.

"You're full of surprises, particularly when you feel insulted."

"I wasn't insulted by your remark."

"You weren't?" he asked with skepticism.

"No, I wasn't."

"Well, somehow it's hard for me to believe that."

Button your lips. I actually followed up on my own advice—for all of about five seconds. "That's because you wrongly assume that I care about your opinion." Great. Why couldn't I just hold my tongue? I was ready to blurt out another apology, but it stayed in my mouth when I noticed his expression. He was staring at me strangely, as if he was trying to decipher me.

"You know, you can be really unpredictable. It's actually quite...refreshing," he said. Was that sort of a compliment? Or was he being sarcastic? I almost asked him, and then thought better of it.

"I should get going." I started to stand, but he caught my arm, gently bringing me back down onto the sofa. The spot where our skin touched became warm and sensitive.

"What did you want to say?"

"I-i-it's nothing."

"Nothing doesn't make you think twice about whether or not you should say it." He removed his hand from my arm, and I could breathe again.

"Uh...I was wondering if you were being sarcastic," I said.

His lips curved into a ghost of a smile. "No, I wasn't. You need to understand something about me. I'm really good at reading people up to the point that they bore me. You, on the other hand, seemed so utterly predictable that when you turned out to be quite the opposite, it feels...different, in a good way." The display on his cell phone lit up. Nate was calling again, but with a quick glance at the caller ID, Ryan sent the call to voice mail.

"You were right about Josh. I like him, but more as a friend. I'm going to talk to him."

"Good, but don't take your time on this. He's a strong believer in relationships and monogamy, all that bullshit stuff. He won't date others even if he only had one date with you." The word "monogamy" came out of his mouth similar to the way the word "virgin" had.

"What's wrong with monogamy?"

"Besides being against human nature?"

"If it were against human nature, people wouldn't get married, choosing to be in a committed relationship for the rest of their lives," I retorted. He settled his elbows on his knees and looked at me.

"Yes, they get married, and then they seek solutions to a problem they themselves have generated. One of the solutions is cheating."

"Not everyone cheats."

"It doesn't mean they don't want to or that they're just too afraid to do it."

"Have you even tried monogamy, before writing it off as against human nature?" I doubted he was ever faithful to Thea, so it surprised me when he nodded.

"Yeah, one time, and it ended badly." His tone expressed just how badly.

"That bad?"

"God, yeah. I'd rather die than go through that again. It ruined everything between us, and after the breakup nothing went back as it was before." He leaned against the back of the sofa. I mirrored his action.

"Maybe she wasn't the right girl for you." I bit my lower lip, then said hesitantly, "Did you love her?"

"No. Or any other girl, for that matter." His voice held a strong note of bitterness.

"Could it be that a girl did break your heart? Leaving you bitter."

"Oh, I am bitter, but not because some chick broke my heart, but because none of them could do it," he said. What? He wanted his heart to get broken? My brows crumpled with confusion. "I'm not afraid of love," he clarified. "And though it's only a bunch of chemicals the brain produces, a pure illusion, I still want to feel it, but I'm just not capable of feeling it and getting my heart broken."

"If you think it's only an illusion, why would you want to feel it?"

"Because I hate living in a world where there are things that people can experience, but I can't."

Things, plural? "What other things?"

"Like tears," he said casually, as if it was normal. My eyes grew wide.

"You've never cried?"

He took a deep breath and let it out slowly. The room got cold. "Let's just say I lost that ability years ago."

The murder of his family must have numbed him inside greatly, and I identified with him. After my own tragedy, numbness had slowly filled me, but it wasn't as strong as this. I could still believe in love. "I hope one day you do feel love. Maybe it'd alter your perspective on commitment, and everything else."

"If I ever experience love, that's all it'll be for me—an experience. No more, no less. It won't change the way I perceive monogamy, or anything else."

"You're wro—" The ring of his phone cut me off. He leaned forward. I mimicked his movement, and my eyes went down to the glowing display. Caller ID: Kirsten Palmer. He thumbed ignore.

His gaze swung to me, his elbows on the knees. "You were saying?"

"That you're wrong. It's a very powerful emotion. It *can* affect your way of thinking."

"What about anger? Is it as powerful as that?"

"Yes, it is."

"Yet, it didn't affect my way of thinking, not when I woke up one morning to a text saying my family was murdered, and not now." His expression grew colder. So that was why he never checked his texts. How could someone deliver the message about the death of his family over a text? A tremble shimmered through me as I watched him. He had so much coldness in him. I was the one who was wrong here. No amount of love had the ability to thaw the ice coating his heart.

The intercom buzz pierced the silence. I tore my gaze from him and grabbed my backpack, slinging it over my shoulder and turning to him.

"The day you stop treating love and anger as the same emotion that brings the same outcome is the day you change the way you see things," I told him. A faint smile played at his mouth, warming his face. When I reached the front door, he called my name, and I cast a glance over my shoulder.

He got to his feet as the intercom buzzed once more. "See you next week, Emma," he said. I nodded once and walked out of his apartment.

Chapter 10

On Saturday, after catching a movie, Josh and I went to a coffee shop, where we sat near the window overlooking the Blue club across the street. He'd called me this morning. It turned out that we both liked each other but as friends and also that we were both suckers for science fiction movies, so we'd decided to go see one playing in the theater downtown.

"The book is so much better than the movie," Josh complained, taking a gulp from his cup.

"Yes, but isn't it in most cases?" I dug into my strawberry pie and took a bite.

"I guess you're right."

Chewing, I held my mug of tea to my lips, smelling the mint coming from the steamy drink while my gaze drifted to the window. A familiar-looking black bike pulled into a parking spot near the Blue club. The driver, in a dark brown leather jacket and jeans, dismounted. His female companion followed suit and pulled off her helmet. Ashley. She finger-combed her blond, abundant hair as she handed Ryan, the driver, her helmet. I sipped my hot tea and looked back at Josh. He was watching them too. No, not them. Her.

"She's really beautiful," I said.

He jerked his head back to me as if I'd caught him doing something bad. "I'm sorry, uh...I wasn't...I..."

I chuckled over the rim of the mug. "It's okay. We're not on a date, and even if we were, no one could blame you. Girls like her are a magnet for attention."

Smiling uncomfortably, he nodded in agreement.

His phone on the table buzzed. He glanced at the screen, and his face lit up like a Christmas tree. "Sorry, I need to take this."

"Sure, go ahead," I said and put down the mug to dive my fork into the strawberry pie. Three bites later, he hung up.

"Who was she?" I asked. Whoever it was, he definitely had feelings for her.

"Just a good friend." His smile diminished. He didn't like to refer to her as merely a friend.

"Does she know how you feel about her?" I circled the cup with both of my hands to warm my fingers. He seemed surprise that I'd figured out his secret. "The expression on your face when you talked to her gave you away," I explained.

Pink splotches decorated his cheeks. "No, I haven't told her, but a month ago when she flew in from New York, I came pretty close to saying something."

"What stopped you?" I sipped my mint tea.

"When she arrived, I thought we'd have some time alone, you know, so we can talk, but she arranged a small get-together at Ryan's place. Thea, Tristan, Nate, and Ryan were there. I came too, but when she's with them, she's different, always trying to impress Thea. It pissed me off. I left and that was it. She went back to the city the next day, and I never told her."

I lifted a brow. "She's friends with Thea and Tristan?"

"Doesn't say a lot about her, I know." He took a long drink from his coffee and then continued, "But before she idealized Thea, she was close friends with Nate. He introduced us, and I got to know the real Sadie. She's truly amazing, always full of life, even after what that...that pedophile did to her when she was only ten." His face darkened.

I swallowed the last of my tea, set the cup down, and covered his hand with my own. "Josh, that's awful. I'm so sorry to hear what she's been through."

"Thanks, but she's strong, despite not getting the support she needed from her mother." Anger hardened his features. "What kind of mother lets the neighbor molest her own child and then sends her to live with her father in Manhattan to avoid the gossip?"

My lips parted and my blood drained from my face. No, it couldn't be.

"Emma?" he asked, concern tingeing his tone. "What's the matter?"

"W-wwhat's Sadie's full name? Is she originally from Brooklyn?" My voice wobbled.

"Yes, she is. Her full name is Sadie Conner. You know her?"

Oh my God. Yes, I did. "No, I don't," I lied, forcing a smile. "The Sadie I know has a different last name. Hmm, I have a bit of a headache. I think we should call it a night."

"Yes, of course," he said, apparently believing my excuse. After he drove me back to my dorm and we said goodbye, I let my mind drift to the past when Sadie and I had once been best friends. We'd been ten years old and lived in the same apartment building. We'd always played together, having so much fun, but gradually she'd started to behave strangely, distancing herself from everybody. Then, one day, she'd accused my uncle of touching her in a sexual way. At that age, I hadn't understood what being touched sexually really meant, but I'd known it had been something grave since my father banned my uncle from the house. I cried for hours.

Uncle Will had never harmed me. If anything, he'd been so kind and generous, and to not be able to see him again crushed me. Two days later, I'd overheard my parents talking about Sadie's mom. Because of her new boyfriend, she decided to send her only daughter to live with her father in Manhattan and forget about the whole thing. The day she'd left, we'd run into each other in the stairwell of our building.

"You don't believe me," she said, infuriated.

"No, I don't. Why did you do it to Uncle Will? Why?"

"I hate you." She raised her voice and started to cry. "I hate you. I hate you. You're not my friend. I'll make you suffer for thinking I'm a liar. You'll see." The look she gave me was pure vengeful, and that was the last time I saw her.

I shook my head, returning back to the present. *No, I won't think about Sadie again. She is in my past. And there she'll stay*, I thought and went to sleep.

The rest of the weekend, I spent reading and hanging out with Hannah. I filled her in about me and Josh being only friends. She was disappointed but hopeful that I'd find someone else soon. She also talked about a guy she was dating, Dylan, and I wished he wouldn't be like the other awful guys she tended to date.

On Monday morning I could barely wake up. I threw a murderous glare at my beeping alarm and pulled the cover over my face to block the light. *The snooze button won't press itself*, I reminded myself. With a grunt of exasperation, I tossed the cover off and opened my eyes. The bright light was effective as a bucket of ice-cold water. Wide awake, I got out of bed and started the day.

The morning passed uneventfully, but in the afternoon, I got an unexpected phone call from Ryan, asking where I was. He wanted to give me a list of changes he'd made to the website, and since he wasn't going to be in the apartment when I'd be there, he needed to make sure I saw them.

We agreed to meet at the student union coffee shop, where I'd wanted to buy a cup of coffee before class. I got there first and found Hannah and Jenna waiting in the long line. Hannah waved me over. Reluctant, I came up to them. Jenna spent the next ten minutes chatting up a storm about some party she'd gone to yesterday at the Beta Kappa House. Her voice evoked a mental image in my head—me snapping my fingers and poof, no more Jenna. Instead, Ryan arrived just as Hannah received a text from Dylan saying he'd stopped by her dorm room for a surprise visit. She left me with Jenna just as Ryan spotted me and walked in our direction. *Terrific—just terrific.*

"Hey, Ryan, craving a coffee?" Jenna said when he reached us, flipping her straight, cherry-red hair over her shoulder. I held back my eye roll as he gave her a quick once-over. Without answering, he shifted his gaze back to me, handing me two sheets of paper as I moved up in the line.

"Here are the changes. It's important you work on it today. If you have any questions about them, call me."

"Ewww, you know this *weirdo*?" A combination of genuine surprise and disgust covered Jenna's face. He moved his head to her, and a slow grin lifted the corners of his lips. She had his attention now.

"Yeah, actually I do, and how about you? How do *we* know each other?"

A smile spread over her mouth. "We talked at the party yesterday."

He looked like he was trying to remember her, and then said, "Right, Jenna, is it?"

"Yes," she said, unable to hide the excitement in her voice.

"Jenna, would you be kind enough to give me your opinion on something?" he asked, and I inched forward in the line.

"Sure, about what?" Her tone sounded like he'd just asked her on a date, not merely her opinion.

"About a small matter. I've always had this idea that girls who talk to guys they've known less than a few minutes about their future babies are pathetic, but now that you brought up the word weirdo, I think it can describe them better. I'm not quite sure. What do you say? Which describes you the best? Is it pathetic or weirdo?"

Did he really just say that? Stunned, I turned to look at Jenna.

Her eyes were huge with shock. "What!" she yelped, outraged. "How dare you? Go fuck yourself."

Ryan chuckled. "Thanks for the suggestion, sweetheart, but I don't really think I need to. You see, your generous offer to rock my world last night wasn't the only one I got. Though, your concern for my sex life is truly touching."

A girl behind me coughed away a laugh, which only made Jenna angrier. Lips pursed, she glared at me, as if I was responsible for her humiliation. She took two steps toward where I was standing, ready to insult me, but Ryan smoothly planted himself between us, his back to me. "If you've got something to say," he said, his tone turning hard, "say it to me." She huffed and stormed off. Ryan waited a moment, then spun around to face me. Something was bothering him. Was that regret for coming to my defense on his face? Why had he done that, anyway? The only explanation I could come up with was that Jenna really got on his nerves. "See you tomorrow," was all he said before he walked off.

The next day, after I finished working, I took off my headphone and heard Ryan's muffled voice outside the office room. I grabbed my backpack and the report and stepped into the living room. Ryan was leaning against the floor-to-ceiling window, a cell phone to his ear. "...but I already told you yesterday, she's out...no, Thea, for the last time, it's off...yeah, I know I told her that, but it's over. She's out."

I sneezed and his gaze turned from the window to me. With his eyes on my face, he headed for the sofa. "It's not up for discussion. It's over. I gotta go. We'll talk later." He hung up and sank into the sofa. I gave him the report. "Sit," he said. I did, and he went over the sheet of papers, then set it on the coffee table and closed the distance between us. A hint of expensive cologne touched my nose. "You know"—he reached for my ponytail, and suddenly my hair cascaded over my shoulders—"I don't think I've ever seen you with your hair down." I experienced a jolt of unreasonable fear in my stomach and had a flashback of Heather and Kate shoving my head down while shaving it bald in a high school bathroom stall.

"P-p-please g-g-ive me back m-my hair-thing." His expression was unreadable as he inspected me for a moment, and he dropped my hair tie in my lap. I swiftly tied my hair into a messy ponytail and stood, grabbing my backpack from the floor. "Tomorrow is my day off, so I'll work on the rest of the changes on Thursday." He nodded once, and I walked out, returning to my dorm. When I went to sleep that night, I had nightmares about Heather and Kate. For years, they'd bullied me, and for years, I had been terrified of them. Being far away from them, I'd thought the fear was gone. I thought they couldn't scare me anymore. I was wrong.

Chapter 11

Ryan wasn't home when I arrived at work on Thursday, and he still wasn't back after four hours of coding, so I left the report on the office desk. When I reached the front door, it opened, and Ryan, holding the keys and helmet in his hands, filled the doorway. "Hey, I completed the changes and the report is in the office room," I told him.

"Okay," he said, but he didn't move from the entryway. Instead, a sexy smile tugged at his lips. "Emma, I got to thinking about you, and I'd like us to become friends."

Huh? My eyes widened a bit. Was he serious? "Friends?"

"Yes. You and me, friends." God, he *was* serious.

"Okay, friends." But I wasn't. No way could, or should, we be friends.

"Good." His expression spoke volumes; *yes, I know you just blew me off.* He stepped aside, clearing the way. I went past him and heard him shut the door behind me. I glanced back. He was standing outside the door, watching me. My face was drawn tight with confusion, but I said nothing. Maybe he'd forgotten something on his bike and was headed back to it. Inside the elevator, he stared down at me. "You live on or off campus?"

"Why?"

"If I'm gonna drop you off, it might be helpful to have an address." He flashed me a dimple. Great, he wasn't going to give up.

"You don't have to," I said to his chest, which got closer as he took a step forward. I backed up until I hit the elevator railing.

He closed the distance, standing a breath away, and said, "But what if I want to?"

I slowly raised my gaze to his.

"What i-i-f I don't want you to?" I challenged back.

He leaned in, and my blood pressure jumped. "I, of course, will accept it, but as my friend—and you did just so nicely agree to that offer a few minutes ago—I expect you to explain your reluctance." The smell of his black leather jacket blended with the scent of fresh mint coming from the gum in his mouth.

"I..." I was looking for a good excuse, but it was almost impossible to concentrate with him standing so near me.

"You?" He pressed, and the dimple deepened.

"Consider motorcycles to be a very unsafe means of transportation." There, I found an excuse, and it was even a good one.

"That's the only reason?" he asked. I nodded. "You sure?" My chin moved up and down again. "Okay." He backed off. Basking in my small victory, I smiled slightly. He pressed the elevator button. The door slid closed, but he stayed inside. Why didn't he return to his apartment? When the door opened, he gestured with his hand. "After you." Instead of stepping out to the lobby, I stepped out to the parking garage.

I glanced up at him. "Why are we in the parking garage?"

Standing beside me, he pointed to a new, sleek, black BMW parked next to his bike. "That's why." Great, why hadn't I thought about the possibility that he could also own a car? He was a millionaire. Of course he also had a car. Once inside, he put the helmet in the backseat and turned to look at me, smirking. "So, off or on campus?" Detecting a note of triumph in his voice, I gritted my teeth. I gave him my address, and off we went.

On Monday morning I walked into the lobby of the Art & Architecture building to find Hannah waiting for me near the staircase. She was with Kayla and two more friends. I wove through small, scattered clusters of people to reach them. Hannah introduced me to the girls I didn't recognize— Kelly and Nikki—and we exchanged polite hellos.

"Look." Nikki, in a Sigma Omega Delta tee, nudged Kelly with her elbow and nodded to something behind me. "Ashley's here," she said, and I turned around. Ashley and Ryan were standing not far away from me, talking with some people.

"Hey, Ash, over here," Kelly called, and I winced, not wanting to face Ryan. The last time I'd seen him, he'd offered me friendship. His new attitude toward me was uncomfortable and confusing. I thought I liked him better when he'd been mean to me. Things had been clearer and less awkward.

"Hannah, I need to go. I have..." My voice faded away. Hannah didn't hear me. She was laughing at something Kayla had said. *Oh, never mind.* I turned to go, moving my stare down to my pen, and it was suddenly gone. I jerked my head up. Ryan stood in front of me with my pen in his hand. "My pen—"

"Will stay with me, and I'm sure everyone in your way will thank me." A subtle grin touched his lips. Fine, he wanted it? He could have it. I let out a miffed breath, stepped around him, and headed up the stairs to the mezzanine floor. At the top step, I rounded the corner and was walking along the glass railing overlooking the lobby downstairs when a hand grabbed my arm and whirled me around. I tipped my head back, and my eyes met Ryan's bright blue ones. I dropped my gaze to his chest, avoiding his stare. He tucked his fingers under my chin and lifted it until we were eye to eye. "You should really get rid of your habit of looking down."

"There is nothing wrong with me looking down," I said defensively and cringed inwardly at the stupid thing that had just tumbled out of my mouth. I blew an annoyed breath.

"Please, let me go."

"You know what? I'll do just that if you give me one conclusive argument for why there is nothing wrong with you watching the floor rather than people." He dropped his fingers from my chin, but not from my arm.

"Because I don't have to look at people." It was a lame argument, of course. I didn't care. I tried to walk away, but I couldn't dislodge his hand from me, even though his hold was gentle.

He turned me back to face him. "Not so fast. When I said one conclusive argument, my main focus was on conclusive." Why was he doing this? Was he trying to ridicule me? I carefully studied his expression. It held no hint of mocking. He seemed genuinely interested in what I had to say. "Why the surprised face?" he asked, and a couple of students hurried past us, reminding me that my class was about to start.

"I have to go. I don't want to be late for class."

"Excellent, that means we both want something from each other, and the best part is that we both can get it. I'll stop bothering you and let you get back to your businesses, and in return, all I ask is an answer."

To save me time, I decided to go with the honest truth. "I was, uh, surprised because..." I cleared my throat. "Because you seemed like you truly wanted to hear what I have to say, and people...well, they don't usually show interest in me as a person."

"Then why are you surprised?" Um, didn't I just give him the reason?

"Like I said—"

"I know what you said, but did you? Because to me it seems you forgot the fact that the word usually doesn't mean never, so it's not as if it's the first time someone has shown interest in you."

"No, but it doesn't happen a lot."

"According to what scale exactly? Is there some kind of universal scale that measures when it's a lot and when it's not? If there were, by the way, usually still doesn't mean never." I was silent. What could I say? The fact was, there had been people who had wanted to befriend me, and Hannah had been among them. He withdrew his hand from me. "Yeah, Emma, you're not as invisible as you wish to think of yourself." Why did he care? What was his agenda? The words "charity case" sprang into my head.

"Look, I don't need your advice about where my eyes should be or any of your help. I'm not your charity case," I said, my voice a thin thread of sound. *Speak up!*

He leaned closer, holding my gaze. "Do you think you're a charity case to me?" He enunciated the words slowly.

I turned away at the sound of girls laughing with each other and strolling by us. Then I dragged my gaze up to his face, reluctant to meet his eyes. "Why are you asking me that if I said I am not?"

"Because I didn't ask what you said, I asked what you think. Sometimes there is a big difference between the two. So, do you *think* you're a charity case to me?"

Discomfort surged through me, and I had no doubt that the truth was written all over my face. My head tipped down. To lie was not an option, but neither to answer truthfully. Silence resolved my dilemma and then was broken by a soft gasp slipping from me when he caught my chin. He guided my gaze to a specific group of people who we had just left downstairs in the lobby. "Look at her." I knew who he was talking about. Ashley stood out from everyone else around her, and her good looks were only part of what made her the center of attention.

He released my chin, yet I kept watching, noticing that Hannah and Kayla weren't there anymore. Two guys had replaced them, one of whom was talking to Ashley. Focused on her fingernails as she bit them, she appeared inattentive to him. All of a sudden, Ryan's breath caressed my ear, warming the inside of it and causing shafts of electricity to course through my body. "Hypothetically, let's say that the guy speaking to her right now leaned in and advised her to get rid of her habit to bite her fingernails. Would she think he did it because she was a charity case?" Of course not. She had confidence in spades. It would never allow her to consider herself a charity case. The warmth of his breath in my ear faded and then disappeared. I turned to stare at his mouth, which just a moment ago had been inches from my ear.

"No, she wouldn't," I admitted.

"Even if he'd done it because he did see her as a charity case?"

I didn't have to deliberate on it; the answer was the same. "Even so, she still wouldn't."

"Emma, in the end, it all comes down to how *you* see yourself, not others. You can be your best supporter or your own worst enemy. You want to be the former? Start by considering yourself more than someone's charity case."

"Ryan?" A girl walked up behind him, and he turned to talk to her.

"I better go," I said and scurried off. This time he didn't stop me. As I dashed down the corridor, I turned over his last words in my mind until I reached the classroom's closed door. I stared at it for a while. It was the first time I'd been late for class since I'd started college. I took a deep breath and slipped in through the back door.

Later that day, after I got back to my dorm room from spending the afternoon alone in Ryan's apartment, I decided it was time to do laundry. The laundry room in the dorm basement was empty, probably because the football game was on and everyone was watching it on the big lobby TV.

I stuffed my clothes into the washer, put quarters in, and pushed the start button. Now I had to wait. Waiting was always easier with chocolate, so I headed to the lobby vending machine. The room hummed with voices and laughter, and the occasional tinny cheers from the enormous TV. I dug a pen from my pocket and focused on it as I crossed the room. A sudden loud scream and a string of curses shot into the air. The room fell quiet, and I glanced up to find all eyes on me. And Jenna. In the wake of me crashing into her, she was drenched with orange juice that had been in the red cup in her hand.

While she kept swearing at me, my roaming gaze found Justin. He was looking at Jenna, but then he transferred his stare to me. Embarrassed, I averted my head and spotted Ryan near the front door. Ashley, her sister, and Nate were with him, and they were all searching for the source of the commotion. Ryan's eyes landed on me. He said something to Ashley and started weaving through the crowd, moving in my direction. I turned back to look at Justin. He took a sip of his drink, watching as Jenna yelled at me. Wishing for the ground to swallow me up, I whirled back toward the stairs, threading my way through the people.

In the basement, I heard the sound of footsteps coming in. I swirled and faced Ryan.

"Ryan, I want to be left alone," I told him, but he stepped deeper into the room.

"Yeah, sure, but before I do that, I wanna let you know that I'm not satisfied with your progress with the website. A ten-year-old with basic coding knowledge could do better and faster work."

I felt like I'd been slapped. Hard. "I'm sorry, I thou—"

"Sorry? You're sorry? Who gives a shit? I'm paying you to give me results, fast and good, not to be sorry. How did you end up majoring in computer science?" His tone was acrid and his words stung me. It was important for me to be good at what I'd been studying so hard, and he wouldn't let it go. "Computer science is for those who can actually code, not for those who think they can. Oh, look at you. What's wrong? Did I piss you off?" *No, and that's the problem.* If I were angry, I'd tell him he was a jerk, like I'd done the last time he'd been mean to me, but instead, I was hurt and needed the protection of my imaginary shield.

He came closer to me, and his eyes were probing. "No, you're not pissed. You're hurt. Good. You're so useless that it's just sad. You're a nobody." I wasn't going to endure another humiliation, so I stepped around him to exit the room, but he caught me by my elbow and pulled me back against the wall. Suddenly, I was caged between his arms, his palms flat against the wall on either side of my head. He looked down at me. "Oh no, you're not running away from it.

You're gonna deal with it. Yeah, I know you're itching to tell me what an ass I am, and that I should go to hell. Well, guess what? All this wanting is meaningless if you're not saying it aloud.

"Your silence doesn't protect you. It protects the people who treat you like shit, people like Jenna, like me. Who's gonna stop me right now? Huh? You? You're weak. You're a nobody, and what was it that Jenna was screaming about up there? Oh, right, you're a pathetic excuse of a human being, and yo—Emma, open your eyes," he demanded. I refused. What Jenna couldn't do to me in the lobby, he did now. Every word cut bone deep. Darkness was the only escape I had. As if picking up on the direction of my thoughts, he said, "The darkness can't help either. Don't you get it? Nothing can help you but yourself. I'm not going anywhere any time soon, and why would I when I have the perfect punching bag right here, in front of me?" The insults he hurled at me sounded like fingernails across a chalkboard. It was unbearable. I needed to stop them. I needed to do *something*. Anything.

I willed myself to open my eyes and tilted my head up to look into his eyes. Determination shadowed them. I glanced around. I was alone with him down here. No one could help me. No one but...me. I raised my chin. "Go ahead, can me already but stop wasting my time. I've got more important things to do than listen to you complain about something I know I did good. And, Ryan, if you decide to do the smart thing and keep me in the project, you better change the way you talk to me because if you think for one second that you have the right to speak to me like this, think again and again until you get it into your head that you have no right, not even as my boss." My eyes fastened on his.

Something I'd never felt before spread inside me and gave me strength, strength to fight back. Preparing myself for his next nasty words, I squared my shoulders and mentally pushed up my sleeves, but in lieu of getting mad, a satisfied smile played across his lips.

"That's right, Emma. Nobody has that right. Not me, not Jenna—nobody. And don't you ever let it slip outta your mind." He pulled back, freeing me. At the doorway, before he left the room, he glanced back over his shoulder. "And since it would be stupid of me to fire a damn good coder, I'll see you tomorrow." Alone in the room, with only the sound of the washing machine, I could name without a doubt the strong feeling still bubbling inside me. Confidence. It felt great.

Chapter 12

It was nine-thirty a.m., and I was already late for class. I quickly grabbed the first shirt I pulled out of my closet while zipping my jeans and pushing my feet into sneakers. It was only when I was outside that I actually noticed which top I was wearing under my thin coat: a juvenile one my mom had gifted me on my last birthday. I hadn't had the heart to inform her that I'd never wear it, so I'd packed it up for college, along with everything else. Unfortunately, I didn't have time to change, so I was stuck with this shirt for today. After my last class, I headed to Ryan's apartment. When I arrived, I opened the front door and walked into a very awkward situation. Ashley was sitting on the left side of the half square sofa; Ryan, on the long side, near her. Her eyes were bloodshot from crying, and tear streaks stained her cheeks. I closed the door behind me, and he glanced at me over his shoulder. His face, in contrast to Ashley, was devoid of emotion.

"Sorry...I'll just..." I trailed off, slinking past the sofa and into the office. I sat in the chair and booted up the computer on the desk. The wall being thin, I could still hear them.

"Ash, I'm sorry, but I've been upfront with you this whole time. I've never sold you some crappy fairy tale about love and a happy ending." His voice was level.

"And I've never meant anything to you, have I?" Ashley sounded broken. There was silence, until she ended it after a short moment. "You're just gonna sit there without saying anything?"

"Do you really want me to state the obvious?" The tender tone he used softened his words.

"So what? Now you suddenly care about not hurting my feelings?"

"Ash, c'mon, let's not do this."

"I can't believe you. You're really going to end this because I told you I loved you?" I heard a snort of frustration, then her voice again. "God, why can't you just grow up and stop pushing everyone away? And you know what? Yeah, you didn't bullshit me this whole time or lie about your intentions, but I wasn't an idiot either. I knew exactly what I was getting myself into.

"It was so apparent from the beginning you were trouble with capital T." She sniffed and continued, "To be honest, the *only* reason I let you into my life was because you were the first goddamn guy who didn't care, who didn't even try to impress me. Yeah, I loved it, and I was drawn to it, and I fell for you."

There was a short silence before Ryan's emotionless, flat voice interrupted it. "I appreciate the honesty. You might, though, reconsider who between the two of us *really* needs to grow up." A loud cell ring followed Ryan's sentence.

"You can be a real asshole sometimes, you know that?" she responded and answered her phone. Then I heard the front door slamming shut. I shook my head. How could a person be so cold? She was hurt and crying, and he didn't care. He was so indifferent to her. I glanced at the computer. It was on, waiting for me. I sighed and got to work. The next four hours passed quickly and without disruptions. I printed out the report and went to the living room.

He was on the sofa, reading from a textbook in his lap. He glanced up from it, and I held the report out to him. He closed the book and leaned over to deposit it on the coffee table, where a spiral notebook and two other textbooks lay. Then he pushed to his feet, took the sheets of paper from my hand, and put them down next to the spiral. "Aren't you going to go over it?" I asked.

"I will, after I get back. I need a break. We can hit the Mighty Coffee"—we?—"and grab something sweet to eat with a cup of coffee or a shake." He stepped to the dining table, grabbed his keys from it, and walked to the front door. He looked back at me. "Coming?"

After coding for the last four hours, his offer actually sounded good. "Yes," I said, and we left. During the ride to Mighty Coffee, I learned that he had a large collection of Rolling Stones music in his car. "Have you always been a Rolling Stones fan?" I asked as I sat down at a table in the back of the coffee shop.

"Yeah, they have great music." He settled into the chair opposite me. There was a pile of napkins and two menus on our table. He picked up one of them and flipped it open. I took the other. My eyes automatically searched for something that had strawberry in it. I had an addiction to this fruit. It was my favorite. And I found the perfect item from the list to order—a Red milkshake. It contained an abundance of strawberries, as the menu claimed. A waiter came over. "Hey, I'm Mark, ready to order?" he asked, holding a pen and notepad.

"Yeah, I'll have the apple pie and a cup of strong black coffee. She'll have the Red milkshake." Ryan turned to me. "Anything else?"

Brows slightly lifting up, I answered, "Um, no." Was he a mind reader?

Mark jotted down our orders. "Okay, it'll be right up," he said and walked off.

I looked at Ryan. "How did you know I wanted the Red milkshake?"

His eyes flickered to my shirt, and his lips hitched up at the corners. "I played a hunch," he replied, amusement in his voice. Oh, God, I forgot about my shirt. I glanced down and sure enough, under a picture of a giant strawberry, the caption read, *strawberry girl*. Heat filled my cheeks.

"Uh, it's not, um, really mine. I just borrowed it." Really? That was the only big, fat lie you could make up? Of course he wasn't fooled. He gave me a full grin, and his dimples upgraded it to dazzling. I wondered why he didn't smile more often.

"You don't smile a lot, do you?"

He leaned his elbows onto the table, one eyebrow arched at me.

"That's what you think of me? That I don't smile a lot?"

"Honestly? Yes. I won't be surprised if your middle name is Ice. But to be fair, when you listen to music your face does get softer. You like music." It wasn't a question.

"I do, yeah," he agreed. "And sorry to disappoint you, but my middle name is Kevin," he said, quirking a corner of his mouth. Mine did the same.

"Not disappointed at all. Do you play an instrument?" He drew his elbows from the table and rested his forearms on the arms of the chair, relaxing in his seat.

"Guitar. I taught myself and since then I've been playing occasionally, mostly to myself."

"Did you teach yourself how to fight, too?" Curious, I had to ask.

"No."

"How long have you trained? Who taught you?" He didn't seem willing to elaborate, so he gave another terse answer. "I started my training in Kung Fu when I was five. My master taught me till I was seventeen." His face hardened and darkened, and I felt guilty for forcing him to revisit the past. Seventeen. That had been his age when his family had been murdered.

"What about you? Why not date the guy you actually want?" He changed the subject and had me blinking at him in surprise.

He couldn't be talking about Justin, right? "Who are you talking about?" I took a napkin from the pile near me and fiddled with it.

"C'mon, we both know who I'm referring to." Yep, he was talking about Justin. How in the world did he know about my crush on Justin? "I'm not blind. I saw the way you looked at that guy yesterday," he said at my expression.

"Okay, I like him. He's not, however, interested." I wasn't blind either. To not sound bitter, I added, "But that's fine. I'm okay with it."

"If you feel like you need to sell this BS to yourself, be my guest, but save your energy when it comes to me."

I uttered a sigh. "Well, even if it bothered me, I can't do anything about it."

"You always give up so easily?"

"What am I—" I broke off. Two guys and a girl passed us to get to a table near the window. I continued, lowering my voice, "What am I supposed to do? Force him at gunpoint to date me?"

He rolled his eyes. "He's a guy, not a complicated science project. Figure him out, then change his mind about you, but personally, that guy doesn't seem worth the trouble."

I put the napkin I'd managed to ruin back on the table. "First of all, his name is Justin. Second, why do you think he isn't worth the trouble? You don't even know him."

"And you do?" He shifted in his chair, seeking a more comfortable position, and the muscles across his chest, under a tight, black shirt, bunched and rippled with the movement.

My eyes darted up to his face. "Yes. He's charming, funny, kind, and sweet. Definitely worth the trouble."

"Correct me if I'm wrong, but shouldn't a person who does nothing to assist his friend, who is being dissed, be considered a jerk rather than charming, funny, kind, and sweet?"

I gnawed at my lower lip. He had a valid point, but I still wracked my brain to find something to say in Justin's defense. Thankfully, with perfect timing, Mark arrived with our orders and set them on the table. When he was gone, I put the straw to my mouth and gulped. My taste buds instantly recognized the strawberry flavor, jumping and bouncing in excitement.

"Maybe he had a good reason," I finally said.

"Yeah, being a jerk, but I wouldn't call it a good one."
Wow, he'd made up his mind about Justin pretty fast.

"Is it a regular thing for you to form an opinion about people based only on one incident?"

He took a sip of his coffee and put the cup back down, looking at me. "No, but in this case, my estimation of him was mainly derived from you."

"From me?" I gave him a puzzled look.

"You know him better than I do, right?" I nodded, drinking from the straw, enjoying the taste. "Then it's only rational that I'd interpret the fact that you're unable to correct me about him being a jerk as a stronger confirmation than mine that the guy is indeed a jerk," he said smoothly and tipped the glass up to his lips.

While he drank, I couldn't help but think I might have been wrong about Justin. Ryan was right. I'd known Justin for over a year, and yet I had nothing to say in his defense. If he was all the things I'd claimed him to be, wouldn't it be easy to find something to prove Ryan wrong? I turned my stare to him, and my eyes fixed themselves on his sensual lips as he put a forkful of apple pie in his mouth. For a moment, I mused about how they would feel against mine, and I almost choked on a piece of strawberry.

Oh my God! Did I really just think that? I subtly shook my head in shock and quickly looked up at his eyes, which were lit with humor. Great, he'd caught me ogling him. He sliced another piece of pie with his fork, but instead of raising the forkful of apple pie to his lips, he brought it to mine.

"Here, taste this. It's delicious." Fully aware of where this fork had been a few seconds ago, I opened my mouth. The taste of cinnamon, caramel, and apple exploded on my tongue. I chewed in delight, eyes closed, and a sound of pleasure hummed in my throat.

"Enjoying yourself?" There was playfulness in his voice, but there was also something else. Was it a sexual innuendo?

"It's very tasty."

"Want some more?" The way he said it made me think we weren't talking about pie anymore.

"Um...no, thanks. I reached my sugar limit for today." And the maximum temperature to which my cheeks can go before burning me alive.

"That's too bad. Well, maybe another day when you're willing to stretch your limit."

He cut another piece of the pie, stuck the fork in his mouth, slowly slid it between his lips, and finished his thought. "And let yourself accept the rest of what I think you should taste."

Heat exploded over my face, and my saliva went down the wrong pipe, making me choke and cough. Breathing again, I blurted hastily, "The Red milkshake is good, too."

"And it also matches the color in your cheeks." Humor flickered in his eyes, and the right corner of his mouth teased up. Then he drained the last of his coffee.

"It's probably the cold," I lied, rubbing my cheeks with my palms.

"Sure it is," he said, but the amusement vanished from his face when four teenage girls gaped at him as they trod past us and sat at a table behind me.

"I told you it's him. It's Ryan Damon," one of them whispered not so discreetly.

"Oh my God, it *is* him," her friends agreed, and they giggled with glee.

Ryan tensed, and his eyes skittered to my empty glass before looking back at me.

"We good to go?" His face was set in a grim mask.

I nodded, and he motioned for our waiter to bring the check. We got it a minute later. I bent to pull my purse out of my bag. By the time I straightened, Ryan had paid the check and left a generous tip, and he was already on his feet. "My treat, c'mon," he said, not glancing once in the titters' direction.

As soon as we got in the car, his tension drained off, and some of the sternness left his face. For some bizarre reason, I wanted it to leave completely and to bring his smile back. Achieving it was actually easy, and by the time we reached my dorm, he was in a good mood again.

"Thanks for the milkshake," I said as I opened the door, ready to get out.

"Emma." I turned to look at him, and his lips shaped into a small smile. "It was my pleasure."

I grinned at him and hopped out.

The next day, Hannah waited with me at the bus stop. The main topic of our conversation was Dylan. She insisted that I meet him. "I'm free this Friday," I told her.

"So, this Friday. It's settled then. You, me, and Dylan at the Blue club." Satisfaction filled her features, and her lips went up in a curve.

My bus pulled up. "It's settled," I confirmed and got on it.

Four and a half hours later, Ryan walked into his apartment, holding a bag of takeout, just as I was about to leave. He set the bag on the dining room table and looked back over at me. "Hope you like Italian."

"Yes, but—"

"Great." He pulled the food out and placed it on the table, then grabbed some silverware from the kitchen. The smell of fresh pasta, garlic, and basil reached my nostrils, and every protest I had vanished, luckily, since it turned out to be the best pasta I'd ever had.

"Wow, it's really good," I said for the third time.

"Yeah, they have real Italian food. I love this restaurant."

"Hannah, my friend, is crazy about Italian food. She wants me to meet her boyfriend this Friday night at the Blue club, but maybe I'll be able to persuade her to go there instead."

He took another bite. "What's wrong with the Blue club? It's a great place for alcohol and dancing."

"It might be, but I don't dance, and drinking isn't really my thing." I filled my fork with the last bite of pasta.

"Don't dance? How come?"

I shrugged. "Me dancing is not a pretty sight."

"Right." A glimmer of humor shone in his eyes, and I realized he'd already watched me dance—that silly, joyful dance after seeing my linear algebra grade.

"Okay then, that's gonna change," he announced and put his fork down on his empty plate.

"What? No, no, no, no it doesn't have to change."

He stood and went to the sound system in the living room. When he returned to the dining table, slow music was playing. "No, no, no." I shook my head vigorously. "I really don't know how to dance."

"Then it's a good thing this isn't an audition." He held out his hand. With a sigh, I took it. My skin tingled at his touch, and I tried to ignore the sensation as he guided me to the living room. He'd already moved the coffee table aside, creating more room.

"Take off your shoes."

Huh? "Why?"

"You'll see in a minute."

I slid my shoes off. The floor under my socks was cold.

"Your socks, too." Not objecting, I took them off and stuffed them in my sneakers.

"What about you?" My gaze dropped to his black, heavy boots.

"I'm not the one who needs to learn how to dance." His lips quirked, bringing out his dimples. God, he oozed sexiness. The slow song was over and a fast one came on when I went to stand in front of him. "Now, I want you to do something for me." His voice was mild.

"Okay, what?"

"Close your eyes." I did as he asked. I was surrounded by darkness, while the music engulfed me. "Breathe in and out slowly, and just listen to the music. *Feel* it." I breathed deeply and focused on the vibrations from the music as they ran through the floor and up through my body, pulsing in my veins, touching my bare foot. Now I understood why he'd wanted me to take off my shoe. I let the rhythm guide me as I started to move. "Yeah, good. Move your body. Now open your eyes." They flew open, and I saw that he was dancing with me, close. His body moved to the pounding beat of the music. Next to him, I looked awkward and clumsy.

"No, no, no, don't stop. Keep dancing," he said and scooted closer, putting his hand on my waist. My heart fluttered. "Here, move your body with mine." His palm molded to my hip, directing me. "No, don't try to match your movements to mine. Let me match yours. You just listen to the music, to the rhythm. Move to it." I did as he instructed. "Yeah, good, exactly like that." He removed his hand from me. We danced through song after song until a slow one started. Hands on my waist, hunching over, I breathed heavily as if I'd just run a marathon. "You did great, a natural dancer," he said. My breathing finally evened out. "Now, I want you to do one more thing for me. Can you do that?" I nodded. "Good. The trust you have in me, I nee—"

"Trust?" I cut him off, stiffening. Trust was not something that came easily for me. It had taken me a long time to believe that Hannah didn't have ulterior motives for being nice to me. "I never said I trusted you."

He edged closer to me, closing the gap between us, and all the muscles in my body tightened at once. "Close your eyes again," he cooed, and I complied. In the darkness, I could feel the heat radiating off his body and caressing me. "You didn't have to say it. Emma, it's the second time I've asked you to close your eyes. You never hesitated. You left yourself vulnerable to me. You do trust that I won't hurt you, and I want you to focus on that now." I gasped as I felt his hand wind through my hair. A quick tug, and my hair tumbled over my shoulders.

I jerked my eyes open. "Emma, it's just you and me here, nobody else. Don't be afraid." His words didn't abate the fear that spread through me. "Tell me what scares you." The music stopped, and the room was soundless. I went to sit on the sofa. He joined me. Oddly, his proximity toned down my anxiety and fear. "Whatever it is, it can't hurt you here," he said gently. I raised my head and looked at him. To talk about what had happened was difficult for me, but something in his nearness helped me, and I was ready to speak about them—to him.

"In junior year, two of my classmates, Heather and Kate, who had constantly bullied me, decided one day that my hair must always be pulled up in a ponytail. They warned me that if I didn't do it, they would shave my head bald. I believed them, so I was terrified to slip up and forget to tie my hair back.

"One day, some boy pulled out my hair tie. I begged him to give it back, but he wouldn't. Later, I found out that Kate and Heather had asked him to do it. It was all a game to them. When they saw me in the hallway, they dragged me to the bathroom, shoved me into one of the stalls, and they..." I couldn't continue. My mind conjured up the painful memory of how they had forced me down to my knees and started to shave my head. It brought up the sound of their laughter mixed with my cries and screams. I shook my head to banish the echoes of those sounds from my mind.

"Did they get punished?" he asked.

"No, I lied to everyone and told them that I'd done it to myself."

"And they believed you?" I detected a note of anger in his voice.

"They didn't have a choice. I wouldn't talk about it, not with anyone"—not even with Dr. Miller—"and wore a hat until my hair grew back." Silence fell over the room until I broke it. "Anyway, even though it's not rational, I feel no fear when my hair is pulled up."

"You don't look scared now," he said, and I jerked slightly when he picked up a strand of my hair and slowly ran it through his fingers. Our eyes locked. One minute of quiet passed, then two, then three. Then a ring of his cell phone disturbed the silence.

"I-I-I should get going." I was on my feet before he could say a word. I pulled on my socks and shoes and grabbed my backpack from the dining room while he answered the phone.

"Hold on a sec," he said to whomever was on the other end of the line when I was at the front door. "Emma."

I glanced back over my shoulder.

"See you tomorrow."

"See you tomorrow," I echoed and stepped out.

Chapter 13

Thursday began as a quiet day at work. I put in my four hours of coding and was getting ready to leave when I heard the front door open, and the voices that soon filled the apartment. As far as I could tell, they belonged to Ryan, Nate, two females, and a guy Nate referred to as Tye. I printed out the report, organized the desk, took the two sheets of paper from the printer, and went out to the living room. Nate and Tye, I presumed, were slumped on the sofa in front of the TV. Kirsten, the topless girl I'd found straddling Ryan in the guest room, was seated next to Tye and beside...oh God, Mia, my mean neighbor from across the hall. There was no sign of Ryan anywhere.

"What's that freak doing here?" Mia gave me a look of disgust and turned back to Kirsten, who regarded me with the same revulsion.

"Oh her, yeah, she's a total freak. I think Ryan hired her. I'm not sure." She swung her gaze to me. "Remind me what exactly you are doing here?"

I moved my eyes from her to Mia and gave her a sardonic smile. "I've got a name. It's Emma. E-M-M-A, Emma. You might have noticed that I spelled it slowly. That's because I figured you probably have difficulties in the spelling department since I don't recall you ever using my name correctly, but hey, no need to be ashamed. We're all friends here. Just repeat my name every morning and evening until you're finally able to say it right, and if you need me to spell it out for you even slower, ask and I'll do it.

"You know me. I'm always happy to help a friend with...special needs." I shifted my gaze from Mia's dumbfounded expression to Kirsten. "What am I doing here? I come here to get paid for a service I provide, which is to write a website. You know, almost like what you do when you come here, except for the writing code part. Oh, and I didn't get the chance to apologize for walking in on you while you were...well, working, so I'm sorry. Won't happen again."

Nate and Tye chuckled lightly, and a silvery laughter emanated from behind me. I spun. Ryan stood at the bottom of the steps to the second floor. There was a look of...pride on his face. Kirsten complained to my back, sounding outraged. "If you're implying that I'm a whore, I—"

"I believe she didn't imply anything, sweetheart," Ryan said, walking toward me.

"The report," I said and proffered the sheets of paper to him.

He glanced at them, and I turned to the door and, not missing the angry look Kirsten shot Ryan, swept out of the apartment.

At the dorm, thoughts of Ryan occupied my mind. I couldn't understand why he'd want to spend his time with Kirsten. Ashley, I understood. She was beautiful, smart, and nice, but Kirsten? She was stunning, yes, but she wasn't as nice or smart. How could she be? She was socializing with Mia.

The next day, noises from the residents outside my room woke me up, and then kept me from getting back to sleep. After staying up all night reading the new fantasy novel I'd bought yesterday, I was bone-tired. Heaving a frustrating sigh, I dragged myself out of bed. After I brushed my teeth and got dressed, I checked my missed calls. Surprise twisted my face when the caller ID popped up on the display—Ryan.

Why had he called me at eleven-thirty last night? It couldn't be work related, and hadn't he been with Kirsten at that time? Ugh, her name irked me, and what I did next caused me to smack my hand against my forehead. *What have you done? Are you insane?* I glanced down at my cell phone in my hand, reading the text I'd just sent him: *Is there a good reason why you called me last night at eleven-thirty?*

Or were you bored with Kirsten and looking for someone to grouse to about it?

Just as I was about to hit my forehead with my palm for the second time, I remembered that he never checked his texts. That was what he'd claimed. I exhaled a breath of relief, but it was cut off when my phone vibrated. I glanced heavenward. *Please, please, please let it be Hannah.* Then my gaze crept down to my cell phone. "One new message from Ryan Damon." I grimaced. Great. Just great. I slid the text open.

Ryan: So, you're pissed off about the hour or about Kirsten? ;)

What! Was he suggesting that I was jealous? "I'm not angry!" I tapped out but quickly deleted the message; the exclamation point didn't exactly convey the idea that I wasn't aggravated. I typed out a new message: *Didn't you mention once that you never check your texts?* And I hit send. The display lit up again a few seconds later.

Ryan: Why? U were counting on that? :)

I puffed an errant wisp of hair from my eyes with a sigh, and then read the next message.

Ryan: As much as I'd love to continue this, I've got something to take care of here. C u later.

See me later? It was Friday, my day off for this week. When exactly did he plan on seeing me later? He'd probably mixed up the days.

At ten p.m., Hannah picked me up outside my dorm. Dressed in a black, short dress, red sandals, and my hair pulled up in a ponytail, I slipped into the passenger seat of her sedan.

"Wow, check you out, girl. You're hot," she complimented me, and I blushed.

"Thanks, Hannah. You look great, too." And she did, wearing a blue skirt, black top, and her chocolate-brown hair down. She gave me a thank-you grin and pulled out of the parking space. When we arrived at the Blue club, Hannah introduced me to Dylan, and we waited in line to get in.

Inside the crowded club, we settled in a booth tucked away at the back of the room. The not so loud volume of the music and our booth's location enabled us to have conversations without the need of straining our voices over the noise.

Dylan was everything I'd expected him to be: handsome, arrogant, and disrespectful. And I was almost certain he was also a womanizer. She had a thing for that kind of guy. They always treated her badly, and Dylan was no different. For the next three hours, his gaze wandered to every girl in the club. Even when Hannah, sitting next to me, leaned over the table to kiss him, his eyes were on the female server that brought our next round of drinks.

"Wanna dance?" a male voice said to Hannah.

Good, let's see if Dylan shows at least a bit of jealousy. I carefully inspected him, anticipating his response. Of course, instead of telling the guy she's taken, he did nothing. I felt so bad for Hannah that I was about to say something to him, but she spoke first.

"Sweetie, I think he's waiting for an answer," Hannah said, amused.

"What? Who?" I looked at her, my forehead crumpled in confusion.

She looked up past my shoulder and smiled. "She'd love to," she told the guy standing behind me, and then she turned to me. "Go ahead, dance with him."

Dance with him? Wait. He was asking me? Still perplexed, I turned and gazed up at him. "Yes, uh, sure," I said and was rewarded with a bright grin. I rose to my feet, and we went to the dance floor full of twisting bodies as colorful lights swirled around them. My dance partner was of average height and medium build, pleasant, with an elongated face and a crew-cut hairstyle. His dance moves weren't nearly as sexy as Ryan's, but he was quite a good dancer. We were dancing to the music pumping on the dance floor when I registered Ryan sitting on a high stool at the edge of the bar. At the seat next to him, a raven-haired girl leaned toward him, her body language openly flirting with him.

"You okay?" my dance partner asked above the music.

"Yes, I am." I dragged my stare back to his, but then quickly glanced at Ryan again.

At that moment, Ryan slid his gaze over to where I was as if he had already known I was there.

"I'm Kyle, you?" He danced closer to me.

I moved my head back to Kyle and backed up a bit from him as I continued dancing.

"I'm..." I looked back toward the edge of the bar. The girl was still there, but Ryan was gone.

"Let's try this again. I'm Kyle, you?" I returned my eyes to Kyle.

"I'm Emma," I answered.

"I've always had a weakness for that name." He closed the distance between us again and settled a palm on my waist. It remained there for a split second before my body was swirled around so fast that his touch was torn from me. Two hands steadied me, and they weren't Kyle's. "Yo, man, we were dancing," Kyle protested behind me.

"Exactly. Past tense. Glad we're on the same page here." Recognizing Ryan's voice, my head snapped up. He wore a subtle smile, but his expression let Kyle know that he really didn't want to find himself on a different page. Apparently, it was enough to drive him off because now Ryan looked down at me, and his body began to move to the throbbing beat of the music, but I stayed immobile. "C'mon, move your ass like I know you can."

"Ryan, what are you doing?" I asked.

"Trying to dance with you."

"No, I mean, wh—" He drew me in close to him. His hands set off a million tiny explosions throughout me, and all of the questions in my head disappeared. My body, shamelessly craving his touch, started to move with him. We danced for a couple of songs, and then he grabbed my hand. "Let's get out of here."

"I can't. I'm here with a friend, Hannah," I said as he led me through the maze of wiggling bodies.

"I know," he replied and walked us right to my table.

Eyes popping, Hannah's gaze locked on our linked hands. "Hey, I'm Ryan," he introduced himself to Hannah, who still looked shocked. "You wouldn't mind if I steal her away, right?"

Dylan nudged her, and she moved her stare from our hands to Ryan's face. "Huh?"

"No, by all means, she doesn't mind," Dylan answered for her, and she finally snapped out of her shock.

"Oh! No, no, go ahead." Her eyes slipped from Ryan, taking my jacket off my seat, to me. The message written on her face said, *You've got a lot of explaining to do.* My look told her, *It's not as it seems.*

Outside the club, the sight of his sleek, black BMW in the parking lot stopped me.

"Why didn't you ride your bike? And how did you know where I was sitting? And where are you taking me? Wh—"

His steps faltered. "You don't regard bikes as a safe mode of transportation," he said, his slightly mocking tone suggesting he knew I'd lied about that, "and I saw you when you arrived. As for your last question, that's a surprise. Now, let's go." I followed him to the car and opened the door. A brand-new, white coat was settled across the passenger seat. I carefully moved it to the backseat, where it joined a pair of new women's boots and socks, slid inside, and closed the car door.

"You might want to put it on before we get there," Ryan said.

"It's for me?" My brows drew together.

"That, the boots, and the socks. If I guessed your size correctly, they should fit."

"What's wrong with what I'm wearing now?"

"Nothing, but it's cold where we're going."

He started the engine, and I glanced at the backseat. The warm-looking coat and the boots were high-end. If I damaged them, he couldn't return them, and there was no way I could afford that coat and boots. "Thanks, but I'll take my chances with my jacket and sandals."

He shrugged. "Suit yourself."

The ride took about forty minutes. We pulled up in front of a big house in a remote, rural area. When he opened his car door, a surge of freezing, cold air blasted in. I zipped up my jacket and unfolded myself from the car. Oh. My. God. If I were stripped naked and tossed into the water of the Antarctic Ocean, I'd probably be warmer than what I was right now. My teeth chattered uncontrollably, and my feet were numbed by the cold. I jumped back into the car and snatched up the coat, socks, and boots. Yep, not my finest moment. After switching from my jacket and sandals to what he had bought, I stepped out of the car, and the only thing I painfully needed right now was my pride. Hearing a soft chuckle, I grudgingly slid my gaze across the hood of the car and looked over at him.

"Okay, okay, you were right. Happy?"

A puff of laughter escaped him. "Oh, you have no idea. We've got some walking to do. Prepare yourself." This time, I did listen, and I readied myself for the twenty minutes of hiking through the woods behind the house we'd parked in front of.

"Who lives there?" I asked as an isolated cabin came into view.

"It belongs to my grandparents. That and the house where the car's parked. They're currently vacationing in Europe." We walked up to the cabin, and he unlocked the wooden front door. A cozy living room with rustic furniture welcomed me. "My mother grew up here. She loved this place," he said as we crossed the room. He led me to the back exit of the cabin, and we were outside again. Not far up ahead stood a dome-shaped glass house. We stepped up to it and got in.

"Wow," I whispered, taking in my surroundings. I was inside an enchanting flower garden. All kinds of flowers perfumed the dome with various smells, but the scent of roses overpowered them all. A waterfall produced a relaxing sound of falling water, and a beautiful angel statue was situated in the middle of the small waterfall pool. Two benches faced it. The glass ceiling of the dome had a clear view of the night sky and the stars twinkling in it. I looked back at the waterfall. "It's amazing," I said, watching the stream of water falling into the pool.

"My mother loved this place. She used to bring me here a lot when I was younger."

I turned around. He was seated on one of the benches opposite the waterfall pool. His elbows rested on his knees as he held a red rose in his hand. I headed for the bench he was on. The temperature here was comfortable, so I shrugged off the coat and laid it next to his jacket across the bench, then sat beside him. He straightened and set the rose between us.

"Red roses are such beautiful flowers. I love them," I said, staring down at it.

"They are," he acceded. Taking my eyes off the rose, I glanced around.

"The dome is breathtaking with all the colorful flowers in here."

"It has the same structure as one of the glass houses in Nunobiki Herb Gardens in Japan. My grandparents love the gardens there. Speaking of colors"—his eyes went to my hair tie—"where do you find these hideous hair ties?" he teased, amusement in his tone.

"Hey! They are not hideous." I was about to playfully smack him, but in a blink, he intercepted my hand before it could even near his shoulder. God, he had an incredibly fast reflex.

"Don't, not with your hand angled like this. Your wrist is delicate, and you can easily harm it hitting something this way." He adjusted the position of my palm so that the back of it faced his shoulder. "Do it only like this, and if you really want to cause pain, the shoulder is not the preferable target."

"I didn't mean to cause any real pain."

"I know, but it doesn't matter. You need to learn this stuff. Have you ever taken a self-defense class?"

"No, I don't have time."

He let go of my hand. "Find the time. It's important. The path from the university to your dorm passes by any number of frat houses. It's not safe for you to walk by yourself late at night like you did that night I saw you when those douches attacked." He rose from the bench and strode to the middle of the open space between the waterfall pool and the bench. He turned around and beckoned me over with a jerk of his head.

"Come over here. I'm gonna teach you a few practical self-defense moves." He would? That would be so useful. I pushed to my feet and went to stand in front of him.

"Okay, let's say that I'm the attacker," he said and brought his fingers toward my throat. I sucked in air, jolted backward as a scared cat recoiling from human touch, and my hand jammed protectively to my neck. I quaked, and my breathing became erratic. It took me a few seconds to regain control over my body and to realize he was watching me carefully.

A breath of awkward laughter escaped me as I looked at him. "Um...so where were we?" I asked, embarrassed.

"Who was it?" he asked, ignoring my attempt to act like nothing had happened. He took one step forward; I, two steps backward. The fear inside me drove me crazy. Why did it make me behave like an insane person? He held his hands up, assuring me he wouldn't come any closer.

"I'm sorry. I don't know what came over me. It's silly." I nibbled at my bottom lip.

"Emma, silly is when you insist on wearing a thin jacket and sandals even though I'm telling you it'll be cold. When someone, however, makes you act the way you just did, that's not silly, that's serious. Was it Kate and Heather?"

"Yes."

"They used to strangle you?" His voice was tinged with fury.

"From the beginning of freshmen year, yes." His expression asked me to explain, so I did. "They forced me to help them study, so every time they failed a test, they dragged me to the bathroom school and punished me by grabbing me by the throat and...strangling me. Just before I lost consciousness, they always released me. I fought back every single time, but they were so much stronger." My vision blurred as tears pricked my eyes. I blinked them away and turned my head aside, wiping my cheeks, but the tears just kept coming no matter how hard I willed them to stop.

I heard light footsteps and then felt the touch of his fingers under my chin. He moved my head to look up at him and brushed his thumb over my tears. After a while, they finally stopped flowing, yet he didn't pull back or drop his hand from me. He stared down into my eyes, and for a fraction of a second, I had the oddest feeling that he was about to kiss me. When he didn't, a twinge of regret shot through me. *What's wrong with me? He's the last person I should have those kinds of feelings for.* I stepped back, disengaging myself from his touch. He remained in his place, and when he spoke, his voice was soft.

"Show me how they grabbed your throat."

What? "Why?"

"Because I wanna know exactly how they did it."

"They used the hand that you—"

"No. *Show* me."

I took his hand and guided it toward my neck. Halfway there, I paused, hesitant. I slowly dragged air into my lungs and let it out, then watched my fingers curl around his unmoving forearm, which lulled me into the feeling that I had control over his arm, and I finally brought his palm to my throat.

"Like this," I said, my voice trembling.

He pulled his hand from me and a sense of relief washed over my body.

"Do it again." Was he serious?

"Why?"

"Because I asked nicely." A hint of a smile was on his lips. "Now, do it once more."

I did—five more times.

"Why do we keep doing this?" I grumbled before doing it for the sixth time. In reply, he swiftly moved his hand to my neck, his fingers around my throat.

"How do you feel?" he asked.

"Confused, what is—" Understanding dawned on me. I wasn't scared anymore.

"Now I can work with you on how you can defend yourself against it."

Step by step he taught me how to protect myself against this kind of attack, and after some practice, I was successfully able to block his hand from my neck. "Yes! I did it!" I bounced with excitement.

"Yes, you did." He grinned, and then walked me through some basic self-defense principles. After I mastered the moves, he glanced down at his watch and sauntered to the entrance of the greenhouse. There, he withdrew a rolled-up, gray blanket from a bag near the door, whipped the lights off, and walked back to where I was. He unfurled the blanket on the floor and settled on it. He gazed up at me and patted the spot next to him.

I sat beside him and he lay down, long legs stretched out and crossed at the ankles, arms folded under his head. I leaned down on the blanket too, legs bent at the knees, hands resting across my stomach, fingers clasped together.

I turned my head to look at him. He was staring up at the glass-domed ceiling. "There is something I want to show you," he said.

"Show me what?" I asked, and I went back to looking up at the night sky.

"Wait and see." The moon spilled soft light through the dome and the sound of dripping water lulled me. My eyelids grew heavier until darkness engulfed me. The next thing I knew, a deep, velvet voice said, "Wake up, sleepyhead." Was that voice part of a dream? Probably. I yawned and opened my eyes, expecting to see my dorm room, not a gorgeous face smiling at me. Ryan! My eyes got huge. Oh, God, I fell asleep! I sat bolt upright. "Easy, there." His hand on my body gently pushed me back down. I rubbed my face and moved my head to look at him lying beside me. He was in almost the same position as before, but his crossed hands were now on his flat stomach.

"I'm sorry. I can't believe I fell asleep. How long was I out?"

"An hour or so, but it's okay. I could handle your snoring." His lips curved into a playful smile.

I gasped audibly. "Hey, I don't snore." Was I snoring? No, he was joking, right?

He laughed. "Kidding. You sleep soundlessly and peacefully, not even drooling." His stare swung to me, and I suddenly noticed that the glass house was dimly lit and not with moonlight. I tipped my nose skyward and was amazed by the view. The sky, clear of clouds, was magnificent. It was painted in pink and orange like watercolor, nature at its best.

"It's...wow..." Fascinated, I watched the beautiful sunrise.

"I know. That's why I wanted to show it to you," he said. When the sun rose fully in the sky, bringing a new day, he shoved to his feet and extended his hand to me. "It's time to get you back to your dorm."

I let him pull me to my feet, and I grabbed the coat from the bench. Back in his comfortable and warm BMW, I succumbed to the tiredness again and slept the entire ride. I woke up to Ryan's sexy voice once more. Yawning and stretching, I glanced through the window. We were in the parking lot behind my building. I began to take off the coat, but he stopped me.

"No, keep it and the boots. They're yours."

"Thanks, but I can't afford them."

"Just accept them as a gift, okay?"

Before I could argue, he opened his door and stepped out of the car. I sighed and climbed out into the chilly morning air. He rounded his BMW and stood in front of me, taking my jacket and sandals from my hands. I rubbed my hands together, warming my fingers with my breath, then started to protest.

"I can't—"

"You can and you will." His tone conveyed that arguing with him further would be useless. Too tired, I gave up.

"Okay. Thank you."

The dorm was relatively quiet, most of the residents still asleep. Reaching the door to my room, I thanked him again. Before stepping inside, I said goodbye, and he handed me my stuff back, wishing me a good sleep before he walked off. I closed the door and set my sandals and jacket on the desk chair. I was sliding off the coat when something fell out of the pocket. I looked down near my feet. A red rose lay on the floor. I picked it up and brought it to my nose, inhaling its sweet scent. I broke into a wide smile. It was nice of him to sneak the flower into the coat pocket, probably when I'd slept in the car. I loved red roses, as I'd told him in the greenhouse. Maybe being friends with him wasn't such a bad idea, after all.

Chapter 14

My cell phone's ring jarred me into wakefulness. Squinting my eyes, I scrambled out of bed, wobbled to the desk, and answered my phone. "Hey, Hannah," I rasped.

"Don't hey me. What the hell was last night? You forgot to tell me something?"

"Morning to you too." I went back to the bed, plopping on it.

"Morning? It's five o'clock, and the fifth time I've called you." What? I'd been sleeping for over nine hours? "I'm waiting. What's going on with you and Ryan?"

"There is nothing going on between us. He's my boss, and we decided to become friends. That's all."

"Friends my ass." She snorted. "Em, he held your hand," she said slowly, emphasizing each word. "Ryan's not the holding-hands type of guy. He's the I-never-do-dates type of guy."

I rolled my eyes at the absurdity of the notion. There was nothing between us, other than the annoying reaction of my body whenever he was near me, which was understandable seeing that he was gorgeous. "He also goes for a certain type of girl, and you and I both know I'm not it." I was far from it. Silence filled the line.

"So you two are really just friends?" she finally said.

"Of course we're *just* friends."

"You're right. I might have jumped to conclusions." Finally, she saw reason.

I heard a whispering male voice in the background and then the unmistakable sound of a kiss. So she was with Dylan. I had to tell her that he wasn't good for her, but clearly this was not the best time.

"Em, I gotta go. Dylan's here and his friends are coming over, so we'll talk later."

"Okay, but, Hannah, when you've got time, we need to talk. It's about Dylan." No response. "Hannah?" Still nothing. Great. She'd already hung up, or maybe Dylan had done it for her, the jerk.

For the next five hours, I cleaned up my room, showered, and studied. At ten o'clock, there was a knock on the door. I looked at it in confusion. Hannah was with Dylan, and nobody else came around here. I opened the door, and my eyes widened. "Ryan? What are you doing here?" My eyes skimmed him from top to bottom, and I almost forgot to breathe. He, being beyond gorgeous, was wearing a battered, leather jacket over a tight shirt, and black jeans.

"Aren't you gonna invite me in?" By his amused tone and expression, I realized that I was bluntly staring. Well, it shouldn't surprise him. I couldn't be the only girl who had stared at him like that. Walking down the hallway toward my room, he probably had—wait.

"How did you get in without an ID card?" Had someone swiped him into the building? But of course someone had. There was a considerable number of girls in my dorm.

"I have my ways." He grinned, flashing dimples as he invited himself in, stepping past me.

"Yes, please do make yourself at home," I muttered sarcastically and inhaled the fragrance of sandalwood and jasmine he'd left behind him. I closed the door.

"You didn't answer me. What are you doing here?"

He fell onto my bed. "Waiting for you to get dressed." An idle smile drifted along his lips.

"What? What for?"

"For a house party."

"I'm not going to a house party. I'm sorry you bothered yourself coming all the way over here, but if you had *called* before, I would've saved you the trouble."

"If I'd done so, I would've lost the advantage of convincing you in person, which is always a better approach."

I went to sit in the desk chair. "Ryan, I'm not going with you. I won't even know anybody there. I'd feel out of place."

"You know me, and you'll meet new people. And anyway, I won't leave you alone. I promise." His bright, blue eyes shone with persistence.

"You won't take no for an answer, will you?"

"What do you think?"

I released a breath. "Okay, I'll get changed."

I grabbed a dress from my closet, and he turned around while I put it on. "You can look now."

He pivoted around. Eyes sweeping over me, lips hitching up, he said, "It's perfect."

As I slipped on the sandals I'd worn yesterday, I made a mental note to go shoe shopping. In front of the mirror, I tugged out the hair tie and my straight, light brown hair fell in a curtain down past my shoulders. I wasn't afraid. Kate and Heather couldn't hurt me. Not anymore.

"I'm ready," I told him, turning from the mirror to face him. Satisfied, he stepped to me, taking a strand of my hair and threading it through his fingers. My heartbeat grew faster.

"You look lovely." His breath caressed my skin, and the muscles in my lower stomach clenched.

"Thanks," I responded, and then we left the room.

Outside the house where the party was, a short line to get in stopped us on the porch steps, but not for long. One of the guys guarding the front door called out to Ryan, and we climbed up the steps and walked past the line.

"Ryannnnnn, my man, what's up?"

Ryan nodded an acknowledgement, and the guy opened the door, motioning us inside. The living room was filled with partygoers. Some were dancing to pop music, others were busy talking, and a few were in the middle of a make-out session near the stairs to the second floor. Close to the presumed kitchen, there was a long table filled with alcohol. Like I'd predicted, I didn't know anybody, so Ryan had found himself introducing me to a lot of people, and all the talking with them had me thirsty.

"Be right back." Ryan crossed the living room and disappeared into the kitchen to get me a glass of water.

"Emma? Is that you?" a male voice asked over the music. I turned my head to my right.

"Justin?" I said, looking at him. At about five feet seven, he was a bit taller than me.

His eyes traveled slowly down my body and back up to my lips, nose, and eyes. "Wow, Emma, you look...your hair...wow, you look great."

"Thanks." My lips stretched into a slim smile. Strangely, for over a year, I yearned to get his attention, and now that I had it, I wasn't even a bit stoked.

"You're here with Hannah and Kayla?" He glanced around, like he expected to see them somewhere in the room.

"Uh, no, I'm…" The rest of the words escaped my mind when I detected Ryan across the room, a small bottle of water in his hand. He had been stopped by a tall, beautiful girl in a skintight dress that hit her mid-thigh, and black, strappy high heels. Even with the dancing people in the center of the room, I could see how close she was standing to him, talking and giggling.

"Emma?" Justin said.

I snapped my head back to him. He was looking over at where I had been gazing a second ago.

"Yes, um, I...sorry, what was the question again?" I asked.

"You came here with Hannah and Kayla?" He turned his head back to me, bringing his red cup to his mouth.

"No, I'm here with Ryan."

"Ryan?" His face screwed up in surprise. "Ryan who?"

"Ryan Damon, Ashley's friend. You know him, right?"

He blinked. "Let me get this straight. You're here with...Ryan Damon?"

His expression said he thought I'd had a little too much to drink and lost contact with reality, so I explained, "I'm working for him on a project. We're just friends."

He rolled his eyes at my words. "Just friends? Emma, don't be naive. He doesn't have female friends and, no offense, you look great and all, but that hot chick"—he nodded in the direction of Ryan and the girl speaking to him—"over there, talking to him, is more his type." I turned to look over at them again. Raking his gaze over Justin and me, Ryan's attention seemed to be fixed on us rather than whatever she was saying. I swiftly averted my face, and my eyes were back on Justin.

"You're right, which is why in my case he is only a friend." And like Hannah before him, after processing it, he concurred and took another drink from his cup.

"This party's dead. I'm zoning out here. Wanna take off and grab some ice cream down the street?" he asked and chugged his drink. I'd dreamed of the day Justin would offer me something like this, so why in the world was I hesitating? But I didn't have to come up with an excuse not to go, because Ryan chose that moment to wedge himself between us like it was the most natural thing in the world. He wrapped an arm over Justin's shoulder. What was he doing?

"It's Justin, right?" Ryan's lips formed a smile. Bewilderment covered Justin's face as he leaned slightly forward to give me a "what's going on?" look. I shrugged helplessly at him.

Eyes on Justin, Ryan said, "Oh, I'm sorry. Am I interrupting something here?"

"Actually, yes. I was just asking Emma for an ice cream down the street and we—"

"Really? Damn, what a coincidence. Did you hear that, Casey?" Ryan cast his gaze to the left. I followed his stare and saw the brunette who had been talking to him standing in front of us. He trained his gaze back on Justin, who from that point on couldn't take his eyes off Casey. "Case suggested the same thing just a few minutes ago." He paused, clucking his tongue, then said, "No, wait. Come to think of it, maybe it was her dorm room, not ice cream." With one smooth move of his head, he faced Casey once more. "Case, how about going for an ice cream instead?"

Her plump lips twisted into a smile. "Sure, I love ice cream, especially when you use it to do that thing where you lick it from my—"

"All right then, and you already know Justin here, right?" She glanced at Justin, and her pretty face contorted in disgust, so Ryan said, "No? Well, my bad, Case, I want you to meet Justin. He's charming, funny, kind, and sweet." The adjectives I'd used to describe Justin that day in the coffee shop were delivered with a hefty dose of sarcasm and mocking. Justin hadn't noticed it since he was too busy drooling over Casey. Eyes on him again, Ryan continued, "Justin, this is Casey, and as you probably figured out, she adores ice cream. Now, you two crazy kids have fun." He withdrew his hand from Justin, grabbed my palm, and steered us out of the house.

"Why did you do that?" I asked once we were in the car.

"Trust me. I did you a favor. The guy's a loser." He decidedly didn't like Justin, and I could understand why; Justin was not charming, funny, kind, and sweet, as I'd always thought him to be, but he wasn't a loser.

"He's not a loser," I contradicted him.

"Yeah, he is, and he's not the guy for you, not if a pair of boobs can easily draw his attention off you." He was right. Justin wasn't the guy for me. He was a mere fantasy I'd created in my head and all because he was the first guy who had remembered my name and hadn't laughed at me. Yet I didn't agree with the last part of his sentence.

"What did you expect? He's a guy, and Casey's absolutely stunning. Every guy in his place would have reacted like him."

"He wasn't just checking her out. He was willing to ditch—no, sorry, he *did* ditch you the minute his eyes fell on her, and for the record not *every* guy is blinded by a pair of boobs and long legs."

I snorted.

"Don't give me that." He threw me a short glance before looking back at the road. "You can be damn sure that if I were in his place, she wouldn't have taken my focus off you."

"Yes, of course, a girl you've already seen naked how many times before? I bet it's way more than once. Unlike Justin, I fail to see how she could have posed any real challenge to your attention."

"That's because you're seeing it the wrong way." He slowed to a stop at a red light and looked at me. The heat flaring in his eyes burned me in my seat. "Emma, when a guy is into you, truly into you, it's *you* who poses the real challenge to *all* the girls for his attention, not the other way around." Silence. My speechless state was enough for him to conclude that I agreed with him. He gazed back at the road and drove when the light switched to green.

At the door to my room, I broke the silence. "Good night."

"Night, Emma," he said with a tender voice, and when he walked down the hallway, I stared at his back, thinking about what he'd said about Justin, and I was glad that my crush on him was over.

Chapter 15

On Monday noon Ryan called and asked me to grab lunch with him. Since we were both in the vicinity of the Legal Research building, part of a complex of four buildings creating a big grassy quad, we decided to meet up there. Five minutes later, I was walking through one of the wide, arched entryways leading to the quad, and I came to an abrupt stop. Ryan stood in the middle of the grassy quad, but he wasn't alone. There were two guys and Kirsten with him. No way was I going to eat lunch with her around.

I placed my backpack on the ground, bent down, and tucked my cell phone into the bag, rehearsing an excuse in my head, something like, "Sorry, my phone just broke, gotta take care of it, like right now." Straightening up, I looked over at Kirsten, and all I wanted to do was to put into practice the moves Ryan had taught me in the greenhouse on her. Dear God, was it jealousy I was drowning in? When my eyes moved to Ryan, I forced a smile, but the curl on my mouth felt stilted and thus awkward. He returned the grin and stepped closer to her, saying something into her ear. Whatever it was, it caused her to throw me an arrogant, victory smile like she'd just won his affection over me.

Why on earth would she think we were in some kind of a competition? I only worked for him, and we were just friends. *So why are you jealous?* a faint, inner voice asked. Angry, I tuned it out, pushing it away. He nodded a goodbye to his friends and walked toward me...with Kirsten. I brushed my hair behind my ear and kept the ungainly curve on my lips. When they came within earshot, I rolled my shoulders. *Okay, here we go.*

"Um, sorry, I can't join you for lunch after all. My cell phone broke, so I need to go and fix it," I said to him, and my eyes slid to her. She walked beside him with a haughty expression and annoying smile. I shifted my gaze back to Ryan's, and I was ready to utter another short apology, throw my backpack back over my shoulder, and take off. But he didn't stop.

Confused, I stepped back, retreating deeper inside the arched entryway, but he kept coming. What was he doing? Whoa! Way too close! "Ryan?" I managed to say before his right hand snaked around my waist and turned me so that my back was to the wall. Then he thrust me against it in three strides. His left hand set itself behind my head, protecting it from the impact, fingers buried in my hair, and his mouth crashed down on mine, his lips moving passionately. At once, the intoxicating smell of his cologne hit me in one big wave. My body temperature jumped up at an alarming rate, and not even the cold of the wall could cool me off.

I wanted so badly to lose myself in the incredible sensation that his skillful mouth had aroused in me from head to toe, but every part of my body had frozen. Noticing it, he slowed his lips until they only grazed softly over mine.

"Shhhh, relax," he whispered into my lips, and his warm breath sent a shiver across my skin. He opened his eyes. A spectacular show of bright blue greeted me, and I felt like I'd been pulled into a crystal-clear, blue sea in the Bahamas. He slipped the hand behind my head to the side of my head, cupping it as his thumb gently toyed with the lobe of my ear. His lips began to caress mine back and forth, and he slowly closed his eyes. The hand cupping my waist started to trace over the side of my body, calming me down.

Relaxed, I closed my eyes and started to move my lips against his. He growled mildly, and the hand on my cheek pressed me to his mouth. I parted my lips to get more of him, and his soft tongue darted inside, stroking mine. Heat pooled low in my belly. He pulled himself closer to me as our tongues tangled together. I needed to touch him, to get even closer to him. As if reading my mind, he deepened the kiss while guiding my hands to his waist. Then his hands returned to where they'd been, one cupping my cheek, the other over my hip. The force of the kiss increased as my fingers went to his stomach tentatively, lightly touching the hem of his shirt and stopping there. He drew his head back and moved my hand between our bodies underneath his shirt, placing my palm flat against his hard, rippled stomach.

He coaxed me in a raspy voice. "Emma, touch me." He went back to kissing me, leaving me to explore his body in whatever way I wished. The direct contact with his bare, smooth skin warmed my hand.

I ran my fingers over the lower ripple of his six-pack abs, up and down, and his tongue caressed the roof of my mouth, eliciting a moan from me. I didn't want this kiss to ever end. The world around me ceased to exist; it was only me and him. Nothing else. I had no idea how long his tongue drove me wild, but when he broke the kiss, I could tell it was not a short time from the puffiness of my lips.

He leaned into my ear, his lips grazing over my earlobe, igniting goosebumps on my skin. "I'm glad that *I* got to be your first kiss." His voice was low.

Muddleheaded by the kiss, I pulled back from him. "Why did you kiss me?" I asked, and the words had unintentionally come out half angry, half irritated, as if I hadn't wanted him to kiss me. I was about to rectify the incorrect impression I might have given him, but he was already coldly answering my question.

"To get rid of her, of course." He retreated from me. Something changed in his expression and it became dark. My heart wondered if what he'd said was really true, yet my brain reminded me that it was Ryan Damon. Him using me to get rid of Kirsten sounded much more reasonable than him kissing me because he wanted to.

"So you kissed *me*? Did you really think she'd believe you'd kiss me and mean it?"

How I wished he'd correct me, telling me that he meant it. But he didn't.

"Hey, it worked, didn't it?" he answered dryly, waving his hand at the empty spot Kirsten had occupied before the kiss. He'd used me, and this realization felt like he'd just pushed me off cloud nine straight to the ground, where harsh reality waited for me, and the pain of the imaginary fall didn't feel imaginary at all. It hurt—deeply. I did my best to hide it. "Yes, it worked, congratulations, and I have to tell you it feels great to be used on my first kiss." I was mad, and the sarcasm just flew out of my mouth.

"Hold on, it's not as if I knew it was your first kiss."

"But you just said you're glad that it was you." He was probably glad that as my *friend* he got to teach me how to do it.

"Yeah, well, after my lips landed on yours, it didn't take a genius to figure that out." Ouch! Did he just imply that I was a bad kisser? He was about to continue, but someone called out his name. We both looked to our right. Nate approached us—perfect timing. I took a few steps to my backpack and picked it up from the ground.

"You dog, spill it. Does she taste the way she looks? Like heaven?" My eyes got big, and I almost chocked on my saliva. "Don't look at me like that. Brian told me he saw you here making out with some chick. Hailee, right? So that's why you dumped Kirsten on Tye the other day? You've already replaced her. Damn, coming to the Red Rock party with her on your arm. God, I hate you, man."

Ryan didn't look as cheerful. "Hailee? What the fuck are you talking about?"

"What the fu—are you fucking kidding me? I'm talking about the freaking super hot Hailee Walsh. She's gossiping to everybody about you taking her to the Red Rock party."

Ryan rolled his eyes. "I've already told you, I'm not going with her or to that damn party. End of story, and now it's not the best ti—"

As if he'd just noticed me standing there, Nate said, "Oh, Emma, you're here. Great, maybe you can talk some freaking sense into him."

"No, she won't, Nate—"

"Nate's right. You should go to the Red Rock party with Hailee, and who knows, maybe after your lips land on hers, it'll erase all of the bad past experiences you've recently had with kisses." I switched my gaze to Nate. "Sorry, gotta go. Bye." I walked away from them without a backward glance.

Later that day, as I was finishing up work at Ryan's, I heard his and Nate's muffled voices outside the office when they entered the apartment. With my bag over my shoulders and the report in my hands, I went out to the living room. Nate slouched on the sofa, turning on the TV. Seeing me, he tipped his chin up to say hello. I smiled at him, then looked at Ryan near the front door and holding his car key. He walked over to take the report from my hands and set it on the coffee table. "I'm dropping Emma off at her dorm. I'll be back later."

He stepped toward the front door, like he expected me to follow him. Being alone with him was the last thing I wanted, but to refuse in front of Nate would cause some eyebrow raising. Besides, I didn't like riding the bus.

"Yeah, fine," Nate said and went back to watching the game on TV. I sighed and trailed Ryan out the door.

The ride to my dorm was quiet. When he pulled up in front of my dorm building, he finally broke the silence. "Look, I'm sorry, okay? I was an ass." Yes, he was. "I shouldn't have said that I kissed you to get rid of Kirsten."

My eyebrows drew together, and I felt frowny lines forming on my forehead when I looked at him. "You know, I really thought you wanted friendship from me, but the truth is you never did. You only wanted another girl in your life you could use." My hand swept down the seat belt to unsnap it, but he fixed me with a hard stare, keeping me in my seat.

"And what about you? What do you want?"

"What?"

"You clearly seem to be sure about what I want from you. Now, I'm curious. What do you want?"

"From you? Nothing," My tone was full of anger. But right after I said it, shock fell on me like a thunderbolt as I realized that it was a complete lie. I did want something from him, and it wasn't nothing, and it wasn't friendship.

I had feelings for him. The signs I'd been attempting to dismiss had been there all along: the swarm of butterflies loose in my stomach every time he was close, the constant thoughts about him, the fact that his lips could cause my heart to beat fast and my knees to go weak. He'd made me feel things I'd never experienced, physically and emotionally. Before he could read the lie in my eyes, I looked away and jammed my hand against the seat belt buckle button. Naturally, the clip got stuck. I tugged at it until a hand clamped on mine.

"Emma." There was calmness quality to his voice. I lifted my gaze to his. He was leaning over the gearshift, his eyes on mine, his body too close, its warmth touching me. My stomach bottomed out. "What if I tell you plain and simple that these lips"—he brought his hand beneath my chin and ran a gentle thumb over my mouth, spiking my pulse— "gave me the best kiss I've ever had, and getting rid of Kirsten was not the reason I kissed you. Would that make you change your answer?"

Click.

His hand over mind had depressed the seat belt buckle button. I was free from the seat belt, and he pulled his hands from me, moving back to his seat, eyes not leaving mine. Yes, I could buy that I was the best kiss he'd ever had and change my answer from nothing to everything. But if I did, I'd be a fool. He wasn't Wesley, the popular boy in high school; he wouldn't laugh at me because I trusted him, yet there was no way I'd make the same mistake of believing the impossible. I wouldn't accept that out of all the girls he'd kissed before, I was his best. That was unrealistic and his obviously weird way of apologizing, which lessened my exasperation.

I finally said in a calmer tone, "No, and I'd appreciate it if you don't try to kiss me again." I grabbed my backpack, opened the door, and climbed out of the car.

Without looking back, I stepped to the main entrance of my building. In my room, I dropped the bag to the floor, flopped onto the bed, sank back down against the mattress, and stared up at the ceiling. I needed to stay away from him. How else would I get over my feelings for him? Feelings he'd all but told me he was incapable of, much less for me.

I let out a breath, angry at myself. How could I let myself get attached to him and to develop feelings for a guy like Ryan? I spent the next ten minutes admonishing myself until a knock at the door interrupted me. I jolted to a sitting position, and the door popped open. Hannah walked in, closing it behind her. Her eyes were puffy and red, tears streaming down her cheeks.

"What happened?" I asked.

"Dylan, he…" She sobbed and dropped on the bed next to me. "He…" She sniffed and continued, "That bastard! I caught him cheating on me."

I leaned to my nightstand and opened the top drawer, pulling out a tissue box. I handed it to her. She plucked a few tissues and blew her nose.

"Hannah, I'm so sorry. He doesn't deserve you or your tears. You'll find someone else. Someone better." I put a comforting hand on her shoulder. "Forget about him."

It was time she met a nice guy, for a change. Someone who would treat her with respect. But who? Nate's name popped up in my head. He was nice and exactly her type, but was he faithful? I couldn't consider him as an option until I checked that with Ryan. After an hour of crying, she calmed down and, for the next hour, we went through a dozen revenge scenarios.

"You know what? I think that the best revenge is you being happy with another guy," I told her, and she agreed, feeling much better.

Chapter 16

Tuesday morning I promised myself to talk to Ryan about Nate, but in his apartment later that afternoon, after I'd finished working, he cast me a sexy smile and those dimples of his made me forget all about my mission. He was seated on the sofa, laptop on his lap. I handed him the report and sat next to him, observing his body. He was clad in blue, faded jeans and a short-sleeved, white T-shirt showcasing his bulging biceps and tattoo. After glancing through the pages, he moved the report and his computer to the coffee table.

"Which would you prefer for dinner: Chinese or Italian?" he asked, settling back in his seat.

"Neither. I have to go, so—"

"Without dinner? You must be starving."

"Yes, but I'll have dinner when I get back to my dorm room."

"Even if I really want you to stay and eat with me?" He threw me a dazzling grin.

I flung him back a smile, a teasing one. "As a fan of the Rolling Stones, shouldn't you already know that you can't always get what you want?"

He chuckled, brushing his fingers through his thick, dark brown, spiky hair. When the phone on the coffee table rang, Nate's name came up on the glowing display, reminding me of my mission. Ryan leaned over and silenced the device, and I pushed to my feet, walking to the refrigerator and pulling out the small bottle of water I'd put there when I came in. My mouth was dry, and I anticipated that our next conversation would be long. I pivoted around and found him leaning against the edge of the breakfast bar.

"Okay, what is it?" he asked, and I had no idea how he'd figured out that I needed something from him. I took a long drink and placed the bottle on the black breakfast bar next to him.

"I was curious about Nate," I said.

His brow winged upward. "You were?" he asked crisply.

"Yes, for Hannah."

His expression softened. "I see. Isn't she sorta already dating someone?"

"She did, but he cheated on her."

He folded his arms over his chest. "And you want to know if Nate's a cheater too."

"Yes, and also to make sure he doesn't share your wonderful opinions about love and relationships."

"My wonderful opinions?" He appeared genuinely confused.

"Yes," I confirmed and started listing them. "That he won't, obviously, be against monogamy, that he believes true love exists, that he doesn't consider it to be an illusion, that marriage is not against human nature and that—" I paused.

"That?" he prompted.

"We're not talking about me, so the last one is irrelevant." I tucked my hair behind my ears and grabbed the bottle of water from the counter, taking a sip.

"Still, what is the last one?"

"You don't remember?" I placed the bottle back down.

"No, I don't."

"Okay, the last one is that he won't think virgins are boring as hell." I used his exact words, which made his lips draw up into an amused smile.

"I said that?" His brows rose, and I nodded. "Let me rephrase it, then." Rephrase it? He pushed himself from the breakfast bar, taking a step toward me. "What I really meant to say was that if I were the lucky guy who deflowered you"— whoa, what?—"there'd be only one thought looping through my brain again and again the whole time, leaving no room for feelings like boredom."

I blinked at him and swallowed hard. I had to steer this conversation back to Nate and fast! "W-what's the thought?"

That was not redirecting the conversation! I didn't have time to get angry at myself since in a flash I was a few inches shy of his body after he unexpectedly had grasped my elbow and tugged me to him in one fluid motion.

Keeping his fingers curled around my arm, he put his other hand on my lower back to steady me. His head descended toward mine, and his lips hovered a breath from mine. The fragrant scent of soap and cologne invaded my senses. I waited for the kiss to come—no, I craved it. But only his warm breath touched my lips as he spoke.

"Emma, am I going to be the guy who deflowers you?" The seduction in his voice caused my legs to go weak. The hand on my back glided down to my bottom and pulled me against his groin. My eyes widened, and I gulped air. His intention was clear: *say yes, and it'll happen right now, right here.*

I finally found my voice. "N-no." Since my head turned subtly to the right to avoid the intensity of his stare, my breath caressed the right side of his mouth, at his upper lip. He pushed out his tongue, licked that same spot, and slid it back inside his mouth, as if my breath was a smudge of chocolate above his lip. Then, that particular edge of his mouth lifted in a lopsided smile, which not only revealed a deep dimple but also that he was only teasing me.

"So it doesn't really matter what the thought is, now does it?" His tone was playful, and he suddenly released me. I swayed on my feet, and he stepped past me to the refrigerator, pulling out a can of Coke. God, he seriously was not going to tell me. He couldn't do this to me! My curiosity was nearly killing me.

"No, it doesn't matter. But I want to know anyway."

He closed the refrigerator and smirked at me. "Well"—he clucked his tongue—"that's too bad, because as someone was kind enough to point out earlier, you can't always get what you want." Winking at me, he pulled the tap and swigged from the can as he headed to the living room. There, he picked up his phone, tapped on it, and brought it to his ear. After several seconds, his voice filled the room.

"Hey, turns out I'm going to the Red Rock party after all...no, not with Hailee...look, I need you to be there without a date...yeah, you heard me right, no date...just trust me, will you?...okay, good. We'll talk later." He ended the call, shoved his cell phone into his front jeans pocket, placed the can of Coke on the coffee table, and gazed over at me. "This Saturday, bring Hannah with you to the Rock Party at the Beta Kappa House. I'll take it from there."

"Wait, what about Nate, you didn't say—"

"Don't worry. Nate would never screw around on his girl, and he doesn't share my *wonderful* opinions about love and relationships." His light eyes sparkled with humor.

"Just one more thing." I nibbled my bottom lip. "Um...I kind of don't want her to know I'm setting her up."

"I'll be damned. Emma Winstead, are you manipulating your own friend?" His smile widened.

"No, I...I just don't want her to feel pressured and..." I fumbled for a lie. The truth was that she hated set-ups. "And I...also...don't—"

"Yeah, of course you don't. Now, could you continue working on your off-the-cuff excuses while coming over here?"

I sighed and stepped over.

"Just don't tell her," I warned him, grabbing my backpack from the sofa.

"Not a word," he reassured me and made a gesture of sealing his lips closed with his hand. After he dropped me off at my dorm, I ate dinner and studied for the Algorithms test I had next week. In bed, before falling asleep, I wished that Hannah would hit it off with Nate. She deserved happiness, and I hoped he could be the guy to give her that.

The next day, I suffered from an itchy pain in my hands. The skin there was so dry that there were cracks and breaks everywhere, blood seeping from some of them. My hands looked like something out of a horror movie. My body's tendency to take everything to the extreme irked me. All it took was a windy, cold day like yesterday to wreak havoc on my skin. Normally, I protected them with moisture cream and gloves, but I'd run out a while ago and with everything going on, I'd forgotten to replace them. Luckily, the pain wasn't severe, and I managed to endure it until the American Lit class, where I'd been using my hands by writing a lot of notes, so when Professor Fields had finally dismissed us, I was ever so glad. Packing up my backpack after the rest of the class had left, I noticed Ryan holding a cup, walking into the room.

"Hey." He smiled at me. I could smell the rich aroma of the coffee. "As I remembered, or should I say my shirt remembered, you take your coffee strong." He handed me the cup, and I grinned. The professor's lecture had dragged on forever today, and I was in desperate need of caffeine.

"Wow, thanks, and not that I'm not grateful, but how did you know I'd be here?" My fingers curved around the cup, and he stared at them, his features twisting with concern.

"Jesus, what happened to your hand?" He took the cup back and set it on a desk.

"Nothing." I whipped my hand behind my back, but he pulled it to him so that he could pore over it. Embarrassed, I yanked at my hand, yet he didn't release his grip. After a moment, he pushed my sleeve up, examining my arm in order to see if the damage reached farther up. It didn't, so he slid the sleeve back down and took my other hand, then shook his head, an expression of perturbation on his face.

"I'm taking you to see a doctor right now."

"No, I'm okay. My skin is highly sensitive. That's all. I just need gloves and moisture cream, and it'll pass."

"Okay, then why haven't you been using them? And where the hell are your gloves? Emma, for God's sake, you're bleeding." I looked down at the blood staining my fingers.

"I forgot to buy them, but I will, maybe tomorrow." He took a deep breath and closed his eyes for a short moment, as if to gather patience.

"Where are you headed now?" he asked, sounding angry at me for neglecting to take care of myself.

"The library. I gotta study. I have a really big test next week."

He leaned forward and picked up the coffee cup from the desk. "Here." He reached out, and I took the cup. "Go to the library. I'll see you later," he said before leaving the classroom.

In the library, I placed myself behind the last, long bookcase, sitting at a table at the far corner of the room. Alone at the table, I buried myself in a stack of textbooks for the next half hour, until I heard my name. Raising my head from a textbook, I saw Chris. I recognized him from my Algorithms class, but we hadn't ever spoken before.

"It's Emma, right?" he said.

I nodded, a faint smile on my face as my eyes flicked to the textbooks in his hands, the same as the ones on my table.

"Are you studying for the Algorithms test, too?" I asked.

"Yeah. It's unbelievable the amount of things we need to know for this test, and I can't understand half of it."

"It's not that bad. I can help you, if you want," I offered.

"That would be great. Thanks."

I moved my stuff aside, clearing some space on the cluttered table, and his average-looking face wore a slightly disgusted expression as he caught a glimpse of my hands. I blushed as he pulled up the chair next to me. "I know, not an attractive sight. It's the weather," I said, pulling my sleeves down over my fingers.

"Don't worry about it." He grinned awkwardly and smoothed a hand over his ginger hair. We got down to studying. Half an hour later, I received a text from Ryan asking which library I was at. I texted him back the details, wondering what was so important that he had to see me right away. My plans to stay away from him had turned out to be rather unviable. He showed up ten minutes later. His smile, when he spotted me, quickly shifted to a scowl as his eyes found Chris. He walked up to our table.

"Get lost." Ryan's tone was icy, and he didn't even spare him a glance.

Chris lifted his head. "What?"

Ryan sighed with impatience and glared down at him. "You're sitting on my chair, so..." He jerked his head in a 'get away' gesture.

"No, I'm not. The chair was empty when I got here. You weren't here."

"And now I am, so get lost."

"You can't make me." His voice cracked a little, and Ryan rolled his eyes.

"Let's save us both some time and skip the part where you're trying to convince yourself that I can't, and go straight to where you know I actually really can, shall we?" Not waiting for a response, he continued, "Since I'm a nice guy, I'll ask you one last time. Get. Lost."

No doubt in his mind that he'd go, Ryan placed a plastic bag on the table in front of Chris, ready to take his seat.

"Whatever." Indignant, Chris swept his notebooks from the table and pushed his lanky frame to its feet. Astonished, I wasn't able to form words in order to stop him from leaving. Taking his place, Ryan sat next to me. He turned the plastic bag upside down, spilling its contents onto the table: two tubes of moisture cream, gloves, and aloe vera gel. He picked out one of the moisture cream tubes and poured a generous amount of the substance into his palm, then took my hand. When he started to massage the cream into my dry skin, I finally found my voice.

"Why did you scare him off?" I demanded.

"He was hitting on you." His eyes remained on my hand as he kept moisturizing it. The cold substance, which was to my skin what rain is to mushrooms, soothed the itchiness.

"No, he wasn't, but even if he was, what's the problem with that?"

"That you deserve better than someone who just hit on three different girls before he tried his luck with you." He switched my hands and gently smoothed the lotion over the back of my other palm, alleviating the pain.

"Wha—how do—three? How would you even know that?" I asked. He let out air as if he had more important things to do right now than elucidate it, things like taking care of my skin. Nevertheless, he explained himself while his eyes still concentrated on his fingers kneading mine.

"Behind me, the table across the room parallel to ours, see the redhead?" I leaned to the side to see past him. A girl with short, curly red hair was sitting and studying alone. "Near her textbook, at the edge of the table, there is a simple origami flower. An iris." My eyes caught the paper flower.

"Okay, so?"

"Now, look two tables down behind her. Notice the brunette sitting across from two guys?" I did. She was reading from a heavy-looking textbook, and a similar origami iris flower was lying carelessly aside, this one blue. It looked familiar, and I was suddenly sure I'd seen it before. But where? The answer abruptly hit me, and my head jerked to look down at my table. A blue, origami iris rested between the textbooks near Ryan. I'd been so focused on flow charts with Chris that I hadn't registered that he'd put it there. Obviously, Ryan had interrupted us before he could give me his work of art.

"So, he planned on dating the three of us?" I asked, aggravated. He was done with my hands, and his gaze moved up, at last, to my face.

He rubbed his cream-soaked hands together and said, "No. They weren't into him. If they were, they wouldn't have treated his origami flower like it was litter and put it carelessly aside. He only approached you after they turned him down. Now, as to your skin, you need to smooth this lotion over them twice a day, morning and night. The aloe vera is to help calm the redness, so use it, too." He slipped the products back inside the plastic bag and set it next to me.

"I'm flying to New York later today, and I'm gonna be there till Saturday. There are things related to the martial arts studio that I need to take care of in person. Can I trust that you'll follow the instructions and that you won't forget to wear the gloves?" He looked at me, and I was suddenly aware that he'd purchased me all this stuff.

"You shouldn't have bought me anything." I sighed. "How much do I owe you?"

"Nothing."

"Then I can't accept it." I moved the plastic bag over to his side of the table. He pushed it back and gave me a pointed look.

"You're really going to argue with me over this? You only insult me by thinking I give a damn about the money. Emma, I gotta go, but I won't unless you promise to take care of your hands. Will you do that?"

After deciding that arguing with him was futile, I replied, "Okay, I'll take care of my hands."

"Good, see you on Saturday," he said and rose from the chair. Watching him walk away, I had this irritating feeling I'd miss him.

Chapter 17

When I told Hannah we'd been invited to a frat party, she was so stoked she didn't even suspect that I had an ulterior motive. We got ready in my room before the party.

Wearing a tight black dress and high heels, she looked great.

"I love those heels on you," she said. A thank-you smile spread across my lips. Yesterday, we'd gone shopping. I'd ended up with four new dresses, four pairs of high heels, and a black skirt that I was currently wearing, along with a red top and a black cardigan over it.

When we parked in front of the Beta Kappa House, the sound of rock music blaring through the open windows welcomed us. Inside, the party was in full swing. A chant of, "Drink! Drink! Drink!" blended with laughter, chatter, and music. We passed the drinking contest some frat guys were having next to a beer pong table. We inched through the partygoers until we got to two free stools at a wraparound bar tucked into a corner.

After a half an hour, Ryan and Nate showed up. Ryan reached us first, dressed in a long-sleeved T-shirt and jeans that molded to his strong legs. He grinned at me as if to say, "Don't worry. It'll work out," and he introduced Hannah to Nate. Three days had passed since I'd seen him, and as they were talking, my eyes roved over him. I studied every inch of him, marveling at his profile, his fashionably spiky hair, and his muscular frame. I'd missed him, and had been excited to hear from him yesterday, when he'd asked me to send him a picture of my hands to see if I'd kept my promise. I had. My skin was almost healed, and he'd been glad.

"Why aren't you drinking?" a male voice, pulling me out of my reverie, asked above the music. I looked at the guy sitting between me and the wall.

"Didn't order yet, maybe later," I answered and was about to turn my attention to the conversation behind me, to see how Hannah and Nate were hitting it off, but the guy spoke again.

"I don't remember ever seeing you here before. You're a freshman?"

I shook my head. "A sophomore." He had short, blond hair, an aquiline nose, green eyes, and he was unequivocally handsome. Behind me, Nate said something and Hannah laughed. I smiled. Great, it seemed that things were going well.

"You have a beautiful smile. Are you here with your boyfriend?"

"No, with my friend," I answered.

"I'm Matt." He held out his hand, and I shook it and gave him my name.

"You have gorgeous hair, Emma." He picked up a strand of it, starting to rub it between his fingers. All of a sudden, his knuckles were violently pressed together by a hand. It took me a few seconds to realize the assaulting hand was Ryan's. He forced Matt to release my hair. Ryan let him go, but not before Matt's face scrunched up with pain and he cried out. My eyes opened wider, and my lips parted. Thrusting his hand to his chest, Matt snapped his head to Ryan, who was standing at my side. "What the hell, dude! You almost broke my fingers!"

"Wrong choice of word here, Matt. *Almost* can suggest that I missed, which I never do, by the way, so let me be succinct. That was a warning. The next time you put your filthy hand on her, I won't *choose* to leave your bones unbroken. Am I clear?" Ryan's jaw clenched. Matt stared at him like he'd lost his mind, which right now, didn't seem far from the truth.

"Since when do you care which slut I'm—" Ryan's hands shot out, and he grabbed Matt by his shirt collar. He hauled him off the stool, and in one slick motion, slammed him against the wall behind him, pinning him there with a forearm locked across his throat. I gasped and slid from the stool to calm him down, but Nate beat me to it.

"Whoa, Damon, chill, man." Alarm crossed Nate's face. Curious onlookers around us stopped talking and dancing to watch the drama play out.

"Relax, Nate." He didn't break eye contact with Matt, who was white as a sheet. His voice was calm but his face—seething. "He'll leave this place in one piece because after all, it was my mistake. I should have been clearer. Matt, Emma is off-limits for you, and that means you don't touch her, you don't insult her, and you don't treat her like she is one of your chicks. If you ever do one of the above again, I'll make you my personal problem, and when I solve it, you'll find out firsthand that there are much worse things than physical pain. Now, did I make myself clear enough for you?"

Matt nodded, and Ryan released him. Matt doubled over, coughing, and then ran out of the house. Ryan looked at Nate. "See? One piece." When he turned to me, his features softened.

I pondered whether I should try to act like nothing had happened, or step outside to calm myself down before I said something I'd regret. Decision made, I glanced at Hannah, who seemed shocked as well. "I need fresh air. I'll be back in a few minutes." She nodded, and I stalked out of there. A whoosh of chilly air hit me when I stepped outside on the front porch. I hugged my midsection and heard footfalls behind me. I spun. Ryan was outside the front door, coming closer to me, not even a mild look of contrite on his face, only calmness.

"You had no right to do that. Did you see his face? He was terrified to even glance in my direction when he walked past me," I said.

"Good, now he won't dare put his hands all over you again." His tranquil expression contorted with ire.

I spat out air in disbelief. "All over me? All over me? He was only touching my hair!" I raised my voice with anger and shook my head, astonished. "And it's not any of your business who touches me."

"It is when it's right in front of my face, and I don't give a shit which part of you he touches. That dickhead shouldn't have even been seated so close to you." His eyes glittered with rage. Whoa, was he jealous? Flabbergasted, I almost gasped. Hannah opened the front door and loud music spilled out of it, along with a couple of drunk guys leaving the party.

"Em? You okay?" She stood next to Ryan.

"Yes, I'm fine, but I think I'll call it a night."

"Okay, let me just go fetch my things, and we'll leave," she said, and I stopped her before she turned to go back into the house.

"No, Hannah, I'll walk—you stay. Have fun with Nate." I grinned, wanting her to get to know him and not be worried about me.

She looked at Ryan and then back at me. "Are you going to walk by yourself?"

"Yes, it's only a few blocks, no biggie," I said, and she put her hands on her waist.

"It's midnight. Do you think it's a good idea to go by yourself after everything that happened with the robbers?"

"Unfortunately, yes, she does, but she won't. I'm walking her to the dorm," Ryan answered for me.

"What! No!" I scowled at him, but he was impervious to it.

"Emma, at this hour, you'll get to your dorm in one of two ways: by walking beside me, or by being carried over my shoulder, and if you pick the latter and have the urge to scream and kick, don't stop yourself on my account; really, I don't mind," he said, and the look on his face added, "Don't test me—I mean it."

I let out a resigned sigh. "I'll *walk*." I looked at him, then shifted my gaze to Hannah, who pressed her lips together to keep from laughing, and went on, "As you can see, I won't be by myself, so you can stay with Nate."

"Okay, Em, call you tomorrow." She smiled and blew me a kiss, then disappeared back inside the house.

Ryan gazed at me. "Civilized it is, then." He waved me forward. I expelled an angry sigh, and we strode to my dorm in silence. When I unlocked the door to my room, he said my name. Hand on the door handle, I turned to face him, waiting for an apology. It wouldn't be enough, but it was the least he could do. That scene he'd made was unacceptable. He didn't own me. We weren't even dating. How could he—

"Matt's last date found herself starring in a sex tape all over the Net. It's his thing, filming them in his room without their knowledge and posting it online."

The anger drained out of me, replaced by horror at what could have happened. That could have been me. "That's awful." I pulled my hand from the handle and crossed my arms over my chest. Ryan wasn't jealous, he was protecting me, and I appreciated it.

"Why hasn't he been expelled from the university or at least from the fraternity?"

"Don't know." He shrugged with indifference.

"Did you report it to anybody?"

"No, why would I? It's not my concern."

Taken aback by his cold answer, my anger slammed back into me.

"What's wrong with you? They're human beings. What that psycho did to them is revolting. He hurt those girls, and they have families—people who care about them. What if they stumbled across those tapes? How could you not report it? He should get punished. God, you're so callous." Aggravation twisted my face, and he suddenly looked so disturbed, so wounded by my outburst that I wanted to take my reaction back.

"Ryan, I—"

"It's okay. Sleep tight," he said, and he was gone. For a few moments, I stared aimlessly down the hall. Then I went into my room, ready to go to sleep and forget about everything, if only for tonight.

Chapter 18

The next day, Hannah called me in the morning. Holding my cell phone to my ear, I listened to her jolly voice reporting everything that had taken place after I'd left the party yesterday. She and Nate had clearly hit it off, and I was happy for her. I half-listened as I was getting dressed. Then she said something that locked me in place. "What?"

"I said Ryan came back to the party and talked with the Beta Kappa president. Something about advising him to kick Matt out of the fraternity over some sex tape business. Can you believe that?"

"Are they really going to expel him?" My voice was hopeful.

"Yeah, Nate told me about it. He also said that Ryan talked to one of Matt's victims and convinced her to press charges. I can't believe I didn't notice that that pervert, Matt, was hitting on you. Thankfully, Ryan saw it and stopped him."

"Yes, me too." I was proud of him for doing the right thing.

"Anyway, you're coming with me to Nate's birthday party at the Beta Kappa House tonight, right?"

"His birthday's today? Aren't they a little worn-out from last night's party?"

"Beta Kappa guys are never worn-out. So are you coming with me?"

"Um, I don't know, Hannah, what about Kayla? Can't she go?" After the incident with Matt, I didn't feel like going to another party tonight.

"She can't. But even if she could, I really want you there, too."

"Okay. I'll come," I said and pulled the phone from my ear when she shrieked with excitement.

"I'll pick you up at nine. The party theme is his favorite color, purple, so wear something purple, like that gorgeous dress you bought at the mall."

"Okay, see you at nine."

The Beta Kappa party was in full swing when we arrived that night. Music poured out of the house, and along the second story balcony a purple banner read: *Nate's 22 birthday party, bitches.*

Inside, everything was in Nate's favorite color. The entire living room was decorated in purple balloons, purple banners, purple streamers, and everyone was dressed in varying shades of purple. They flooded the space, dancing and drinking. The music throbbed around me as we crept through the crowd. Nate, towering over most of the partygoers in the room, spotted us from the center of a makeshift dance floor in the living room. His eyes fell on Hannah, and he beamed. A purple birthday cone hat with elastic string keeping it in place rested on his head. He got rid of it before he began to move in our direction.

"Glad you guys could make it," he yelled over the noise when he reached us.

"Happy b-day, birthday boy," Hannah shouted back and plastered a bright smile on her lips.

"Happy birthday, Nate," I wished him, then turned to Hannah. "Your song is playing, go dance." I nudged her toward him. Neither of them needed any more coaxing. He took her hand and they disappeared into the crowd. I was happy for her. Nate seemed like a good guy who would treat her right. Shouldering my way to the wraparound bar, I searched the room for Ryan. There were no empty stools at the bar, so I propped my back against the wall and scanned over the people, but there was no sign of Ryan. I was about to step to the bar to order a drink when a sudden jolt, weakening my knees, traveled through my body.

Bang. Bang. The sound of a gunshot starting the next rock song continued, fanning my anxiety. No, no, no, no, I couldn't have a panic attack, not here, not in front of all these people. *Just breathe, in and out, breathe.* My vision became blurry, and my chest hurt as if it had been pressed hard. I started to breathe fast and heavy. Everything began to spin around me. *Breathe, breathe calmly, in and out, breathe slowly.* But I couldn't get enough oxygen. It was like someone had shoved a thick fabric against my mouth and nose. I was suffocating. Knees buckling, I dropped to the cold floor, my entire body trembling as I curled into a small ball and rocked back and forth. A surge of fear crashed over me. My heart galloped hard, and the pain in my chest got stronger. I dissolved into tears while I braced myself for an imminent heart attack. Like being inside of a bubble, I heard muffled voices circling me.

"Dude, I think she's having a seizure or something."

"Is she okay?"

"What's wrong with her?"

"Whoa, look down there. Is she on something?"

I couldn't endure their stares and comments. The shudders in my body became painful.

"Get the fuck away from her! Move away!" An angry, loud male voice barked at the blurry, curious people around me, and then someone flung himself to the floor beside me. Two strong hands pulled my shaking body into protective arms, enveloping me, sheltering me from prying eyes. "Baby, I'm right here, and I'm not going anywhere. Just inhale slowly and let it out, in and out. Breathe and relax your muscles." I knew this cooing voice. Ryan. He pulled my head into him, and my wet cheek was pressed against his hard chest as he cradled my body in his arms and stroked my hair. I wasn't cold anymore.

"What's happening to her?" Hannah said, alarmed.

"She's having a panic attack," Ryan told her.

"What? A panic attack? Are you sure it's a panic attack?" Hannah asked.

"Yes. Nate, get them the fuck away before I do it, and it won't end pretty," Ryan shouted.

"C'mon, guys. There's nothing to see here. Move away." Nate was the last person I heard before I closed my eyes and was pulled seven years back into Dr. Miller's office.

"And you can't blame yourself. What happened was not your fault. It was *not* your fault." Dr. Miller had assured me twice, but it hadn't helped. I still had felt that it'd been my fault. On the sofa, I closed my eyes and revisited that night a month ago in my head. It had been late, maybe after midnight, when I woke up from a bad dream. Thirsty, I went downstairs to get a glass of water from the kitchen. Reaching the bottom step, my dad's work room door had been cracked open, sending out a shaft of light. I padded to it.

"Dad?" I peeked in. He wasn't sitting at his desk, so I walked inside the room. "Dad?" I glanced to my left and found him looking out the closed window, his back facing me. Why was he shaking? "Dad, are you okay? Are you sick?" He slowly turned around. Confusion distorted my face. He held something black in his mouth. "Dad? What are you..." Tears escaped his eyes. I stepped closer and recognized the black object—a gun! In that exact moment, millions of possible actions had run through my head, but in the end, I hadn't done any of them. Instead, I'd frozen. Paralyzed, voiceless, I stared at him. His eyes begged for forgiveness, and there was a loud sound. *Bang.*

Warm blood splattered on my face, on my hand, on my PJs, on the carpet floor. Blood everywhere. Everywhere. I'd stared down at my father's lifeless body, and an earsplitting scream ripped through the entire room. Mom? I couldn't turn to look at her. I'd been paralyzed—useless.

"Honey, don't look," Mom had shouted and swerved me around, hugging me tightly, crying.

"Emma, tell me, how do you feel?" Dr. Miller had jarred me back to her office. Opening my eyes, I'd repeated.

"I-I-I f-f-feel g-g-uilty."

"That's it. Breathe. Ease your muscles." Ryan's voice was back, pulling me to the present. I drew in a deep breath. It was easier to breathe, and my heart returned to a normal rate of speed. Finally, I opened my eyes, studying my surroundings. I was in an unfamiliar room on a comforter next to Ryan.

"Where am I?" I sat up.

"Easy." Ryan palmed my waist, helping me to adjust my position.

"Upstairs, in Nate's room," he replied, and it all came back to me. I dropped my head to my hands and squeezed my eyes shut, abashed. God, I had a panic attack downstairs in front of everybody. I turned my head to him. "Did you bring me up here?"

Sitting, legs stretched out before him, crossed at the ankles, he leaned against the headboard of the twin-sized bed. "Yeah." He brushed my hair behind my ear. "Was it your first episode?" I curved my arms around my bent-up knees, chin resting on them, looking straight ahead at the wall across the room.

"No, it wasn't. It started after my father committed suicide in front of me when I was twelve." Somehow, I felt the need to explain why he'd done that. "My mother told me, when I was older, that he'd made a bad investment before he killed himself. We lost nearly everything and were drowning in debts." I moved my gaze back to his. He was listening carefully, eyes on me. I returned to look at the wall opposite me and went on. "My dad's mom was the one who bailed us out, after my dad's death. My grandfather has money in abundance, but he'd never approved of my father, who'd just graduated college, and all he had was student loan debts. In spite of his threat to cut her out of his life and off from his money, my parents eloped, and he didn't speak to her again, not until a few days after the suicide. We desperately needed his help. Swallowing her pride, my mom took whatever he offered." His palm touched my back, caressing it. I looked back at him.

"Why are you blaming yourself for your father's death?" Catching me off guard with his question, I opened my mouth and closed it, saying nothing. How did he know that? At my silent response, he explained, "There is a distinct guiltiness in your eyes. You've got to stop holding yourself responsible for what he did."

I crossed my legs, lotus style. "I did nothing. I could have screamed for my mother to come. I could have begged him to pull the gun out of his mouth. I could have changed his mind by telling him that everything would be okay...but I just froze."

"Tell me, what kind of a person kills himself in front of his twelve-year-old daughter?"

A few seconds passed, and I answered, "A desperate one."

"And can you talk sense into a desperate man who has lost everything, including hope?"

"No," I answered without doubt and felt like some kind of weight was lifted off of me.

"Listen to me. Even if you had screamed, even if your mother had dashed to the room, it wouldn't have stopped him from pulling the trigger. He'd already made up his mind a long time ago, and at that moment in that room, nothing could have changed his death, not even you." He drew me into his arms, hugging me. I breathed him in and wrapped my arms around his back. All bad thoughts faded away. We stayed that way, holding each other, until someone knocked on the door.

"Damon, how's Emma? Hannah's kinda freaking out downstairs. What do I tell her?" Nate asked through the door. I withdrew from Ryan's arms, scrambled to my feet, and opened the door.

Nate looked surprised to see me standing.

"I'm fine," I told him.

"You sure?"

"Yes, I'm okay, thanks," I said and stepped past him. "I'll go and calm her down." I tossed over my shoulder. After I reassured Hannah that I didn't need an emergency room and that I was truly fine, Ryan drove me to my dorm room. Later, in my bed, I thought about him. I was dangerously close to falling in love with him more and more every day. In one week, the project would be over, and I made up my mind to cut all contact with him after I finished with the website, for the sake of my heart.

Monday evening Hannah swung by my room to check in on me, and she had company—Justin. Her eyes sparkled with enthusiasm as she pranced in, still thinking I liked him. "Justin wanted to tag along when I told him I was heading to your room. Anyway, I just remembered that I've got this thing I have to do, so I'll leave you two alone." With her back to him, she winked at me and walked back out of the room while Justin stepped inside and sat on my bed.

"Hey," I said with a faint smile and joined him on the bed. He grinned, and I got the feeling it was supposed to be sexy and seductive, but it fell flat.

"Hannah said you went to a frat party last night. What happened to you over there? Ashley mentioned that you had some kind of a breakdown." Ashley was there?

"Nothing happened. Just felt a bit dizzy is all. I'm fine now." No way was I going to talk to him about my panic attacks. I gave him a wider smile.

"Okay, good to hear you're fine now. So what's really the deal with you and Ryan? Yeah, you said you were only friends, but according to Ashley, he's definitely naili—" He broke off, cleared his throat, and finished his sentence. "Sleeping with you."

"What! No! Why in the world would she assume that?"

"She saw him sweep you up in his arms and take you upstairs, and he told some dude not to let anyone in the room."

"And she concluded that he slept with me? With the condition I was in?" I winced.

"I guess so." He shrugged.

I shook my head in disbelief. "Well, she's wrong. We're not sleeping together. We hang out sometimes as friends, that's all." I looked straight into his eyes. He studied me for a moment and smiled, satisfied to see that I meant what I'd said. Then, he suddenly cupped my cheek, leaned forward, and shoved his tongue into my mouth. Fighting for air, repugnance surged up in me. Unfortunately, the choking noises erupting from my throat weren't enough to make him stop. Someone rapped on the door. I wrenched my lips from his and launched myself to my feet, dragging a sleeve across my mouth. Grinning, he moved from the bed and went to stand at my side. He curled an arm over my shoulders and pulled me up against his side. Another knock. "Yes?" I said.

The door opened before I could knock his touch away. Ryan stood in the doorway, eyes sliding from me to the hand over my shoulder, and his expression swiftly shifted from calm to murderous.

Fuming, blue eyes fastened on Justin. "Don't you think you're a tad too free with your hand over there?"

Not moving his hand away from me, Justin straightened his spine and answered, "No, I'm not." He watched the ripple of the muscle under Ryan's jaw as Ryan clenched his teeth together.

"Would you like to rethink your answer before I *show* you the right one?" The way he stressed the word show delivered his intention loud and clear; violence would be involved in the showing process. To diffuse the tension, I ducked beneath Justin's arm and faced him. "Justin, could we continue this uh...conversation next time?"

He look at me, insulted. "Just friends, huh?"

I refrained from commenting on that, and he snorted, then stalked out of the room, shouldering past Ryan. After Justin was out, Ryan closed the door and walked over to the bed, falling on it. I sat next to him.

"What did he want?" Disdain creased his chiseled features. He clearly didn't believe Justin was the right guy for me, so repeating Justin's words would do nothing but anger him more.

"He just dropped by to see how I was doing."

He shot me a look of incredulity, and I said, "Let's just drop it, okay?"

He let out a short sigh. "Okay...Emma, I came here to tell you that I need to fly out to New York again. I'm leaving today and won't be back until Friday."

"Oh, okay." Almost a week without him. It was exactly what I needed to keep my distance from him, and yet sadness filled me.

"I'll be in touch," he promised, and over the next half hour, we discussed subjects related to the end of the project. At my door, before he said goodbye, something dark flashed across his face, bringing back the cold, distant Ryan I'd first gotten to know. I was about to ask what bothered him, but he was quickly gone and the question stayed in my mouth.

Chapter 19

He hadn't called. Not Monday, not Tuesday, not Wednesday, and not Thursday. Nothing. I was mad at myself for constantly checking my cell phone display throughout the course of every day like an idiot, hoping to hear from him. On Friday when I arrived at his apartment, he wasn't there. Disappointment filled me. I began to work, and after the last four hours of the project passed, the website was done. Just before I shut down the computer, I noticed a folder that wasn't related to the website. I opened the folder, and a series of videos popped up. *China, Ryan, lesson number ten*, was the caption under the first video. Intrigued, I kept looking through the folder. The same description was beneath each media file, except for the numbers, which had gone in sequential order from lowest to highest, and also except for the last three videos, which had been marked differently.

I clicked on *China, Ryan, lesson number eleven*. A large training room decorated in Chinese style had shown on the screen.

Younger Ryan, about ten years old, faced a Chinese man in his fifties. Barefoot, they wore white shirts and loose white pants. They bowed to each other and started to fight. The man, obviously his trainer, beat him in a matter of seconds, and in the second video, the third, the forth and so on, but from lesson number twenty, Ryan started to improve, more and more with each media file I opened. The last three videos in the folder had been named: *China, final contest part one, China, final contest part two, A rose by any other name...*

The final contest videos showed him at about the age of seventeen. There were two different contests: part one with long battle swords, part two without. Those fights weren't in the training room but outside a house surrounded by mountains and green gardens. He succeeded in beating his teacher in both fights, and I didn't miss the astonishment that flickered over his trainer's face when his student won, as if Ryan was the first who ever defeated him.

The last video, *A rose by any other name...*, displayed an adorable five-year-old Ryan sitting on his mother's lap, inside a greenhouse that looked exactly like the one he had taken me to. Jasmin, his aunt, filmed them on the bench across the waterfall. His delicate and beautiful mother held in her hand a bunch of red roses, her opposite arm wrapped around her son's body.

"Ryan, say hi to the camera," Jasmin said from behind the camera.

"Monkey, wave hi to Aunt Jasmin." His mother looked at him with a loving smile.

Ryan looked over at the camera and waved, then asked, "Aunt Jasmin, why do you need so many roses?"

"It's for her good friend David. He wants to surprise Chelsy, the girl he loves, by giving them to her," his mother explained.

He turned to glance at her and wrinkled his nose. "But why red roses? Why not candies?"

Jasmin chuckled and the camera shook. "You know, monkey, one day you'll find a girl who will make you feel something wonderful in here"—she put her palm on her son's small chest—"and you'll bring her to this greenhouse, cut a red rose, and give it to her. By handing it to her, you're telling her that she is a very special girl for you because red roses mean love." Ryan seemed so mature for his age, listening to his mother and not showing signs of disgust like most boys at that age would have.

"Would that special girl's name be Chelsy, too?" he wondered.

His mother put the bouquet on the bench beside her and turned to face her son. "Yes, her name could be Chelsy, but it could also be Kelly, or Britney, or Sarah. Her name is not what's important, monkey. What's important is who she is because that's what would make you want to give her your heart, along with a red rose."

"A rose by any other name would smell as sweet," Jasmin added, and little Ryan appeared to try to get the meaning of it.

Lily laughed and kissed his forehead. "You're only five. You'll see when you grow up. Now who wants some hot chocolate?" she asked and playfully mussed his dark blond hair, which over the years would turn to dark brown. The video ended with that.

Was I that special girl for him? Back at my dorm, I picked up from the desk the rose he'd given me that day in the glass house. Although I'd dried it, it had retained its red color. My eyes moved to my too-quiet cell phone resting on my bed. Why hadn't he called? Not wanting to torture myself about it anymore, I laid the flower back on the desk and headed to my bed, dozing off a few minutes later.

Sunday evening I had a terrible feeling that maybe something bad had happened to him, but when I'd called Hannah, she'd mentioned that Nate had met with him in the morning and that he'd been fine, yet in a really vile mood. Right when I hung up with her, someone knocked on the door.

I jumped out of my desk chair and darted to the door. Opening it, my heart skipped a beat when I stood in front of Ryan. With dark circles under his eyes, he looked drawn and ragged, wearing a pair of faded jeans, a black leather jacket, and a slate-gray shirt. I stopped myself from wrapping my arms around him and squeezing. I'd missed him. "You look weary," I said, biting my lower lip and tightening my grip on the door handle.

"Yeah, I'm beat." He pinched the bridge of his nose and rubbed his eyes with his thumbs, drawing a deep breath and letting it out slowly. Then his gaze was back on me. "But I'm still up for watching a movie with you." A small, forced smile appeared on his lips.

"A movie?" My brows knitted together.

"I rented something you love. We can watch it over at my place, and, Emma...I'm sorry I haven't contacted you over the last week."

Without dithering whether to go with him, I grabbed my stuff, and we went to the place I'd been afraid I wouldn't see again, my no longer workplace. The ride was quiet, and he seemed so distant.

"What's going on with you?" I asked once we reached his apartment. I was worried about him.

With a big bowl of popcorn, he came over, set it on the coffee table and after sinking onto the sofa, he turned to me. "Nothing. Let's watch the movie." He tapped the spot next to him.

"Ryan, what's bothering you?" I crossed my arms over my chest, determination in my voice.

"I'm fine," he insisted. I moved to sit beside him.

"The dark circles under your eyes say otherwise," I countered, and it was then that he looked as if something inside him broke.

Letting out a bitter laugh, he looked down and ran his fingers through his messy hair.

"He fucking won," he hissed to himself.

"Won? Who?" He lifted his head, looking at me, and his expression grew darker. "Who won?" I pressed.

"God, I'm sorry, Emma." He heaved a long sigh. "I'm so fucked up right now. I shouldn't have come to pick you up, not yet."

"That's why you didn't call me? Ryan, I don't care what state you're in. Whatever you're going through—" I paused when my eyes caught a picture of a little, cute girl, about ten years old, hugging Ryan's mother, displayed on the laptop he'd left open on the dining room table. A bolt of recognition struck me. Last week, when he'd been in New York, it was the anniversary of his family's deaths. Obviously, he'd been referring to the man who killed his family, blaming him.

I jerked my gaze back to him. "No, he didn't win. He's dead. That's not winning."

"No, not the killer, the man who's buried next to my mother and sister," he corrected me, and I lost him.

"Your father?" I asked, puzzled.

He nodded and sagged a bit down in his seat, as if his last ounce of strength had left him. "I can't cry. I can't. I can't. I really thought that now I'd be able to fucking cry on my mother's and sister's graves, but no. I just can't."

"W-what, Ryan, I—what are you talking about?" One moment he was sitting near me, the next he was standing and pulling off his shirt, then throwing it aside. Horror swept through me. I inhaled sharply as I jammed a hand to my mouth. My stomach nearly regurgitated its contents.

Chapter 20

Two rows of scars ran across his chest. The horizontal line marks in his skin were separated and short. What gave rise to the nausea was not their ugliness, but bearing witness to a cruel, sadistic act. Who had done that to him?

He answered my unspoken question. "A gift from my dear, dear father." The word father came out of his mouth in a contemptuous tone.

"How could it be? He loved you. I could see it in his eyes when he talked about you in an interview."

"He didn't make millions by being a bad actor. It was his job to get into character and fool everybody. It might have sounded heartfelt, but trust me—it wasn't."

I swallowed hard and got to my feet. I felt so sorry for him. My gut twisted at the thought of what he must have gone through. I stood in front of him and reached for the first row of scars, but his voice stopped my fingers midair. "Don't."

I pulled my hand back and gave him a questioning look.

"Emma, every time we meet, you give me something of yourself; it can be your smile, your blushes, your laugh, the scent of your lavender body lotion. All of what you give me, each time, I cherish, but your pity is not something I ever want from you." His voice was blank, but his eyes were full of complex emotions I couldn't read. He pivoted around, and for the first time, I got a full view of his colorful ink as he moved to the floor-to-ceiling windows. The tattoo was a vicious-looking python, evil, red eyes, jaw outstretched, showing scary, sharp teeth and a thin pink tongue. Its wide body coiled up his arm from his right elbow and extended across a large portion of the right side of his back, where the snake wrapped its body tightly around a small, black heart. Ryan leaned a shoulder against the window, looking out it.

"Why did he do that to you?"

His gaze was on me now as he stuffed his hands into his front jeans pockets, crossing his ankles.

"A month after I turned six, my father came to tuck me in bed. He brought with him a small, flat metal box. In it, there were three sheets of paper. As he pulled them out, he told me that it was time for me to become the perfect son a—"

"The perfect son?" I went to sit on the sofa, facing him.

"Yes. The perfect son. His definition of it was typed on the first sheet of paper. I was a quick learner, and at that age, I knew how to read and write. He had me read that page aloud." He paused for a few seconds, took a deep breath through his nose, then proceeded. "The perfect son never cries, is never afraid, never feels sympathy toward others, and is the fastest, strongest, and most fearless fighter there is," he recited from memory and turned his gaze back to the view outside the window. "It was my new bible...that was what he said." A muscle in his jaw worked, and his throat moved as he swallowed. A couple of seconds later, he returned his cold stare to me. "On the second page, there was a set of rules I had to follow in order to become what he wanted me to be. Rule number one, every day before going to bed I must read the definition of the perfect son and then for four hours straight write it down in repetition. Rule number two, twice a month, I had to accompany his men to a room where they tortured people in front of me in order to see if I'd cry or show any sympathy."

"Oh my God. Your father was..." The cruelty of him was indescribable.

Reading the thought from my horrified face, he agreed with a nod and continued. "Rule number three, once every two weeks, I had to face the Fear test, which was changed from time to time. The most common one, though, was to bring me to the roof of a high-rise building, where his men forced me to stand at the edge and look down." Sickened, I closed my eyes. When I opened them, he went on. "Rule number four, the last one, was all about the Fighting contests. They began when I was ten, but the intense regime of training started at five. I was trained by my master, Chao Wáng, every day after school. In the summers, we flew to his house in China to get full-time training from the first light of day till midnight. He requested from Chao Wáng two things: to record his lessons while I was there, and at the end of the summer, to have me compete against someone my age and with the same level of fighting skill as mine. In those contests, I had to win."

He paused, and I asked angrily, "Where was your mother in all this? She must have known. Why didn't she stop him?"

"She knew, yeah, but every time she fought him, it put pressure on her, and since she also suffered from panic attacks, a lot of them, I wanted her far away from him." So that was how he could tell I was having a panic attack at Nate's birthday. "Besides," he continued, "fighting him was pointless. He was a bully with enormous power, and I'm not only talking about physical power." Money. Bruce Damon was a billionaire. It must have bought him power in the right places.

"What was on the third page?" I wasn't eager to hear more about his father's gruesome ideas about how to raise his child, but I had to ask.

"The punishments for failing the tests and contests." Looking at the scars on his chest, a tremor raked through my body. "Failing twenty times on one of the tests earned me a cut with a knife. Losing a contest in China twice meant two cuts. From the day he gave me those sheets of paper, I got two punishment-free years to practice everything, and after that I had to be very careful not to fail."

"But you did fail..." I said, looking at the evidence of what his father had done to him. "You were so young. How was your body able to take all the physical trauma?" I tried to keep my voice steady, but it was hard. He pulled his hands from his pockets, glancing out through the glass while answering.

"I suffered a few infections. Some of them were severe."

"And the hospital didn't think to call child protective services?" Irritated, I raised my voice. He turned his head to me.

"I was never treated in hospitals. He had a friend, a doctor who kept his mouth shut and treated me. Eventually, though, I succeeded in getting almost full control over my body, and there were no more cuts."

"But no one can control fear or tears. It's impossible," I argued.

He pulled in a deep breath and looked as if he was traveling back in time inside his head, remembering things. Heavy silence descended. Eventually, he broke it. "After Chao Wáng noticed my scars, he taught me the art of meditation. Mastering it took me a few years, but in the end, I was able to gain control over my mind, to bring it to other places during the tests, and then I was able to pass them." He scrubbed a hand down his face tiredly and looked over at me. "The one thing I couldn't control was the fear of getting another slice in my skin. The fear was so strong that gradually, I felt how my body started rejecting the urge to cry, and now I just get this paralyzed feeling whenever I have that urge." His hands went back into his front jeans pockets.

"Until this day? Even when you know he can't hurt you anymore?" I asked.

He huffed a mirthless laugh. "Trust me, I've tried so many times. The day I received a text message saying my mother and Camilla were murdered, I was devastated, but I couldn't shed one single tear...he won."

"No, don't say that. What about getting professional help?" Ryan turned to face me fully, his back leaning against the window. Seeing all of his scars sent a jolt through my body. God, what his father had done to him had been pure torture.

"Like I said, I've tried everything. Nothing worked," he said with an emotionless voice. Ryan had been brain-washed at such a young age, and now everything about him was adding up—especially his coldness. His father, on the other hand, I couldn't understand. "Why was he so obsessed with turning you into his twisted version of a perfect son? Was he abused as a child?" Or maybe he'd been just a pure psychopath.

"It wasn't an obsession. It was merely a goal to him."

"A goal?"

"Yeah, to win a bet."

"A bet? What bet?" I'd thought things couldn't get any more disturbing. Turned out I was wrong.

Chapter 21

"My mother got pregnant with me about the same time as his close friend's wife, who was also carrying a boy, Tristan, so their husbands decided to make a wager: who would succeed in raising the perfect son." Tristan? I recognized this name. Josh had told me about him and Ryan's ex-girlfriend, Thea. The three of them were friends. I shook my head, appalled that another psycho was involved in this story—Tristan's father.

"Was Tristan raised the same way you were? With all the rules and tests?" I asked.

He took in a breath, letting it out slowly. The gravity of his expression created gentle lines across his forehead. Talking about his past was obviously hard for him.

"All I know is that we were both trained from the age of five. The terms of the wager were that we start training at five and finishing it at the age of seventeen. When Tristan and I hung out, we never talked about what was going on at home. Also, neither of us knew about the bet."

"How did you find out about it?"

"When I turned seventeen, I had my last fighting contest over two separate days. It was against Chao Wáng." I'd seen the two parts of the fight on his computer. And now, knowing what I knew, I felt a shudder rocked through me. His face darkened before he went on. "Failing was not an option for me. Getting another two cuts was...I just couldn't fail. Even though I never lost a fight, winning against Chao Wáng wasn't something I thought I could pull off. Chao Wáng is the best there is, and he might have taught me everything, but no one can match his fighting skill. He's a rare talent."

"It wasn't a fair fight. You were a kid and he was your teacher. Why did he agree to compete against his student?"

"He didn't see it that way. To him, a fighter is a fighter regardless of his age. If you are skilled, age won't matter. A month before the fight, Chao told me that I was done with the training, and for the next month, I was practicing for the contest by myself, every day, all the time. It was worth it; I won. And then, right after the last contest, he flew me to Alaska, where I first learned about the bet and the Elites."

"Why did your father fly you to Alaska? And what's the Elites?"

"He and Tristan's father were members of an exclusive, tight group that called themselves the Elites. It consists of ten powerful and rich members who have a custom: once a year, every member gathers in a heavily guarded house. The location changes every year. They invite other powerful men from around the world, and the guests and the members of the Elites stay there for two weeks in which virtually everything is allowed: drugs, alcohol, gambling, and also underground fighting, where the fighters fight to the death."

"To the death?" I echoed, a distinct quaver in my voice.

"That's the rule. To win, you have to kill your opponent, without any weapon or help." He paused, maybe to let me process everything he'd dropped on me.

I closed my apparently open mouth and ran a palm over my face, then murmured, "It's terrible." I gazed back over at him. "Who were the fighters? How were those mortal combats organized?" I had so many questions in my head that I felt like it was going to blow up. He seemed to understand and answered each of my questions with patience.

"During the two-week party, there is a fight each night. The winner continues to the next day, and the last one remaining alive at the end of the two weeks wins ten million dollars plus an invitation to the next year's party as a guest. And you'd be surprised to know how many are willing to come and fight, some for the money, some because killing gives them a thrill, and others because they want access to the party, which is in a separate section of the house that no one who's not one of the Elites or their guests is allowed to enter."

"They are killing people for an invite to a party and money?"

"And respect, a lot of it."

"Do the Elites and their guests watch the fights?" I asked, feeling sick.

"Yes, but not in the same room with the others."

"The others?"

"Unlike the closed party, you don't have to be associated with the Elites in order to gain entrance to the fights. You only need to have the right connections, which can get you an invitation, but you'll never have any interaction with the Elites and their guests." His icy eyes were on me when he spoke.

"I don't understand. Why did your father take you to this...this gathering in Alaska? So you would take part in the fights?"

"Not exactly. The Elites' members were supposed to determine who wins the bet. They all agreed that when Tristan and I reached the age of seventeen, there'd be a special gathering. In addition to throwing the usual party, they'd also test us in three different tests: fear, compassion, and fighting. The winner would be the one whose son was still alive at the end of the three tests." It was hard to fathom how a father could risk his own child's life. A thought suddenly jumped into my head: he was alive, and so was Tristan.

"Nobody won? What happened?" I asked.

"Before the tests started, he told me about the Elites and that I had to pass three final challenges in front of them. I didn't ask too many questions. I just wanted to get it over with. During the week I was there, I successfully finished the Fear and Compassion tests. The day before the fight." He stopped. His jaw hardened, and his light eyes simmered with a stark anger. His voice filled the air again. "He came into my room, and that was when I discovered that Tristan was my opponent. Confused, I asked him what the hell Tristan had to do with all this, and he told me about the wager. I was so furious to find out that I was just a bet. I was just a fucking bet to him." He tangled a hand through his hair. "I snapped and for the first time in my life I defied him, yelling that he could go to hell and that I wouldn't fight. In return, that prick yelled back at me, saying that without his money, I'm nothing, that he made his first million when he was only twenty—something I could only dream of because I had zero abilities." A puff of bitter laughter escaped him. "He kept screaming that no college would have me while Tristan had already gotten into Harvard.

"He ended his lovely speech by telling me that even if I got into some college, I'd flunk out since I'm a loser. That day, as I flew back to New York alone, I promised myself three things. One, I'd make my first million before turning twenty. Two, I'd get accepted into Harvard, but I'd attend school here in Michigan, where my mother always wanted me to go, and finish a degree without flunking out." With an arctic look, he snorted in scorn at his father's belief that he would flunk out. "Three, I'd never again use a dime of his money. Never. He was killed soon after he returned from Alaska, and before I could accomplish everything on my list. But it didn't matter to me."

"You weren't there at the time of the murders. Was it because of what happened with your father?"

"Yes. When I arrived back in New York, I immediately packed up my things to get out of his apartment, but my mother begged me to stop and think it through. She said I should clear my head in Europe for a week or two, let things cool off, and if I still wanted to leave, she'd find a way that I'd be able to stay with my aunt."

"How did she expect you to live in the same house where your father was?" There was an edge of annoyance in my tone.

"She was afraid that if I ran away, I'd gradually lose touch with her and become homeless, living on the streets. In the end, for her, although I knew I'd never go back to live in his house again, I agreed to take off to Europe for a week, and she bought the tickets. I said goodbye to my little sister." He paused. I watched sadness spread across his face and my heart constricted. "Before I left, as the elevator door slid open, she...she grabbed my hand, demanding that I promise to teach her Kung Fu when I got back. She loved everything related to martial arts, so I assured her that not only would I teach her, but I'd also one day buy a martial arts studio for her."

And he had, in New York. "It must have been so hard on you. How did you deal with their deaths?" I asked.

"By focusing on the list I'd made for myself. Living at my aunt's, I began to work on number one. It wasn't easy, to say the least, but I've always loved challenges. I found out that although writing songs can bring some good money, it wasn't enough. I had to make a million and fast, so I began to do extensive research about the market and then decided to invest in Nate's cousin's startup. At that time, it was new, but I believed it would be worth a lot of money in the future, and I was right. It was bought for over a billion dollars.

"From this sale, I got more than he could ever dream to have when he was nineteen, and I crossed off number one. Number two, I crossed off in my senior year of high school. The day I received the acceptance letter from Harvard, I went to his grave and threw it there." He huffed with a contemptuous air. "I can only hope he was rolling over in his grave. Number three, I crossed off recently when I got his damn inheritance money. All of it, along with his houses, I gave to the two things he hated the most." A slow, satisfied smile shaped his lips. "Half to charities and the other half to my mom's sister, Jasmin."

Stepping away from the window, he came to stand between the coffee table and the sofa, peering down at me. "Emma, I didn't want you to see me like this, but I screwed up and brought you here anyway. I know this is a lot to dump on you...a lot to take in. If you feel like going back to your dorm, just say the word."

I rose from the sofa and approached him. I tipped my head back to gaze at him and thought about his accomplishments and the way he'd stood up against his father in the end. I was full of admiration for him. My stare dropped down to his chest. If only I could take his pain away with kisses and touch. I outstretched my arm toward his scars until my hand came in contact with them. This time, he didn't stop me. I ran the pads of my fingers over the ridges and puckered skin, closing the distance between us and kissing the deep marks. His chest rose sharply as he sucked in air, and he gently pressed me closer to him, his hand behind my head.

After a moment, I pulled away. I curled my fingers around his left shoulder and circled behind him, studying his tattoo.

Having heard the details of his past, I gathered that the python symbolized his father and the black heart strangled by it was Ryan's. How I wished I could remove the snake from his skin, his memory, his soul. I finished my circle and was back in front of him, staring up at his cold, ice-filled eyes. I touched his cheek, feeling his features grow softer under my palm. Then I got onto my tiptoes, wound my arms around his neck, and kissed him. Warm lips eagerly welcomed mine. While his tongue swept out to meet mine, his hands went to the small of my back, turning me, moving us to the sofa and leaning my body down onto it.

On top of me, he broke the kiss and drew back a fraction. With the thick heat of lust in his eyes, he looked down at me, his thumb stroking the contour of my jaw, then his mouth went to my throat, his hand slipping to the nape of my neck as he tugged it to his lips. I dropped my head back, feeling his tongue over the sensitive skin under my ear lobe, my fingers digging into his shoulders. He kissed a path down my neck, his hand moving to the rise of my breast, cupping and kneading it over the fabric of my T-shirt. A weak sound escaped me. He trailed kisses down the curve between my shoulder and neck. The hand on my breast slipped underneath my top and his thumb teased my nipple through the thin fabric of my bra, then he lifted me slightly, yanking my tee over my head. He pushed the cup of my bra down and his tongue swiftly replaced his thumb as he leaned me back and suckled the hard bud into his mouth, flicking it with his tongue.

I moaned and buried my fingers in the soft, thick hair at the back of his head, pulling him closer.

He turned his attention to my other nipple and gave it a similar treatment, circling, sucking, and nipping. I closed my eyes with a low cry, pleasure racing through me. His hands skimmed over my waist, his lips exploring, his tongue trailing downward. Hands following his mouth to my navel, he caressed the tender flesh right above the waistband of my jeans, searing it with his touch, then slipping down and opening the first button of my jeans. He popped the second button a short moment later, and while he positioned himself back up, his fingers opened the third one. He kissed me deeply, one hand cradling my cheek as his tongue stroked mine, the other going down over my fourth button. I burned with desire and the need for him to pull my jeans off so I could feel his solid body against mine, so I could feel him inside of me. But he pulled away. Breathing heavily, he shut his eyes and shook his head, as if forcing himself to stop. He opened his eyes, and re-buttoned my jeans. *What's wrong? Why doesn't he continue?*

"No, not like this, not on the couch, not with you," he whispered, more to himself, and gazed down at me. "Emma, we should stop." He dragged himself up and sat, rubbing his face with his hands. I quickly righted my bra and put my shirt back on, humiliation killing my horny mood and allowing me to think clearly. If he hadn't stopped us, I would've slept with him, here, on the sofa—my first time. Not so smart when you've got strong feelings for a guy who might also share some of those feelings, but had huge commitment issues, which I'd forgotten about. Ending up like Ashley or Kirsten, with tears and a broken heart, was not something I aspired to.

Having his shirt back on, Ryan settled into the sofa and grabbed the bowl of popcorn and remote from the coffee table, ready to watch the movie he'd rented. When I didn't make any move to lean back against the cushions and relax, his hand shot around my waist and pulled me against his side. I scooted back from him. "Um, Ryan, I think you should get me back to my dorm."

My response didn't seem to surprise him, but he asked anyway, "You sure? It's your favorite movie, *Casablanca*, at least that's what Nate said after fishing it out of Hannah for me." His lips went up in a sexy smile. *Casablanca is* my favorite movie, and I wanted more than anything to snuggle with him while it played on his big, flat screen TV. But I couldn't.

"I'm sorry. I need some time alone."

"I understand." He got to his feet, put the bowl and remote control onto the coffee table, and offered me his hand. I took it. "C'mon, I'll drop you off."

In the dorm, after I unlocked my room and stepped in, he trailed me inside and closed the door. I turned, a multitude of thoughts running through my head and none of them good. "You okay?" he asked, cupping my shoulders. Not nearly. I titled my head up and my eyes were on him.

"Yes," I lied, feigning a grin.

"Okay, I'll give you space, but if you need anything, and I mean anything—call me." He pulled me into his arms.

"What are you doing?" I asked, alarmed.

"I'm pretty sure it's called a hug."

"No, Ryan, I..." I pushed away. His features contorted with confusion.

"What happened earlier...it was a mistake." That I'd made when I had kissed him. The puzzlement left his face.

"Yeah, I agree. I want to take things slow with you, Emma." His fingers gently grazed the line of my jaw, filling me with a pleasant warmth.

"No, I meant…" Fighting the urge to bury myself in his arms, I took two steps back and tucked my hair behind my hair. "I meant it shouldn't have happened in the first place because we are *just* friends. That's all." At his perplexed look, I tried to explain. "I'm sorry for kissing you. I—"

"*That's* what you're choosing to be sorry for? For the only freaking thing that makes me feel sane in this screwed-up world?"

The hurt in his voice broke my heart. But if I was going to hand it over to him, I had to know where I stood with him. "Ryan, what exactly do you want from me?"

Please, please, please say something that has words like commitment in it. With bated breath, I waited for his answer. And waited. And waited. He fell quiet. Only a burst of laughter and muffled voices outside the door punctuated the silent room.

Which, I supposed, was his answer. Silence meant he didn't want anything meaningful with me. Was that how Ashley had felt when she'd asked him if he'd cared about her and he'd replied by saying nothing?

I broke the painful silence and forced my lips to curve into a faint smile. "Well, we're not the first friends who've crossed that line, right? Let's just forget about it." He didn't react. His eyes held a faraway look, like he was staring through me. "Ryan? Are you with me?" I waved my hand in front of his face, but it was my voice that jolted him from his stupor. He shook his head and regained his focus.

"Sorry, what?" he asked.

"Are you okay?"

"Oh, yeah, yeah, I am."

"Um, anyway, I sorta need to do some stuff now so…"

"Yeah, sure, I'll leave you to it." And that was it. He was out of my room and…life?

Hurting, I flopped onto the bed and pushed off my shoes, my mind slowly drifting to everything he'd told me about his father. The queasy feeling in my stomach came back, and it was still there when I woke up the next morning.

I spent the day trying not to mull over the way things had ended last night with Ryan, but by the time Hannah dropped by later in the evening, I was a mess. With bloodshot eyes and a leaky nose, I told her about my feelings for Ryan and how he'd not so subtly evaded my question yesterday. She hugged me and announced, "That's it. No more crying. You're joining me to meet Nate at the Blue club." I didn't feel at all up to going out, but it was better than the alternative: staying in the dorm, sobbing. Unsatisfied with the clothes in my closet, Hannah insisted that we go over to her room to find something suitable for me to wear. And by suitable, she apparently meant a tight, skimpy, blue dress.

My eyes rounded when I peered at the tiny piece of cloth on the hanger in her hand.

"Oh, come on, Em. You've got to show off your assets in order to attract the hotties."

She quirked her lips and rocked her eyebrows up and down. I rolled my eyes and, for the first time that day, I smiled. Not in the mood to argue, I slipped the dress from the hanger and put it on. It was brand new. Hannah hadn't worn it before, but somehow there was still something familiar about it, and while scrutinizing myself in the mirror, I remembered. It was the same dress Ashley had been wearing that day I'd found her waiting for Ryan in the living room, after I'd finished coding. Shoving the compliments he'd thrown her way from my head, I let Hannah put makeup on me and, after she got ready, we went to the Blue club downtown.

Inside the club, we hitched ourselves onto the high stools at the bar. The place was already crammed, and there was no sign of Nate. Hannah ordered us drinks and texted him. "He'll be here in a minute," she told me above the music, and her eyes examined me. "Hey, sweetie, cheer up, every guy here is checking you out, so wipe that my-pet-just-died look off your face, and put on a I-am-having-the-time-of-my-life face." I couldn't help it; I was miserable and going out didn't help as I'd hoped it would. "There he is." She craned her neck and waved, beaming. Nate appeared from behind me and pulled Hannah in for a long kiss. After separating his lips from hers, he turned to look at me.

"Hey, Emma, what's up?" Before I could answer, he drew his brows together in concern. "Everything okay?"

God, did I really look so sad? "Yes. I'm fine." I faked a smile. "Why don't you two go dancing?" I suggested, not wanting my mood to spoil their fun.

"No, I'm staying here with you. We're finding you a hot guy." She was determined, but I was more.

"And how could I possibly meet guys with you sitting next to me?" I grinned and winked at her. She laughed. "I'm serious, though. I'm fine." I swung my gaze to Nate. "Go ahead, dance with your girlfriend," I pressed, and they went to the dance floor. I took a sip from my apple martini. The alcohol burned a path down my throat. I coughed and grimaced. Then I took another drink, and another. For all of the bitter taste, I drank on. Before long, I was buzzed and nodding along to the thumping beat of the music. Two songs later, Hannah came back, by herself.

"Where's Nate?"

"He had to make a phone call. He'll be back in a minute." She eyed me and rested her elbow on the bar. "You look better. Wait." She gasped. "You so met a cute guy! Where is he? Did you give him your number?"

"Nope. No guy." I giggled. Her eyes darted down to my almost empty glass.

"Gosh, Em, you've gotten yourself wasted from barely one drink?" She chuckled. I wasn't drunk. I just felt better, less unhappy.

"I'm not drunk." I closed my eyes and touched the tip of my nose with my index finger, as if doing a sobriety test. I opened my eyes. "See?" Her attention drifted over my shoulder, and I turned to find Nate working his way to us while maneuvering through the crowd. I looked back at Hannah, who had her head tipped back as she swigged from her beer.

When he reached us, he took her hand and dragged her back to the dance floor.

I went back to my drink, taking my time with it, finishing the glass after about six songs.

"How is it that a beautiful girl like you is sitting all alone?" A guy in jeans and a black tee said. He was the fourth guy who hit on me tonight, and that pick-up line was the worst I heard. "Can I buy you another drink?"

I scanned his face. Black hair, brown eyes, long scar bisecting his right brow, and a charming smile with a set of white, even teeth. An outcome of hard work in the gym, his body was larger than the previous guys who had hit on me in the last half an hour. He exuded self-confidence. Great. How was I going to dispose of this one?

"No, thanks," I replied, not showing interest. Unapologetically, his eyes dropped to my cleavage for a moment before going back up. I shifted on the stool, uncomfortable. I needed to get out of there and back to the dorm, so I raised my hand, signaling the bartender for the check, and leaned to my side to look behind him over the packed space of the dance floor, searching for Hannah.

"Leaving already?" This guy was not taking the hint.

"Yes," I said flatly over the loud music. When I got the check, I dug my wallet from my purse and slapped a bill on the wooden counter.

"No, allow me." He drew his wallet out from his back pocket. "Where are you headed? I'll give you a ride." He tossed enough money on the bar to cover my bill.

"Thanks, but I'll pay for my own drink, and go home— alone." I scooted his money away from mine.

"Whoa, why the hostility?"

"I'm not—" I broke off and lied. "Look, I'm sorry, but I've got a boyfriend."

"Don't worry; I'm very discreet. He doesn't have to know." He threw me a smug smile, like he'd just solved our sole obstacle.

I sneered at him. "I'm not interested." I was ready to get up and go look for Hannah, but being awfully persistent, he continued.

"Don't BS me and tel—"

"She said she's not interested. Beat it," a recognizable, deep male voice cut him off.

I whipped my head around. Behind the annoying guy stood Ryan, eyes concerned, assessing my condition. Why was he worried about me? He took a step toward me, but the guy turned on his stool, stood, and blocked Ryan's way.

"You piss off," the guy said angrily.

"I strongly advise you to get the hell out of my way." Ryan sounded infuriated.

"Listen, asshole, go pick another girl or your pretty face won't stay pretty anymore."

Before things could deteriorate, I jumped off the stool and stepped aside so that the guy's body wouldn't conceal me from Ryan. I looked at Ryan, ready to say something, but furrows appeared in Ryan's brow, creating a stern look on his face as he told the guy, "No. You listen to me. This is how it's gonna be: one, you move your sorry ass out of my way. Two, if one doesn't suit you, then your sorry ass will have a painful introduction with my foot. Three—" I gasped sharply when the guy suddenly took a swing at him. In a split second, Ryan's hand jerked forward to clamp the guy's fist before it reached its target, Ryan's face. Then he drove his foot into the guy's shin.

The guy cried out, but Ryan wasn't done. He wrenched the guy's arm behind his back, grabbed his hair, and slammed the right side of his head against the bar top with a loud thud. Glasses shook, and people sitting at the bar near them jolted away. Refusing to relinquish even an ounce of his firm grip, Ryan leaned in to him and resumed talking as if he'd never been interrupted. "Three, I smash your ugly face against the bar top. And that's where you should consider yourself lucky since option number four doesn't have the same gentle approach." He released him.

"Fuuuuuuuck!" the guy screamed in agony when he tried to put weight on his injured leg. Dropping to the floor and clutching his hurt leg, he threw threats at Ryan, who paid them as much attention as one might give the buzz of an annoying mosquito. Looking at me, his blue eyes slid over my dress, providing deep cleavage and reaching halfway down my thighs. With a disapproving look, he shrugged off his black, leather jacket and stepped up to me.

"Are you okay?" he asked as he hung his jacket over my shoulders, covering me. The faint scent of his spicy cologne touched my nostrils.

"Yes, he didn't do anything to me." I gestured down at the guy, who, in between cursing and moaning in pain, leaned his back against a stool, unable to stand.

"I wasn't talking about him, I—" Ryan stopped and took my hand. "Let's get outside. I can't hear myself in here." With my free hand, I grabbed my purse and Hannah's, and as he led me to the back exit of the club, I glanced back in the direction of the yelling and cursing. The guy's face was screwed up in pain, and he still didn't seem able to use his leg. Nobody paid any attention to him, though, and the people who had left their stools during the fight were back at the bar like nothing had happened.

"What did you do to him?" I shouted to his back.

"I didn't break anything if that's what you're asking, but it'll hurt like hell for the next twenty-four hours," he shouted back, not turning to look at me.

Once outside, in a parking lot behind the club, a blast of cold air hit my bare legs. He stood close to me, sniffing my breath.

"Have you been drinking?" His voice was laced with surprise. "You never drink. What's going on with you?"

"Nothing. Since when does trying new things mean something's wrong?" I asked defensively. His gaze went from my high heels to the provocative dress and stopped on my made-up face.

"When it all comes at once," he replied. I removed his jacket. The chilly night froze me, but his smell was too much for me. I needed to distance myself from him and everything connected to the man I'd fallen in love with. A group of rowdy guys opened the door of the club and went out. The music spilled out until the door closed behind them, reducing the noise to a dull sound. As they passed us, all of them fixed me with a look that rendered me uncomfortable. With all the stuff in my hands, I folded my arms across my chest, shifting my weight nervously from one foot to the other. He snatched his jacket from my hand and slung it back over my shoulders.

"Leave it," he ordered.

"I'm not cold," I lied.

"It's not just for warming you up," he said sharply. Unfortunately, the cold night wind overrode my need to stay away from the smell of his cologne, so I slid into his jacket. He seemed content to see me in it. Why was he treating me like I was his little sister? I guessed he didn't regard me as he did Ashley. What should have stayed inside my mind somehow got out of my mouth.

"You know, I seem to remember that when Ashley was wearing this exact same dress, you didn't complain about it. If anything, you were telling her how sexy and hot she was."

Before I could mentally smack myself, he was suddenly inches away from me, tipping my chin up so that my gaze met his. My body instantly stirred from his touch and proximity.

"Did you like it when those douches leered at you?" His eyes blazed when he indicated the guys walking away from us.

"No," I admitted.

"Why?" he asked and dropped his hand.

An image of their stares went through my mind and the unpleasant feeling was back.

"Because they looked at me like I was—" For some reason, it was hard for me to finish the sentence.

"Was what?" he pressed.

I sighed. "Nothing but a piece of meat."

"And how did I look at Ashley when I told her how hot and sexy she was in this dress?" he asked.

The memory of the expression on his face, when he'd complimented her, surfaced in my head and any jealousy I felt vanished in a second. "The same way they looked at me," I finally said.

His feathers smoothed, and a smile crept onto his lips.

"Why are you smiling?" I asked.

"It amuses me that you would actually think I'd remember when or if she wore a dress like this."

"You didn't remember?"

"No, I didn't. I simply made a reasonable supposition that I looked at her in the same way." He chuckled, moistening his bottom lip with his tongue, his dimple on full display. "You're cute when you're jealous, you know that?" He tapped the tip of my nose, and my cheeks warmed. "Emma," he said, and his voice took on a more serious tone. "When I see you dressed like this, the words sexy and hot definitely come to my head, but in a diffident way. Also, I have no desire to share you in this dress with everybody else." He zipped his leather jacket up to my throat.

"Em?" Hannah said from behind me. I spun. She was outside the club, rubbing her arms against the chill, eyes on Ryan, mouth tightly compressed. She turned that glare on me, ready to say something, but I was quicker.

"I'm fine. I'm heading back to my dorm, though. You stay with Nate. Have fun." I handed her her bag. I'd left my coat in her car, so I made a mental note to get it tomorrow.

"No, I'm not leaving you with him."

"It's okay. Really," I promised.

Knowing there was no point in arguing with me, she said, "Okay. Call me tomorrow." At that moment, Nate pushed the door open. He was completely focused on Hannah that he didn't notice Ryan and me being there.

"Here you are. Dave's daring you to a drinking contest. You're totally gonna nail him, right?"

He pushed her inside as she answered, "You bet I will."

I felt hands touching my arms from behind me. They turned me and I faced Ryan.

"My car's right there." He nodded to the parking lot. "Let's go."

The drive to my dorm only took a few minutes. Ryan parked behind my building and walked me to my room. We stopped outside it, and his fingers grazed my cheek. "Sleep tight."

He turned to go, but I caught his arm. "Ryan." He faced me again, a question in his gaze. Instead of offering to return his jacket, I asked, "Can I stay at your place tonight? I don't want to be alone."

Chapter 22

What was I thinking? Was I insane? God, yes, I was, but I didn't care, not about how he might interpret my request or about the consequences of spending the night at his apartment because right now, all I needed was to be close to him. I seemed to have caught him off guard, but after a few seconds, he snapped out of it and smiled at me. "Sure."

I packed up a bag, and we went back to the car. When we arrived at his place, a question popped into my head.

"Why were you in the club?" I asked.

"Looking for you. Nate left a voice mail, saying you seemed really off." Oh my God, he'd called him?

"Why would he do that?"

"He's not stupid, Emma. He's got eyes, and he figured that I'd wanna know if something is wrong with you."

"He shouldn't have done it. I'm fine."

"No, you're not. Something is bugging you"—*yes, you not knowing what you want from me: a real relationship or a passing fling*—"but I won't push you, for now. C'mon, I'll show you where the shower is." He picked up my duffel bag and led me to the second floor. I'd never been up here before. I followed him into a large, modern-looking space that contained three rooms, one of which was the bathroom. The floors were marble, the walls white, and the countertop a deep gray, above which hung a large, spotless mirror. I caught my reflection in it. I had mascara smeared under my eyes, as I had forgotten I'd been wearing makeup and had touched my eyes a few times. I sighed at the sight in front of me and took a shower. When I was done, I brushed my teeth and wrapped myself in a towel that reached my knees.

I stepped out of the bathroom. Ryan's voice drifted down the short hallway. I followed the sound to a half-closed door and nudged it open. He was lying on a king-sized bed, talking on the phone, and motioned for me to step in. What appeared to be his bedroom had floor-to-ceiling windows overlooking the dark sky and downtown. Two guitars and my overnight bag were propped against the closet door. He hung up, swung his legs over the side of the bed, and walked over to me. "I'll let you get dressed. You got everything you need?" I nodded. "Okay then, you'll sleep here. I'll be in the guest room downstairs."

The whole purpose of spending the night in his place was to be close to him. "Why not here? In your bed...with me?"

He looked torn. Just as he was about to reply, I did something stupid. Without thinking, I pushed to my tiptoes and kissed him, my arms hooked around his neck. He groaned low in his throat and kissed me back, pulling me in tight to him.

Not breaking the kiss, he rucked the towel up above my thighs, lowered me onto the covers, and scooted my body up the bed until my feet were off the floor. Hovering over me, he inserted his leg between mine, pushing them apart. His lips left mine and trailed down my neck, kissing my skin as his right leg started to press and rub against my core. At that friction, I instantly moaned and my body began to quake. I clung to him, and he increased the pressure there while his right thigh rocked faster and faster.

My breathing sped up, and I buried my face against his moving shoulder. I clawed at his back, grinding into him, and when he licked the shell of my ear while his body's movements grew even quicker against mine, the climax rolled over me, and I cried out his name. I was breathless as he moved to stare down at me. His lips edged into a small smile while he brushed a strand of hair off my face. I felt his hardness and slipped my hand down between our bodies and reached for the button on his jeans to open it and return the favor, but he caught my hand and brought it back up.

"Trust me, there is nothing more I'd rather do right now than this, but it's not such a good idea. You should get some rest." He kissed my forehead and began to draw away from me.

"Why is it a bad idea?"

My question caused him to slowly return to his previous position, on top of me.

"Because, right now, things can easily get carried away." He skittered his fingers across my cheek. I was in love with him, and even though I probably wouldn't get any commitment from him, I wanted him to be my first, with or without strings attached.

"Good. I'm ready. I want to do this, if you've got...er...protection."

"Emma, I don't want you to do something you'll regret in the morning. We should take things slowly."

"I won't regret it, and it's my choice to make."

After a long, tense moment, he said, "Be right back." He gave me a quick kiss on the lips, shoved his weight off the mattress, and left the room. About three minutes later, he was back with two boxes of condoms. Two! My eyes bugged. He turned off the light and walked in.

"Um, not that I'm skeptical about your...abilities, but two boxes of condoms?"

He chuckled as he stood in front of the nightstand next to the bed, pulling one plastic package out of a box and tucking both of them inside the top drawer. He deposited the condom packet on the nightstand, then reached back with one arm and yanked his shirt over his head, tossing it aside. Next, he stripped off his jeans and boxer briefs. The moonlight illuminated the room, and I could make out his naked body, watching it in awe. My eyes went up to his gorgeous features. A sideways grin crossed his mouth as he crawled over me.

"You better not be skeptical." There was playfulness in his voice, but it was gone when he spoke again. "And I brought the boxes because I can't see why they should be in the guest room anymore."

"You don't keep condoms here, in your room, as well?" I was surprised.

"Up until now, I didn't have a reason," he said, and his eyes darkened with lust. He kissed me hungrily. The pleasure of his kiss seared away any more questions I had. He took the towel off my body and looked down at me. "Emma, if you feel you want to stop, tell me. I can stop at any time and I mean *any* time. Don't hesitate or be afraid to say something, okay?" I nodded, and he cupped the back of my head, lowered his, and slanted his mouth across mine. His tongue slid inside, twisting and stroking, making me soft and shivery inside. I reveled in his taste.

My hands roamed over his chest and back, touching his scars and hard muscles. He worked his hand from my head to my breast while his sensuous lips traveled down my neck and along my collarbones. His skillful mouth, tongue, lips, and hands drove me wild and had me near mindlessness. I writhed beneath him, my entire body igniting. And just before I reached the peak again, he leaned over to the nightstand and grabbed the square of plastic, ripping it with his teeth. He slipped the thin rubber on and, back on top of me, instructed in a guttural voice, "Baby, wrap your legs around me." Baby? Why did I have the crazy feeling he'd called me that before?

He mistook my hesitation. "It's okay. We don't have to go any further."

"No. I want this." I curved my legs around his waist in invitation. "Really want this."

Needing no more coaxing, his hand went down to the sensitive nub between my thighs. He stroked and rubbed it, bringing back the exquisite tension. He braced himself over me and while he continued building the pleasant pressure with his fingers, he pushed slowly inside me, his muscles flexing under my palms. My body stretched to accommodate him.

"I'm sorry, but it'll hurt less this way," he murmured thickly when he encountered my hymen. Then he pulled out and with one quick thrust he was deep inside me. A sharp, burning pain sliced through my body, but his fingers between my legs moved faster and eased the scalding sensation. "Baby, open your eyes. Look at me." His voice shook a little, as if he was making an effort to stay still. I did as he asked. "There is only one thought in my mind right now: Emma, you're mine." He seized my mouth in a deep kiss, his fingers on my nub working magic, and the pain receded. I rocked my hips, and he moaned low in his throat, beginning to move inside me. As he filled me, kissing my neck, I clung to his shoulders, our slick skin sliding against each other. Grunting, he picked up the rhythm of both his hand and hips, faster, vigorously, almost fiercely, and everything inside me clenched. I cried out when suddenly waves of incredible bliss surged through my body. He thrust a few more times and found his release too. Our breathing was ragged as he rolled off me and tugged me against him.

I rested my head on his heaving chest and ran my fingers across his scars while he caressed my hair. My eyes drifted closed, and I fell asleep.

Sometime later, a bright light awakened me. I squinted, looking around. I wasn't in my room and a naked male body, very male, was spooning me. Seconds later, the memory of last night came flooding back to me. I turned to look at Ryan, observing him while he slept. *You're mine.* That's what he'd said. Had he felt possessiveness toward all the girls he'd slept with? I wouldn't know. What I did know was that he'd never answered my question about his intentions toward me: something serious? Or just sexual pleasure?

I glanced at the alarm clock on the nightstand. To try to figure anything out at eight o'clock in the morning without coffee in my bloodstream was rather challenging. I rubbed my eyes and yawned, then maneuvered myself out of bed, careful not to wake him. I went to my bag, pulling out a T-shirt, a pair of jeans, my toothbrush, and took a shower. After washing up, I brushed my teeth and stepped back to the bedroom. He was still asleep and still so amazingly stunning.

I perched on the bed and, leaning over, I caressed his cheeks and kissed him lightly on his lips. His slumber was deep and peaceful, and he didn't even stir.

"I love you," I whispered to his sleeping face.

My first class today wasn't until ten, but to avoid having an awkward, after sex morning talk with him, I took my belongings and left his apartment.

After my ten o'clock class, I headed for the library. On the way, my cell phone chimed with an incoming text.

Ryan: Why didn't u wake me up?

You were sleeping so peacefully, I texted him back, and got a response a few seconds later.

Ryan: Peacefully or not, next time, wake me up, so I can make u late for class ;) Where r u? Still in the classroom?

Staring down at the display, my brows rose. Next time?

No, on my way to the library, I typed out and hit send. After a few beats, another ding from my cell phone.

Ryan: K. C u in 30.

See me in thirty minutes? My stomach did a flip-flop. It was time for that talk. If he was just looking for a replacement for Ashley, then sleeping with him was not something I planned on doing again. It would be a recipe for disaster, and I'd end up with my heart broken. But the fact that he'd transferred the boxes of condoms from the guest room to his sparked a tiny hope in me. Maybe he wanted something more than sex. A new text from him asking for my exact location cut off my thoughts. I sent it to him and resolved to spend the next thirty minutes studying.

Half an hour later, when I was searching for a book in one of the library aisles, two hands slipped around my waist, pulling me back against a strong chest. Ryan's intoxicating smell swirled into my nose as he buried his head in my hair and whispered in a deep, sexy voice, "Hey, beautiful." His warm breath set off an electric charge over my body. He pushed my hair aside and nuzzled my neck, bringing me closer to him. My eyes drifted closed as I relished the feel of his touch.

He turned me in his arms and drooped his head. His mouth molded to mine, kissing me at a leisurely pace, like we had all the time in the world. Eventually, I remembered where we were and pulled away from him, breaking the kiss. I glanced nervously down the aisle, afraid someone had seen us. After Ryan had ended whatever he had with Ashley, everyone in my dorm had gossiped about her. Some had pitied her, and some girls—plus Justin—had been thrilled. I didn't want to be a part of that gossip.

"What's wrong?" he asked. "You look a little worked up."

"Ryan...we need to talk." The sooner, the better. He slowly inhaled and exhaled. His smile evaporated.

"You're regretting last night, aren't you?"

"No." My voice came out louder than I'd intended. I cleared my throat and continued in a lower volume. "I'm not, but we need to talk." Not giving me enough time to protest, he pulled me in and his lips landed on mine, his tongue moving in for a short tease, and he drew back, looking down at me.

"I'll drop by your dorm at seven. We'll talk then, okay?"

I nodded once. He released me and took off.

Hannah called later on, but I didn't tell her about last night, at least not until she came by to return my coat. I was just returning from the communal showers and was wearing a white bathrobe and a towel twisted over my head like a turban when I found her waiting outside my door. I opened the door. The moment it was closed, I turned to her. "I slept with Ryan last night."

She stood motionless next to the door, eyes wide, mouth hanging open, staring at me.

I took my coat from her hands.

"And you're just *now* telling me?" She squealed as she passed me and fell onto my bed. "I can't believe you! Ryan? Why him?" She rolled her eyes and answered her own question. "Okay, yeah, the guy's drop dead gorgeous. Fine. But he's also a giant womanizer." She growled. "I'm so gonna kill Nate for calling him. Ugh, I shouldn't have left you with that manwhore."

"You knew Nate called him?" I unwound the towel from my hair and draped it over my desk chair to dry.

She scowled. "He told me after you were gone."

"Don't blame him. I'm the one who slept with Ryan, and I'm completely okay with what happened. It's no big deal." I leaned against the desk.

"Em, I know that sex *is* a big deal for you. You did it because you love him. I get that, but I just don't want to see you getting hurt. He doesn't do relationships."

"That's why I'm not expecting anything from him. And yes, I love him, but it wasn't like I deluded myself into thinking he'd offer me more than sex. Don't worry, okay? Last night won't repeat itself. I'm going to talk to him, clear things up. In fact, he's coming over here in an hour." Someone knocked on the door. We both cast our gazes to it. "Or less?" I said.

She answered it and greeted Ryan with a glare. "Look who's here. An hour early." She shot him another glower for good measure and stepped past him and into the hall. "If you need me, I'll be in Justin's room," she called over her shoulder and walked away.

Ryan frowned after her, then walked in and settled his long body on my bed. "What's with her?"

"Nothing. She's right. You're early." I approached the bed and stood near him, tightening the bathrobe around me.

"I couldn't wait."

"Couldn't wait? To what?" I asked, and he pushed lightly at my ankle with his foot so that I'd trip and fall right into his arms. He caught me, rolling me down onto my back and lowering his head to me, and his mouth was on mine, tongue swirling around the soft palate at the back of my throat. A whimper of delight escaped me, and when he left my lips, I almost tugged him back to them.

"To this," he answered huskily. *Talk. You have to talk to him!* I reminded myself.

"Ryan, we..." I swallowed. This moment could be our last. "We need...I need..."

"Yeah, to talk." His hand slid to my breast as his lips found their way to the hollow of my throat. His thumb rubbed across my nipple, sending a delightful frisson down my spine. Moving slowly, he traced kisses downward while his other hand clamped around my waist. His mouth reached my breasts, playing with them for a while, and my fingers found his hair. Then, lowering his head, he splayed my thighs wide.

"W-what are you doing?" I uttered between pants.

"Making the conversation a bit more pleasurable," he replied and twirled his tongue around my navel.

"We can't...I really need to talk—" I broke off with a moan when he nibbled at my inner thigh, and then licked it.

"Then start talking. I'm listening." He hooked my knee over his shoulder and his lips went to my other leg.

"Not like that. You can't...you can't..." He can't what? His tongue was causing me sudden amnesia.

"Listen to you?" he offered as he kissed his way up the side of my thigh.

"Yes, that. You can't listen." I sounded like I'd been running laps for hours. I felt his soft chuckle against my skin.

"Oh, I disagree. Baby, my ears are not the part of my body that's about to be busy." His mouth dipped between my legs, lips closing around the sensitive nub. My head fell back, and I moaned, arching my back and grabbing a handful of the sheet. Plucking and tweaking and thrusting, his mouth and fingers brought me to ecstasy. My body convulsed with pleasure as I cried out his name and moaned loudly. Breathless, I watched him move up to face me. What we did next involved plenty of oral activities. None of them, however, included talking.

Chapter 23

After Professor Smith dismissed us, I stuffed my things into my backpack. Normally I enjoyed the Art History class, but today I'd barely written any notes. It'd been a week since I'd promised Hannah that I'd handle the situation with Ryan. Rather than doing that, I'd gotten myself even more attached to him, spending lots of time in his bed and company. In addition, I'd constantly put off The Talk, not wanting to ruin everything.

And now all I could think about was what Hannah had casually announced yesterday, after Ryan had left my room. "He's totally in love with you. It's so sweet."

"What? How on earth do you figure that?" I'd asked, shocked.

"He's so overt about it." I'd raised an eyebrow, and she'd rolled her eyes. "Don't tell me you can't see it. Em, it's obvious." Maybe to her. To me, not at all. We might have acted like a couple around Hannah and Nate the past week, but Ryan had never mentioned love to me. I'd become what I'd been afraid of—Ashley's replacement, save for the display of public affection. To minimize the gossip about us, I hadn't let him touch me intimately outside his apartment or my dorm room. He hadn't liked it, to say the least, but he'd respected my wish.

Jolting me from my thoughts, someone put a hand on my arm when I got out of the classroom door. I jumped nervously. "Whoa, sorry. Didn't mean to startle you." Evan, who hadn't spoken to me before, gave me a smile most girls would have found charming. He sat one row ahead of mine in the Art History class. All I knew about him, aside from his name, was that he was on the football team.

"It's okay," I said, and he withdrew his hand from me.

"I'm Evan. You're Emma, right?"

"Yes."

"Emma, I was kinda wondering if you're free this Friday. There's a great new restaurant downtown." Waiting for my answer, he moved to clear the way for two students exiting the classroom.

"Um, I've already got plans."

"Saturday then?"

"Look, I'm sorry, but it's not gonna work." In an instant, his expression changed from flirtatious to angry. He grabbed my arm and yanked me close.

"You're Ryan's new little bitch, aren't you? So what? Now I'm not good enough for you? You're all the same—whores. Smell money and turn into a shark smelling blood." His strong hold tightened around my arm. He was hurting me.

"Let go of me," I hissed.

"Or what? You'll run crying to him? Hate to break it to you, honey, but he doesn't give a rat about his whores, and everybody knows that." He barked a cruel laugh.

"You should be more worried about my knee hitting your groin than whether I go crying to him. Let go of me." He glanced down at my leg and saw that it was in a perfect position for a kick. Yep, Ryan had taught me a few things.

"Let her go!" Hannah's voice came from behind me.

"You bitch." With a snarl, he cursed and released me, walking off. I turned around. Hannah was darting toward me, down the busy hallway.

"You okay? What did he want from you?" she asked after she closed the short distance between us, sounding concerned.

"Nothing. It was a misunderstanding."

"Is he in your class?"

"Yes, but he won't bother me again. Let's go. They're waiting for us." Ryan, Nate, and Kayla were waiting in the Art & Architecture building. Hannah, having a class in the same building as mine, had texted me at the end of class. She'd wanted to know if I'd join her, Nate, and Kayla for lunch. After I'd agreed, Ryan had called, so I'd asked him to come and eat with us too and to meet me at the Art & Architecture building.

"If he tries anything, tell Ryan. He'll teach him a lesson," she suggested as we walked.

"He won't, so everything's okay," I said, and there was a note of anger in my voice. Evan's words had gotten to me. Ryan's little bitch? Was that how guys regarded the girls who were with him, his bitches? God, it was awful.

"Hey, I'm just saying..." she said defensively.

"I'm sorry, Hannah. It's not you. I'm just a bit tired and all."

We reached the large lobby of the Art & Architecture building. "There they are." She pointed to the staircase leading to the mezzanine floor, at our left. We stepped toward them, but when I noticed a cute coed chatting with Ryan, I came to a halt. She was decidedly flirting with him, giggling at something he'd said and flipping her long, blond hair over one shoulder, hand going to his arm. Jealousy coursed through my veins. "I'd rather die than go through monogamy again," he'd told me in the past.

"Why did we stop? Em? You look sick. What's wrong?" Hannah said.

"I..." My stomach heaved. I was ready to spin around and walk out of there when he took her palm off him. Not giving up, she returned it a few seconds later with more giggles. He removed her hand from him once more, uttering something to her that caused Kayla's jaw to drop and to look over at me. As if sensing my stare, he turned and smiled at me, looking so breathtaking in that dark brown leather jacket and faded blue jeans. I must have seemed pretty off since the corners of his mouth suddenly fell, and he quickly moved toward us.

"Em, you're scaring me," I heard Hannah say.

"Baby?" Ryan reached up, standing in front of me. I snapped out of whatever funk I was in.

"I'm fine," I told them.

"You don't look fine. Does it have something to do with what that creep did to you?" She touched the spot where Evan had grabbed me and pain shot through my arm. I winced.

"What creep?" Voice rising in anger, he trained his gaze on her, demanding a reply.

"Some jerk from her Art History class. I think he's on the football team." Her eyes met mine, and from the set of my face, she must have been able to tell that I wanted her to stop providing more details about Evan. Taking another look at him, she seemed to understand why. With that thunderous expression on his face, it wouldn't be wise.

"He's on the football team?" he asked.

"Uh...I think Nate just called me." She bolted before he could ask more questions.

He sighed and came closer to me.

"It's nothing, really," I said while he carefully pushed my sleeve up my hurt arm to evaluate the damage. Evan's grasp had left me four nasty bruises in the shape of his fingers. He sucked in a sharp breath through his nose, like he was struggling to maintain control.

I raised my stare to him. His eyes spat venom, yet his voice was even when he spoke. "What's his name?"

"It's not as bad as it looks. My body tends to overreact."

"Emma, what's his name?" His voice was still deceptively calm.

"I'm not telling you."

"I'm gonna find out who did this whether you tell me or not, but I'm asking you to save me some time."

"No," I said.

He gently released my arm and sidestepped me. I pivoted around. He was heading for the door.

"Where are you going?" I asked. He paused and turned.

"To find who he is and have a little chat with him."

"Don't do it. Leave it alone."

He strode back to me. His eyes blazed with fury. "The hell I will. Look at your arm. He assaulted you." The calmness in his voice vanished.

"Okay, I understand. You care. I'm your—" I broke off. What was I to him? "Friend." I ended the sentence. To refer to myself as his friend was painful, but now was not the time to discuss our status or for our talk. Before I could continue, he interrupted.

"Friend?" Something I couldn't quite place replaced the wrath on his features. Was it hurt? "Friend?" he repeated, his tone mocking. "That's also how you think of me? As your friend?" I opened my mouth to reveal my feelings for him, but closed it again when I remembered that we were in a lobby with people who were starting to look at us. He misinterpreted this action as a yes. "I see," he said, and he was silent for a short moment. His expression was inscrutable. "If you'll excuse me, I have an asshole to take care of."

"Why can't you just let it go?" My voice stopped him mid-turn. He twisted to face me again, and then, as if he'd just realized something, he shook his head disbelievingly.

"God, you have no clue, do you?"

"Clue? What? I don't un—"

"Emma, please do me a favor and burst the bubble called your world, so you'll be able to see the real one, where you'll find your goddamn answer to why I can't let it go, since in the real world there is a huge sign hanging over my head, screaming with bold letters that"—he stepped backward, spreading his arms to the side as he bellowed—"I fucking love you, Emma Winstead!" He dropped his arms back to his sides. The volume of his voice dropped to normal when he added, "But I guess it's not mutual." He spun on his heel and stalked out of the building. Thoroughly shocked, I glanced slowly around. All eyes were on me. Some stared at me, smiling. Some stared at me, giggling with their friends, and some girls threw me envious looks. I swallowed and looked back.

Hannah, standing next to Nate and Kayla, curled her lips into an I-so-told-you-so smile and motioned with her hand for me to hurry up and go after him. At that instant, I was jerked out of my stunned state and rushed outside the building. He was twenty feet away, walking with long, fast strides. "Ryan!" I dashed toward him. "Ryan!" He didn't stop. Okay. I'd hurt him pretty bad. I'd fix it. "Ryan! Please—" Reaching him, I almost slammed into his back when he stopped short. He turned around, his expression cold.

"What is it that you want from me, huh? You want to hear the whole story? Is that it? You want to hear how I'm sick and tired of hoping you'll stop pushing me away? How I'm trying to figure out how the hell I'm supposed to deal with a situation I've never even been in before?" He dragged his fingers through his hair. "A situation where my heart decided to give a crazy amount of power to one girl. And only to her. Yeah, you can be damn sure there's no way another girl would have made me willing to give up everything for her, including my pride." He ran a hand down his face and went on. "So, yeah, I'd wait for you like a fool even though all I keep getting from you is coldness, but that was okay because I would've given you whatever time you needed before you were ready to let me in." He took a deep breath and let it out slowly. "But time isn't the real issue here, is it?" He paused, then gave me a direct look. "I'm completely yours while you...you don't even let me hold your hand around people, as if you're ashamed of what we have...or what we could have."

"No, I'm not. Ryan, you told me in the past that you'd rather die than be monogamous again. That even if you were in love, you wouldn't change your opinion about it, and that day, in my room, when I asked you what you wanted from me, your only reply was silence, so yes, I pushed you away. I was scared to get close to you."

He seemed to rummage around in his memory, and some of the sternness left his face. "I was speechless after you asked me that question because I suddenly realized that it wasn't what I wanted from you; it was what I needed from you. Love. Emma, I've never in my life needed someone's love. Never. But there I was, standing in front of you and feeling vulnerable. It blew me away. I had no idea how to react or what to say. Though, in retrospect, it shouldn't have come as a shock to me. I should have figured my feelings for you would grow stronger from the moment I first kissed you."

"That kiss? But you used me to get rid of Kirsten."

"The only girl I used that day was Kirsten. You were standing there, trying to hide your jealousy with that smile." The corners of his mouth turned up in a faint grin, and my cheeks warmed. "I liked that you were jealous, so I told Kirsten she was welcome to come with me, and when those lips of yours curved into a wider, disgruntled smile…God, I just had to kiss you right then and there, and it was the best kiss I've ever had."

"Come on, you can't possibly expect me to believe I was your best kiss."

"Yeah, actually I do because it had nothing to do with technique and everything to do with how your lips and mouth made me feel here." He pressed his palm flat over his heart. "I felt alive, and none of the girls before you could cause my heart to pound fast and strong from excitement. It was a rush I'd never imagined I'd ever get from a mere kiss." He stepped closer. "You were right all along. Love did change the way I see things—changed me. Back then, when I told you I'd rather die than be monogamous with someone again, death was a figure of speech, nothing more, but right now, death is a potent painkiller that can end the pain that comes from the fear of turning around and walking away from you—for good, because Emma, I can't do it anymore. It's all or nothing. You need to decide. What is it that you want?"

I stared up at him and cradled his cheek. "You. I love you, Ryan Kevin Damon, and I want it all." A full smile spread across his mouth, and he pulled me in for a passionate kiss. When our lips parted, I asked curiously, "What did you say to the blond girl who touched you earlier?"

A corner of his mouth tugged upward.

"That I didn't think my girlfriend would approve." Hearing him refer to me as his girlfriend did something to my heart. "Like I said, Emma, it's all or nothing."

I laughed softly and stretched myself up to cover his mouth with mine. I was Ryan Damon's girlfriend, and I couldn't be happier.

Chapter 24

Midterms were over and the Halloween party at the Beta Kappa House tonight was a good way to recover from the endless cramming. Dressed up in a fairy costume, I looked at myself in Ryan's bedroom mirror. I'd tied my hair in a braid and had on a white dress that reached my knees and wings attached to the back with elastic shoulder straps.

"Can we skip the party? Mmmm, I've got other plans for us, much more enjoyable." Arms snuck around my waist, careful not to ruin the wings, Ryan hugged me from behind. His shaving soap wafted to my nose as his smooth cheek caressed my temple. I twisted in his arms to face him and traced a finger over his dimple.

"No. I gave Hannah my word that we'd show up, so I can meet Kayla's new boyfriend. We've got to go." He rubbed his thumb along my bottom lip.

"Okay, fine, but then you're all mine." He grinned down at me seductively and went to slip the fake fangs into his mouth. With the tight, black, Lycra shirt showing off his taut abs rippling under it, black pants, and a cape, his Dracula costume looked incredibly sexy. His dark hair was slicked back, emphasizing light eyes.

When we reached the Beta Kappa House, the number of stares and double-takes he received from girls were uncountable.

"Hey, you." Hannah jumped on me and kissed my cheek. She was in a Playboy bunny costume and Nate, standing next to her, was dressed in a red velvet Hugh Hefner smoking jacket, a corncob pipe between his fingers. "I think Kayla's upstairs, c'mon."

"Okay"—I gazed at Ryan—"I'm going with Hannah. We'll be upstairs," I told him, and he nodded. She grabbed my hand and directed me to the second floor. Aside from the few people passing by, it was relatively empty.

"Where are they?" I asked.

"She said she wou—"

"Emma Winstead," a slow, feminine voice called. Hannah and I paused and pivoted around. A tall girl in a red satin corset, a leather miniskirt, and horns stood in front of us. My memory coughed up a name to match the striking face with blue eyes and long, wavy, brown hair: Thea Vanderbilts, Ryan's ex-girlfriend.

Nonetheless, I asked, "Do I know you?"

"No, but I know you." A malevolent smirk curled her heart-shaped, full lips as she closed the gap between us. "Well, at least from what Ryan has told me about you. I'm a very close friend of his. Though, lately, we've grown a bit apart since he thinks he loves you."

"He does, bitch," Hannah interjected, and Thea turned her head to look at her.

"Oh, please." She snorted derisively. "As if he could fall in love with a girl whose cuckoo uncle woke up one morning and slaughtered his precious family." What? Was she high?

"My uncle? You're crazy," I said and was about to pull Hannah by her hand and go search for Kayla, but Thea swung her gaze to me and continued.

"Sorry, that would be your uncle. Speaking of, I heard that mental illness can run in the family. I'd check myself if I were you." Even though she was talking nonsense, an uncontrolled shiver traveled through me. She picked up on it. "Look at you...so weak. No wonder he canceled the game. You don't pose a challenge to him, and he loves challenges. He would've destroyed you so quickly, before the real fun could even begin."

"What the hell are you talking about?" Hannah sounded irritated.

I didn't believe her insane, delusional story, but nevertheless, my body began to react strangely, and I found myself asking, "What game?" Thea's gaze was patronizing.

Her eyes widened, her mouth opened, and she covered it with four delicate fingers as she gasped in mock surprise.

"You didn't know? He didn't tell you about the TRT game?" She chortled. Her voice gushed venom, debilitating me.

"I'm sorry, Damon, she said you know she's here and that you were waiting for her." Nate's apology drew my eyes over Thea's shoulder. He was with Ryan. They emerged at the opposite end of the hallway, where the staircase to the second floor ended.

"It's okay," Ryan replied sharply. Thea looked back, and the ferocity of the expression he shot her scared me. Promising threats that would make anyone sorry they had crossed him were in his eyes. I'd never seen him so dark. Ryan paused in front of her, Nate next to him.

"And I thought you were smarter than that. Making *me* your enemy, Thea? Really? That was not a smart move, or did you forget that you're not dealing with Tristan here, and that I won't hesitate for a second to break you?" His tone was deadly, face earnest and grave.

"It's her you want to break, not me. I was there when you promised her mother you'd do it, so what the fuck happened? You're not in love with her. It's a joke. You cannot be in love with her." She pointed at me, and he shifted his attention to me. The hardness dissipated from his eyes.

"Ryan, what's going on? She's saying that my uncle— that he killed your family, that you want to hurt me," I sputtered.

"Emma, I…" He stopped, looking like he was searching for the right way to complete the sentence. No, no, no, no, no, no. Something was very wrong.

"Ryan, please tell me she's crazy or lying." He said nothing. Why wasn't he saying anything? I felt the blood drain from my face.

"Of course she's crazy," Hannah said, doing what he should have—speaking up. I was cold. Everywhere.

"P-please t-tell m-me she's crazy," I pleaded. He opened his mouth, but no sound came out. Why in the world would he think my uncle had murdered his family?

"R-r-ryan?" I whispered.

"I...we..." he finally said and sighed heavily. "Baby, we need to talk, but not here." He stepped in front of me and reached for my hand. I jerked away, knocking his palm off me.

"D-d-don't t-t-touch me!" I yelled. Thea laughed with relish. "A-a-are you i-i-insane like her?" God, I was a game to him. He wanted to destroy me because he thought my uncle murdered his family.

"I can explain, but not here. Le—" I backed away from him, and Hannah positioned herself between us.

"Leave her," she demanded.

"The hell I will."

"Ryan, look, I don't know whether all this crazy shit is true or not, but it doesn't matter because she's upset—very upset. If you care about her, you have to give her time to settle down, all right?" He didn't object, so she turned to me and took my hand. We passed him, and he let us. I was grateful for that because I couldn't remain there, not for one more second. In Hannah's car, as she attempted to calm me down, my mind began to race. What was the name of the man who murdered his family? What did he look like? Did he have a resemblance to my uncle? Did he have a name similar to my uncle's? I rubbed my face with frustration. I just couldn't find the answers in my head.

I'd been fourteen at the time of the murders, two years after my father had killed himself, which had been a catalyst for nightmares. News of murders and suicides had always augmented the bad dreams. That was why my mother had switched channels every time those topics came up, and whenever I'd been online, I'd steered clear of stories like that. But escaping the story of Ryan's family's murder was impossible due to his parents' celebrity status, so I knew the basics. Then why couldn't I remember the name of the killer?

I needed to be alone, to have some time to think. Fortunately, Hannah understood that. She dropped me at my dorm and hugged me goodbye. Inside my room, I grabbed my laptop off the desk and sat on the bed. Tears blurred my vision as I opened the computer. Despite the fact that I hadn't seen or heard from my uncle since my father had banned him from the house, I knew he couldn't be the killer. The notion that he'd murdered someone was surreal. So why on earth was I crying? Why was the hand pressing the keys on the keyboard trembling?

I clicked the pages I'd surfed the last time I looked Bruce Damon up, but none of them had a picture or the name of the murderer. They all referred to him as "a mentally ill man in his forties." I kept searching, and at last, the killer's picture appeared on the monitor.

A tide of relief washed over me. That man was not my uncle. Bald and skinny, he looked sick. Long, deep scars on his cheeks, chin, and forehead mutilated his face. According to the website, the cuts were self-inflicted, a byproduct of his mental illness. I closed my eyes, pulling up from my memory images of my uncle, and the relief I'd felt slowly left my body. I stared at the man again, observing his eyes...familiar eyes with two different colors.

I swallowed hard and quickly closed the website. After I inhaled and exhaled a few times, I clicked on another result that Google presented on Bruce Damon, and there it was— the name of the killer.

William Epping.

My surroundings grew quiet until all I was able to hear was my pulse drumming in my ears and my fast breathing. I slammed the laptop closed and gradually stood, taking a few steps to the window. Everything around me started to spin. The tiles under my feet felt as if they were quivering. Losing my balance, I crumpled to the floor and slowly crawled back to my bed. With a shaking hand, I reached into my bag near the foot of the bed and withdrew my cell phone. It slipped from my fingers to my lap.

After two tries, I was able to hold it in my hand. I navigated to the contacts list and tapped my mother's name. Four rings in, she answered, sounding worried.

"Honey? It's past midnight, is everything okay?"

"Mom." I sobbed loudly.

"What happened?" Her tone was alarmed. I sniffed and wiped my wet face with the back of my hand.

"U-u-uncle d-did..." I choked on a sob. "Did he kill them?"

"Honey, I can't understand you. Relax, okay? Breathe, just like Dr. Miller taught you, in and out." I breathed in and out, trying to control the tears. After a moment, I started to calm down.

"D-d-id Uncle Will k-k-kill those people? Was he sick? He's dead?" I whimpered.

There was a long silence on the other end of the line before she talked again.

"I wanted to tell you so many times, but after what you'd been through, how could I put my little girl through all that again? I wanted to protect you. Honey, your uncle was a very sick man, and he refused to keep taking his medication. Your father, he had to...he had to ban him from coming back to the house, but it wasn't because of that child, Sadie. Uncle Will would have never touched her in an inappropriate way."

"So why ban him? And why not force him to take his pills?" My voice quavered.

"We couldn't force him. He wouldn't hear of it. Your father was scared for your safety and didn't want him near you." I heard a sniff. My mother was crying softly. "It was so awful, everything that happened. A seventeen-year-old boy was left orphaned. I've been praying for him ever since. I can't blame him for being so mad at me."

"How do you know he's mad at you?" Thea's comment about my mother came into my mind. My mother had met Ryan.

"After that horrible thing your uncle did, I went to his aunt's house. I had to ask for forgiveness for what my brother did." She sniffed again. "His aunt wasn't home. It was only him and some girl...he was so angry at me...oh, honey, I'm so sorry that I kept it from you."

She sounded really upset. Asking more questions about her interaction with Ryan would only disturb her more, so instead, I comforted her. "Mom, it's okay. I'm not mad at you. I understand why you did what you did, and it's all in the past now. Don't worry about Ryan. I'm sure he's not blaming you anymore."

"It means the world to me to hear you say you're not mad at me. I love you so much, honey."

"I love you too, Mom." We calmed each other down for the next few minutes, and after I promised her that I'd come home for Thanksgiving, we hung up. I had no idea how long I stared at ceiling, lying on the bed, but at some point, I had to get outside the room, which had started to feel like it was closing in on me, and clear my head. I opened the door and gasped when my eyes fell on Ryan. He was sitting near my room, his legs thrust out in front of him and crossed at the ankles, his back against the wall. He wasn't wearing the black cape anymore, but he still had the Dracula costume on. He looked up at me and pushed to his feet. I sighed and stepped back in. He followed me inside and closed the door. I moved to the desk and propped my body against it. Giving me space, he stood next to the door.

"Why didn't you tell me about my uncle?" I accused.

"I knew that eventually I'd have to do that, but I couldn't. I was scared. Scared of the possibility of losing you after you found out about the game...and the stuff with your mother."

"What happened when she came to talk to you?"

"She appeared at my aunt's apartment a week after the killings. Her timing couldn't have been worse. That day, I was in such a bad mood that I snapped at her. I looked her in the eye and swore I'd do everything in my power to destroy her family, starting with her children." A chill raced down my spine. "When she left, Thea suggested I plan a new game for...you. I agreed and hired a private investigator to get thorough info on your mother."

"What is this TRT game?" I asked angrily.

He reluctantly began to answer. "On my sixteenth birthday, Thea threw me a big party at her house. When it was over and everybody was gone, Thea, Tristan, and I were hanging out in the living room. She started to rant about her ex-BFF, Audry. I wasn't really listening, but then Tristan proposed something that caught my attention. To come up with a plan that would socially ruin Audry. I was intrigued." He leaned a shoulder against the door. "But mostly, I was bored. I had too much spare time on my hands since my training had been reduced to two hours each day and the tests...well, their frequency had been reduced, too.

"To keep my mind busy, I taught myself how to play the guitar. The learning process was fun, challenging. Then, I began to write songs. It was freeing, but after a while, I needed more distractions, and it came in the form of the TRT game. At least, that's what Thea called it. TRT stands for our initials." A noisy group of residents singing loudly passed outside my room. When the quiet returned, he went on. "Audry was the first victim, but not the last, and that's the story behind the game."

"How did you do it? Break her, I mean."

"Emma, I...do you really want to hear it?"

"Yes," I said decisively.

Sighing, he pushed his fingers through his hair. "In the three weeks after the party, I studied Audry's routine and habits, what she liked, what she hated, everything. That's how I learned that she had a secret crush on Tristan. I told him to flirt with her sister, to get a date with her."

"A date with the *sister*?"

"The goal was to get my hands on Audry's diary. Audry is not the kind of girl who would fall in love with guys like Tristan. After four dates tops, she would've dumped his ass, and four dates wouldn't have been enough time for him to obtain the diary, so I exploited her competitive nature by sending Tristan to date her sister. That kept him closer to Audry and her room, where the diary was."

I shook my head with disgust. He'd calculated every detail in that plan in order to destroy the girl's life. He noticed my reaction, and emotional pain etched on his face. He paused.

"And?" I prompted.

"Why are we doing this?" His voice was low and calm.

"I need to know...everything," I replied. Pulling in a deep breath and closing his eyes, he ducked his head and pinched the bridge of his nose between his thumb and index finger, as if revealing this side of him to me was hard on him. Looking back at me, he continued.

"The next move was to ask Thea to kiss and make up with Audry. Be the perfect friend to her. Whenever she needed her, Thea had to be there, for support."

"Why? The point was to ruin her socially, not to give her friends back."

"An essential part of ruining someone, socially or not, is to hurt them as much as possible. What hurts more than a good friend who betrays you?"

Seeing that I got the point, he went on. "After Tristan took pictures of her diary's pages and sent them to me, I held her private secrets in my hand. And from them, I learned her two biggest fears: her parents getting a divorce, and to be humiliated in front of everyone. To make the first one happen, I sent Thea to get close to Audry's father, to flirt with him discreetly, get information about him. I had a feeling that he was hiding something. They all are. Thea found out what it was. He was secretively cross-dressing in bed. I asked her to film him while he was in lingerie.

"The next day, she emailed me the video. I told her to send it to Audry, Audry's mother, and to Serena, who was famous for her big mouth, and that was it. The whole school saw it. She was humiliated and devastated to find out that her father cheated on her mother with her best friend. Right after, her parents got divorced."

I stared at him, appalled. He was the mind behind the TRT game. Thea and Tristan were just tools he'd used to destroy people's lives. God, who was the man I'd fallen in love with? Who was the man I'd thought I knew?

"You're a monster," I finally said. He closed his eyes. When he opened them, I could see how much my words had hurt him.

"No. I'm not a monster. I'm worse than a monster. What I did to Audry doesn't come near to the awful things I did to other people. People who didn't even go to our school. Emma, I *am* my father. I can't escape it. No matter how much I've tried to feel remorse, or ashamed of what I did, I felt nothing. Then you came and—"

"And what? I wasn't enough of a challenge for you? To put me in your sick game? That's what you told Thea, isn't it? That I'm too weak?" I raised my voice, thick with the tears lodged in my throat. He didn't deny it. We both knew it was the truth, so he made no reply, an apology on his face.

"Tell me what you two talked about me."

"No. I am not doing this. I'm no—" He broke off. His eyes fell on a drop rolling down my cheek, and there was suffering on his face.

"Baby..." He took two steps toward me before I held my hands up to stop him.

"Don't!" My voice was loud. He stilled. Thinking back, I wondered if he'd hired me because of the game.

"Did I get the job so it'd be easier for you to devour me?"

"No. You got it because Ethan, the man who did the interviews on my behalf and who's also Nate's cousin's friend, believed you were the best candidate. When he called to inform me that he'd hired you, it got me thinking—could it be that you're Elizabeth Winstead's daughter? Yeah, I know, it was a crazy thought. I mean, what were the odds that you were her daughter? Right? But still, I had to look into it. I didn't have a lot of information about you, not even what you looked like, so I contacted Emily, the PI, again an—"

“Wait a second.” I swiped at my wet cheeks with my hand. “Didn’t she already do a background check on my mother?” I asked.

“Yes, but when I first hired her, things were different in my life. My sister and mother were dead. He was too, and Tristan was mad at me for not fighting him in Alaska. I was tired of arguing with him and of Thea’s constant questions about why he wanted to fight me, since she didn’t know about the Elites and Alaska.

“Needing time for myself, I kinda grew apart from them, so planning new games was not exactly on my mind. That’s why I called Emily and told her to stop investigating, and in that phone call, she gave me a few details about you. She told me your name, that you’re an only child, that your father killed himself, that after the suicide you and your mother moved to a different neighborhood in Brooklyn, and that you had no idea what your uncle did since your mother kept that from you.

“The second time I spoke to her was to find out if you’re the same Emma, and if you still didn’t have any knowledge about what your uncle had done. Being an excellent PI, she got back to me with the information shortly after that.”

“What about the two times that I slammed into you? You didn’t know who I was?”

“No, only when you said your name, I connected the dots.”

“And the game started anew,” I added sourly.

“At first, yes. I called Thea and told her that Emily had confirmed that it was you, but as the days passed, things changed, and I ended the game.”

“But Thea wasn’t happy with that.”

“No, but I won’t ever let her hurt you. She’ll never come near you again. No matter what, I’ll always protect you. Always. Look at me,” he ordered when I averted my eyes angrily from him. I returned them back to his face and he said, “I love you more than you could ever imagine.” His intense gaze mirrored his words.

I laughed bitterly. "You love me? How can you feel love if you don't even have a conscience?"

"Because you are my conscience. Emma, when I told you that I don't care about the girls Matt had filmed without their knowledge, you gave me a look of such disgust, and that was all it took to make me feel ashamed of who I was. I wanted to be a better man for you, so you would never look at me like that again, ever." He rubbed his face with both hands and moved a hand up to thread his fingers through his hair. "I'm a screw-up. I know that. He stole a part of my humanity from me, but then you came into my life, and you're slowly bringing it back."

He stepped toward me again. "Don't." Still hurt by everything, I held up my hand. Ignoring my gesture this time, he stepped up to me and pulled me into his arms, pressing me against him. I shoved, punched, and pushed at his chest over and over, crying and twisting to get free, but all my efforts were in vain. Escaping his hold was impossible. He just stood motionless, absorbing my blows quietly until I wore myself out. Then he gently stroked my hair and slipped his finger under my chin, bringing my gaze up to his.

"I'm so sorry, baby." His thumb wiped my tears from my cheeks. "I'm sorry that I'm the one who's responsible for them, and for your pain." His voice was soft. He bent his head, lips moving against mine tenderly, but I kissed him back with savagery as my hands, at his lower back, pulled the hem of his Lycra shirt up, trying to shuck it off. A low moan erupted from his throat, and he broke the kiss to reach back and yank his top over the head, flinging the cloth to the floor. He lifted me by the waist and laid my body onto the desk. Some of the stuff on it fell to the ground with a loud thump. He shoved his pants and boxers down his legs. Stepping out of them, he set himself between my legs and brought his lips back to my mouth, his hands all over my body.

Although I wanted to push him away from me, to yell at him, to hate him, I couldn't. I loved him, I wanted him, I needed him. I dug my fingers roughly into his skin and pulled him closer, hearing the sound of my voice begging him to enter me and then my underwear ripping off. As I wrapped my legs around him and felt his bare, damp skin, he plunged deep inside me, filling me. With each thrust of his hips, a pressure started to build inside my body and mounted as he went faster and harder, his muscles clenching and tightening. Warm breath touched my ear. Breathing heavily, his voice was hoarse as he said, "You're my everything." I moaned as waves of pleasure crashed over me, and, still inside of me, he carried me to the bed.

Moving his hips again, he kissed me and thrust with unbridled passion. Another wave of pleasure exploded through me, and with a loud, low cry, he reached his climax too. He collapsed on me, his face buried in my neck. We didn't move or speak. I closed my eyes, listening to our fast and heavy breathing, and succumbed to the fatigue.

When I woke up, Ryan was spooning me, naked. His clothes were scattered over the floor, along with the white wings of my fairy costume and my torn-up underwear.

I turned to him. Awake and looking tired, he moved back a bit to give me more space on the bed and lightly kissed my forehead. "Didn't you get some sleep?" I asked him.

"No." He brushed my hair from my face.

"Why?"

He sighed, rolling to his back and looking up at the ceiling. For a moment I thought he wouldn't answer, but then he turned his head back to me.

"Tell me I didn't lose you."

"Ryan, your world scares me. Tristan, Thea, the game..."

"They are not part of my world anymore. I left them behind me when I fell in love with you. There are no more TRT games, manipulation, playing with people's lives. It's over. It's all in my past." Staring into his eyes, I believed him. My fingers caressed his cheek. I loved him so much. Nothing could keep us apart, not even his past.

"No, you didn't lose me."

His eyes shut in relief. Opening them, he pulled me against him, kissing me softly. I rested my head on his chest, tracing my hand over the scars.

"That was all I needed to hear," he whispered. Listening to his heart beating, I mused about what I'd discovered. Uncle Will was dead, and he'd murdered Ryan's family. I felt like I was going to wake up any minute and find out that the recent hours were just a bad dream. I thought about the genetic condition Uncle Will and I shared—Heterochromia. Right eye green, left eye brown. That had been the color of his eyes as well. Did Ryan see his mother and sister's killer whenever he looked at me?

"Ryan?" There was no answer. "Ryan?" Still no answer. I lifted my head and glanced at him. He was sleeping soundly. I returned my cheek to his chest and closed my eyes, falling asleep, too.

Chapter 25

I looked out the window of my dorm room. The sky was dark gray and cloudy, rain pouring down. After spending a week in sunny Miami for Thanksgiving at my mom's boyfriend's house, getting used to the cold weather again was not easy. I moved to my comforter where my bag was and went back to unpacking as I reflected on Ryan. I hadn't seen him in over a week, but we'd spoken every day on the phone. He'd spent Thanksgiving with his aunt, Jasmin, and his cousins in New York.

While everything between us had returned to normal since Halloween, a nagging question kept creeping into my mind: did he see his mother and sister's killer in my eyes? But with all the drama and emotional truculence we'd had over Halloween, I couldn't bring myself to ask him that. Things between us had been good, and after hours of talks with my mom about Uncle Will and Ryan, things were good with my mom as well. She was happy for us, and he'd even talked with her on the phone, apologizing for what he'd said in the past.

When I was done unpacking, there was a knock on the door, and Ryan opened it. I gasped with joy and, charging in his direction, I jumped on him. He caught me with both hands and closed the door with his foot, mouth crushing against mine as my legs circled his waist. He brought us to my bed, and as we kissed on it, I pulled his short, black shearling jacket from his shoulders. Helping me to get rid of it, he left my lips and took it off, looking at me.

"I missed you so much," he said and leaned forward to kiss me again. When my fingers slid to his back, unintentionally scratching him with my nails, he hissed and winced. Dismissing the pain, he kept moving his head toward mine, but I drew back.

"Did I hurt you?" I asked hastily.

"No, don't worry about it." His lips reached my mouth, but I pulled away.

"Ryan, what happened to your back?"

Although he didn't look as if he wanted to shift our attentions to his back right now, he answered anyway, "Nothing bad, but I hope you like it." He flung off his shirt, putting it aside, then turned around. My mouth opened with shock. The python tattoo had been changed. The artist had done an incredible amount of work on the details. He'd reshaped the snake's eyes. They were closed instead of open, and its body bled. The small, black heart the snake had been strangling had been skillfully altered into a black hand squeezing the python's body. The reptile inked on his skin was dead. On the left side, covering half of Ryan's back, there was a new tattoo. The skin around the ink was a bit red and the tattoo itself was peeling off, but I could see its outlines clearly. It was me! I sat cross-legged in jeans and a tank top, and in my cupped hand, I held a red heart.

"The tattoos, they're..." The words to describe them escaped me. He turned back to me. A warm look on his face, he grazed my cheek with his knuckles.

"What I feel," he completed.

"Your heart...is...not black."

"And in your hands," he added.

"What if you regret doing it?"

He framed my face between his hands, angling it back so I'd look at him. "You might stop loving me and leave, breaking my heart into tiny pieces, but I will never stop loving you or regretting tattooing you on my skin. You'll always be a part of me."

I gave him a bright smile. "I love you, and I won't leave," I said before kissing him deeply and melting in his arms, knowing he too would be in my heart forever.

From that day on, everything was perfect, and the time ticked by all too fast. The end of the fall semester was already here, along with finals, which made me forget what sleeping felt like and what being relaxed meant, but yesterday had been my last final. The feverish studying was officially over.

"Yes, we'll be there." I chuckled as I reassured Hannah for the millionth time that Ryan and I would come to the end of semester party that the Beta Kappa House was holding tonight. I dragged my chair back and stood. I was ready to leave the coffee shop that Hannah, Kayla, Justin, who had finally stopped avoiding me, and I were in. Waving goodbye, I left. Outside, I pulled the early evening air into my lungs and smiled. I was in a good mood. It was unusually warm for December here, and I decided to take advantage by skipping the bus and walking to Ryan's apartment.

A few blocks from it, I got the sense that someone was following me. I flipped around, but there was no one suspicious along the narrow street. I shook my head and laughed at myself. *Paranoid, much?* I kept walking, and then from nowhere a hand grabbed me and yanked me into a dimly lit alley. I was smashed against the wall of a building and my hands were clipped together over my head, my mouth covered by a manly palm. A smell, myrrh mixed with sandalwood and musk, wafted to my nose. Two green eyes looked down at me. I fought against the strong fingers binding my wrists, but his grip was like iron. He didn't put any real effort into keeping me in my place, and his strength scared me. My pulse raced. Rape or murder—I couldn't decide which fate was worse.

"Relax. If I wanted to hurt you, you'd already be in pain," he said. I stood still and breathed fast through my nose. "I'm going to remove my hand slowly. Are you going to be a good girl and stay quiet? Because honestly, I've got this really annoying headache, and your screaming won't help to ease it. So would you be a good girl?" A corner of his mouth went up. I nodded, and he moved his palm from my mouth. Head titled back, I observed his face. With green eyes, a square jaw, and short, brown hair, he was spectacular.

One glance down his tall, large body in high-end clothes and accessories, plus his expensive cologne, ruled out robbery.

"Like what you see?" He bared his white teeth in a grin. He wasn't here to rob me, and it didn't seem like he intended to rape or murder me. My fear waned.

I stared up at him. "What do you want from me?" My voice was firm.

He gave a small laugh. "I'll take that as a yes."

"What do you want from me?" I repeated.

"What? Straight to the point? No foreplay? Where's the fun in that, huh?" When he didn't get any reaction from me, he rolled his eyes. "Okay, if you really insist on getting to the boring stuff right away, fine. Call your boyfriend and tell him his old friend Tristan is here, waiting for him." My eyes widened. Tristan?

"No, I won't." Just as I refused, my cell phone rang. I prayed it wouldn't be Ryan.

"Allow me," he said. With one hand, he opened my handbag hanging over my shoulder and pulled out my phone, checking the caller ID and smiling as he answered the call.

"Well, well, well, it's been a long time, Ryan, and quite frankly, I'm insulted by the way you threw Thea and me out of your life. So why don't you make it up to me and come see me and Emma in this lovely alley." A pause, and then surprise skittered over his face. "The alley is across from the only deserted building near your apartment." Tristan hung up, peering down at me. "Thea was wrong; he does love you. I don't recall ever hearing him so pissed off at me or caring about anything that wasn't his Lily or Camilla." He dropped my cell phone back into my bag, and lips curved slightly up, he swept his gaze over me, sizing me up. "You're such a disappointment. Yeah, I might get why he'd keep you around for a while, but fall in love?" His forehead creased in a genuine lack of understanding. "Choosing you over *Thea*? That I truly don't get." He stared down at my eyes, inspecting them. "You know, I, personally, have no problems with uniqueness, but your boyfriend? He can't tolerate flaws, just like Bruce couldn't. Everything has to be perfect. I'm sure he didn't share this piece of information about himself with you, seeing that he loves you, for some strange reason, but you'll have to trust me on that. I'm positive that every time he looks at your eyes, he sees flaws. He sees your uncle. And deep down, he blames you."

I twisted my body, wanting to get away from him, from his words. His laugh rolled in the space of the alley. "Why would he blame me? I'm not my uncle," I said defensively.

"Funny how the human mind works. How it tries sometimes to convince us desperately that the truth is not the truth, especially when it hurts."

"I didn't kill his family. That's the truth," I sputtered.

"Does it matter?" He released his hold, and blood rushed back into my hands. He took my right hand, then skated his fingers down the inside of my arm. "Don't fool yourself. In these veins runs the same blood that murdered his sister and mother, who he adored so much. For him, you are and will always be a constant reminder of what happened on the night of October 24."

Suddenly, he was gone and Ryan was there, throwing a brutal punch into Tristan's face. The blow knocked him to the ground, onto his back. Ryan's lips pinched into a fierce frown, and he pointed down at Tristan. "You touch her again, and you're a dead man." His gaze slid to me. "Baby, are you okay?" His eyes swept swiftly over me to check for injuries. I nodded.

Tristan pushed himself to his feet. "Whoa, touchy, are we?" He spat blood onto the cement, chuckling. Standing in front of Ryan, he was the same height as him. Tristan dusted dirt from the shoulders of his thin, black coat. "Ryan Damon is in love. Who would have believed this day would ever come? God, I just can't wrap my mind around it, but I'm happy for you, really.

"You remember what you once told me? You said that someone's weakness could always be used as someone else's leverage. Yeah, I listened to you and learned a few things.

And now, here I am"—he turned to look at me—"right next to your weakness—my leverage." He gazed back at Ryan. "You owe me a fight, and if her safety is important to you, and it is, you'll give me that."

"No! Don't fight him. He wants to fight you to the death. Don't do it," I urged Ryan.

"I see you told her about the underground fights. That's not something I would've expected from you," Tristan said and moved to face me. "He will fight me because he can't be around you 24/7, and I hear that deadly accidents tend to happen at the weirdest hours of the day."

Ryan shoved his hand through his hair and clenched his jaw, seemingly helpless against Tristan's threat.

"You're sick. You came all the way here just for a fight? Why can't you satisfy your blood thirst with someone else?" I burst out.

"I'm surprised. Doesn't she know about your reputation?" he asked Ryan, and his gaze shifted back to me, expression growing serious, all amusement gone. "Your boyfriend defeated the great, legendary, Chao fucking Wáng. To prove that I am the best, and that I am the one who my father should respect, I need this fight." He turned back to Ryan. "My father's arranged a special gathering in this area. We are the only fighters for tonight, and they're all waiting for this fight, including my father. You will show up if you don't want to lose her." He gave Ryan an address, and before disappearing out of the alley, he faced me, lips curling into a smirk. "Don't say I can't be romantic. You're welcome to come and watch your boyfriend give his life for you, and since I'm guessing he won't let you tag along, tell the guards you've got a private invitation from me. To confirm this, give them the code: 185WD."

Ryan turned to me, his eyes filled with concern. "Emma, don't even think of coming. I don't want you anywhere near that place. Go wait for me in the apartment. I'll call you when it's over."

"Not if you lose." The thought almost paralyzed me.

"Won't happen."

"No! You can't go there!"

"I have to. If he does something to you, and you wind up—" he broke off, unable to finish the thought.

"We'll go to the police. He won't do anything to me."

"Listen to me." He cupped my shoulders with his hands, demanding my full attention. "Tristan and his father want this fight badly, and they won't stop at anything till they get it. Up to now, Tristan had nothing that could force my hand, but things have changed. He got the leverage he needed—you. His father is a member of the Elites, and he has the power to make murders disappear. Tristan was right. I can't be around you 24/7. The only way you'll be safe is if I go and fight him and be done with it." He took his hands off my shoulders.

"I don't care. You can't go. You promised me you are done with Tristan, Thea and all this...this twisted world."

"I also promised I'll always protect you."

"Even if it could turn you into a murderer?"

"Make no mistake, Emma." My heart leaped at the intensity on his face. "I will become *anything* in order to protect you." His words sliced through the air like razors, slashing any more protest from me. He was going, and nothing I could do would change his mind. Fear of losing him shot through me, sending tears rolling down my cheeks. His face softened, and he brushed his finger over my cheeks. "Baby, I'm sorry, but I have to do this. I know you're gonna hate me after it, but a world where you are mad at me is a world I can live in, while a world where you're dead...that I can't. I won't." He kissed me lightly on my lips, then said, "Go to the apartment. I'll be in touch."

He was insane if he thought I'd obey him and wait while he was out there risking his life for me. As soon as he walked off, I called Hannah. She answered on the third ring. "Hannah? I need a ride."

Chapter 26

Almost an hour had passed before Hannah arrived with Nate's Honda, apologizing for the delay. "I'm so sorry. I lent my car to Kayla and I couldn't find Nate's car key, and he was all busy with the preparations for the party. Please tell me we're not too late." I'd filled her in on what was going on, and she raced us through the streets. Her voice was laced with fright.

"I hope not."

"Gosh, Em, Ryan's crazy! What was he thinking? We've got to stop him."

"I tried! He wouldn't listen to reason." I threw my hands up and let them fall onto my lap and sighed. How Hannah and I were going to foil the fight, that had probably already started, was anyone's guess. The ride felt endless, but eventually, about forty minutes later, we were finally close to our destination. In a remote rural area, we drove for another few minutes along a narrow road through lush landscaping and turned onto a long, gravel path leading to a huge mansion located behind a black, wrought iron fence.

We stopped in front of a large, silver gate, guarded by two big, imposing men in black suits and sunglasses. One of them approached the driver's side window. Hannah rolled it down and gave him a flirtatious smile. The man bent over, eyes quickly scanning me and moving back to Hannah.

"Did you girls get lost?" His face was serious, tone suggesting we should answer yes and make a U-turn.

My pulse spiked, palms all sweaty, but leaning over to Hannah, I ignored the fear and start talking. "Um…no. I'm, I mean we, um—"

"We've got an invitation from Tristan." Hannah cut me off swiftly and threw a wide grin to the guard, but he was not affected by it. His expression stayed severe while he stepped aside and communicated with someone through his earpiece, then returned to us.

"The code?" he asked, voice flat.

"185WD," I replied. He straightened and nodded once to the other guy next to the gate. It slid open electronically, and Hannah drove up the long driveway. We both gasped with awe when the enormous size of the grand, stonewall mansion was fully exposed to us. On each side of the driveway, there were two green, large gardens. Passing them, we reached the main entrance of the manor. To our left, a line of luxurious cars were parked along the perimeter of the house that looked more like a castle. We squeezed the Honda between a Jaguar and a Rolls Royce and got out of the vehicle, careful not to ding them. Aside from the chirp of birds, everything was quiet. My heart skipped a beat when we passed a black, shiny BMW, which I recognized as Ryan's.

"It'll be okay. We'll get him out of there—alive," Hannah promised, putting her hand on my shoulder. We reached the massive front doors, and Hannah knocked. A moment later, they were opened by a man who appeared to be in his forties, wearing a gray suit.

"Ladies." He inclined his head with formality and moved aside, motioning for us to come in. We stepped into a spacious foyer, and I glanced around. The place was empty of people. Where was everybody?

"I'm afraid that the betting is closed," he said.

"That's fine. We only came to watch the fight. Where is it?" Hannah asked.

"Follow me, please." Trailing after him, we passed winding marble staircases, a few rooms, and went through two corridors before climbing down five sets of stairs that took us to a poorly lit room. Across it, there was a door made of steel plates. My skin crawled and my hair stood on end. Scenes from famous horror movies involving kidnappings and torture basements ran through my mind. We stepped forward, our footsteps echoing in the silence of the dim space. The man slid a plastic card through a small, black box mounted beside the steel door, unlocking it, but not opening it. His body blocked the entrance as he faced us.

"Your names?" he said. I swallowed, beads of sweat gathering on my forehead. From the look on his face, I had the sense that if we gave him wrong names, like names unfamiliar to him, Hannah and I wouldn't leave this place alive.

"Emma Winstead, and I brought a friend with me. Tristan said I could," I lied. Instantly, all tension left his expression, and he cast us a warm smile.

"But of course, you're Tristan's private invitation. He notified me of your possible arrival before the fight, and I forgot. Forgive me for my rudeness. Here you go. Enjoy." He cleared the way, and I let out the breath I'd been holding.

The instant he opened the heavy door, a clamor cut through the silence and assaulted my ears. Hannah and I walked into a much larger room that was filled with murky and dim lighting. I looked around. The chaos of people yelling, cheering, and sweating surrounded us. The dichotomy between the peacefulness inside the mansion and the wildness of this separated space was immense.

"Look! The fight has already started!" Hannah shouted above the noise and pointed up at a huge TV on the wall opposite us. She grabbed my hand, and we edged our way through the throng to get a better view. When we finally reached the front, we were standing in front of a twenty by twenty foot, floor-level ring. Inside it, Ryan and Tristan were fighting each other. They wore loose, black pants and black tank tops, their bodies glistening with sweat. I flinched when my eyes fell on Ryan's wounds, but glancing at Tristan's bloody face, I felt a bit better; Ryan's condition wasn't much worse.

"How are we gonna stop this?" I shouted to Hannah. She shrugged hopelessly.

"Yeahhhhhhhhhhhh!" A kick straight to Tristan's chest caused a deafening reaction from the people around us. Fuming, he jutted his chin out and charged Ryan, socking him with incredible speed. Ryan didn't have enough time to dodge the hit. His head snapped back. He licked the blood from his split lower lip and succeeded in diverting the next blow. But Tristan wasn't giving up that easily, and he pressed all four fingers against the thumb and poked Ryan's throat in a specific spot that threw him off balance, and he almost collapsed to the floor. Being an excellent fighter, Tristan's next moves were fast, skillful and deadly, but Ryan's were faster, deadlier, and even more skillful. Ryan was so good, in fact, that the dread I'd felt that he'd lose shifted to dread that he'd win, and become a killer. There is no coming back once you take a life.

"What's he doing?" Hannah's focus was on Ryan. He was standing still next to Tristan's prone body as Tristan was coughing hard. Staring down at him, Ryan wore a look that said, *I'm sorry, but you left me no other choice.*

"He's going to kill him!" I said. Ryan slowly crouched down on one knee, one hand pinning Tristan's body to the ground, the other fisted as it moved back and drove down. Since Ryan had once explained to me how certain blows could be fatal to the body, I knew that if his fist landed where Tristan's heart was located, the lethal blow could cause Commotio Cordis—a severe disruption of the heart rhythm—and death.

"Noooooo!" I howled so loudly that my throat burned. His fist stopped just inches from Tristan's chest. Ryan's head jerked up, feverishly searching the crowd, and then worried and stunned blue eyes locked on mine. "Please, please, don't do it!" I yelled while virtually everybody around me chanted loudly.

"Kill him! Kill him! Kill him!" Over and over. In that second, Tristan thrust his hand into his pocket, pulled out a small, plastic bag full of some kind of gold substance, and called Ryan's name. Ryan, distracted and unfocused, turned to look down at him, and was hit with the small, plastic bag. Tristan rolled over and vaulted to his feet as Ryan reeled back, wiping sand from his eyes. Tristan took advantage of Ryan's disorientation and struck him hard in the stomach.

Ryan fell, and instead of defending himself from Tristan's next assault, his attention quickly went to where I was. He tried to rise, as if to come to me, but a choke hold from behind brought him back down, and he looked over at me with foggy eyes. He couldn't breathe. Hysterical, I launched myself forward to enter the ring and try to save him, but I was jolted backward by two hands.

"Are you insane? He's a mad man. He'll kill you!" Hannah shouted at me, holding me in place.

I turned to her. "I don't care. He can't breathe!" Looking past me, she suddenly paled.

My head snapped back to the ring. What I saw wrung a scream from me, and I squirmed to get out of Hannah's hands. Ryan seemed unconscious. Was he dead? No! Without releasing his grip, Tristan's lips curled into an evil smile as he looked over at me. He bent his head to say something to Ryan. Ryan's eyes struggled to open and then abruptly, like he'd gotten a shot of adrenaline, he threw himself backward, pushing Tristan to his back, popping his feet down and swiftly swinging them aside to roll over, breaking from the choke hold.

With renewed energy, Ryan blocked every blow and kick that came his way, and eventually, Tristan seemed to tire. That was when Ryan took the offensive, throwing brutal back, front, and sidekicks, punching him in the face, legs, and chest, and even spinning in the air to slam his leg into Tristan's wounded body a few times. The crowed went mad, and Hannah's arms fell away. I glanced back. The muscles of her face were slack with shock, mouth ajar, eyes glued to Ryan, who was pummeling Tristan mercilessly. Then her eyes widened and she said, "Oh my gosh, he has another one!" I whipped my head back to the fight in time to see another small, plastic bag in Tristan's hand.

Stumbling, he hurled it at Ryan, who jerked to the side, and the bag of sand sailed harmlessly past him and to the floor. Rounding Tristan, he kicked him from behind, and his opponent pitched forward onto his face. Ryan squatted near him and seized Tristan's hair in his fist, lifting his head back. Both eyes swollen shut, Tristan drooled blood, saliva, and sand over his chin and neck. Ryan's lips moved. The shouting from the crowd in the room was deafening.

I looked back at Hannah. "What is he saying?"

"I can't hear him either," she answered. Tristan replied to whatever he'd said to him, and Ryan let go of his hair. He pushed himself to his feet, looked over at me, and then down at his gory palms. He turned and walked to a towel and a bottle of water in a corner of the ring. He poured water over his face and hands and dried them with the towel. Next, he stepped toward Hannah and me, passing Tristan's prone body. When a man in his sixties and a black, expensive suit appeared behind Ryan, people quieted.

"What do you think you're doing?" he demanded from Ryan.

"Leaving," he answered angrily and kept walking.

"You know the rules. You can't. Finish him." Ryan stopped. His gaze swept the room, settling on the far, mirrored wall.

"Yeah, I know the rules, as well as all of you up there," he said to the mirror, and then turned around to face the man. "One of them is that you can use only your body, nothing else, when fighting. Your son used sand. He broke that rule. He lost." Son? He was Tristan's father? "You and the other members of the Elites"—he jerked his head at the mirrored wall—"got your fight. I'm done with all this shit. You hear me? Done."

Tristan's father nodded once. "You won. Your ten million is waiting i—"

"You can shove your money up your ass." Ryan turned away from him, stepped out of the ring, and swept me into his arms as the crowd began to get loud again.

"Thank God you're okay," he said over my head and released me. "Goddammit, Emma, I asked you to stay in the apartment. It's not a fucking amusement park here. They could have hurt you. Both of you." His eyes moved to Hannah, rebuke in them.

"You're right. I'm glad you're okay and that it's over. This place gives me the creeps. Can we get the hell out of here already?" Hannah pleaded.

"Yeah, I'll just go change, and we'll be out of here."

After Ryan changed, we walked Hannah to her car. She stopped by the driver's door, and her eyes went to his face. A lot of fresh cuts lined it, lips slit in multiple places, and his right eye was swollen.

"I guess you two are a no-show at the party later. Hell, with everything that happened in there, I don't think I'm up to going myself. I'm still shaken up, but Nate's counting on me to be there, so..."

"Hannah, can I trust you won't tell him about everything you saw here?" he asked.

"Ryan, we should go to the police. What they're doing is illegal," I argued.

"Yeah, but going to the police would only put you and Hannah and Nate in danger, and it won't help bring them down."

"Em, he's right. You don't mess with this kind of people." She shifted her gaze to his. "Don't worry, I won't tell." She opened her car door and stopped. "What did he say to you that made you go all Rambo on him?"

He dragged in a breath and looked down at me. "That after I die, there would be no one to protect Emma."

"But the whole point of the fight was to protect Emma from him," she said angrily.

"It was. Tristan wasn't referring to him as being the one who would hurt Emma, he was talking generally." The name Thea sprang up in my head. Hannah looked horrified, then nodded and got in the car.

"I'll make up an excuse for why you guys couldn't make it, and Ryan, your face might not be as busted up as Tristan's, but you should see to it."

"Will do," he said. She pulled out, waving goodbye and speeding off.

Once we were in his BMW, on the way back to my dorm so I could pack a bag, I said, "When Tristan was down and you pulled his head back, what did you say to him?"

He kept his eyes on the road. "Whether or not he understands that he lost, that he would never come near you again." He slid his stare to me. "It's over. Neither Tristan or his father will bother us anymore." He reached over and lightly squeezed my thigh. His knuckles were severely scuffed. I gently put my hand on his, wishing my touch could heal.

"How can you be so sure they'll leave us alone? And what about the Elites?"

"Tristan's a lot of things, but he's a man of his word, and he acknowledged his loss. His father acknowledged it too. All they wanted from me was this fight. They got it, and now it's over. It's behind us, Emma."

Thinking about Tristan, his words came back to me. *"You're a constant reminder of what happened to his family."* I looked through the window. It had started raining. *"Funny how the human mind works. It tries sometimes to convince us desperately that the truth is not the truth, especially when it hurts."* I shook my head, thrusting his words from my mind, and turned to stare at Ryan's profile. His attention was on the road. He looked tired, but happy. I leaned my head onto the headrest, listening to the sound of the rain against the windows. A smile spread across my face as I gazed at him. My eyelids felt heavy, and I let them drift closed. And then I was in the alley again, but everything was darker, scarier. Tristan stood in front of me, his face serious, though at least this time, my hands were free.

"I lost, and now all is good, right?" he asked.

"Right," I agreed.

"Wrong. Emma, why are you lying to yourself? Face the truth because you can't run away from it; you can't be with him. You're a constant reminder of what he doesn't have anymore—his mother and sister. If you really love him, you'll set him free."

"No, he doesn't blame me."

"Do you believe what you just said?" I couldn't answer since I was pulled out of my dream by Ryan's voice.

"Baby?" I opened my eyes and felt like crying. "Hey, it's just a bad dream." He used one hand to caress my cheek. I rubbed my eyes.

"I'm okay." I forced myself to put on a relaxed expression, grinning.

"What were you dreaming about? You were a bit restless in your sleep."

"Can't remember. Just a bad dream, nothing more." Was it? I glanced out the window. It wasn't raining anymore, and we were about ten minutes away from my dorm. In a week it would close for winter break, but we'd decided that I'd spend that week at his place, and then we'd fly to New York, so I could meet his aunt and cousins.

I turned to look at him again. He was bleeding from a cut on his forehead. I clicked open the glove box, searching for the Kleenex he usually kept there. As I shuffled through his stuff, a sheet of paper fell from it. I picked it up.

"Damn, it was supposed to be a surprise," he said.

"What is it?"

"I wrote you a song, and I planned to sing it to you at the party tonight. Now, I guess you'll get a private show, but go easy on my singing, huh?" There was playfulness in his voice.

My eyes skimmed the lyrics. They were beautiful.

I will always love you. One day, far far in the future, you'll see it's the truth. You'll see it's the truth.

I read this line again and again until Tristan's voice popped in my head again. "Don't fool yourself...you are and will always be a constant reminder of what happen on the night of October, 24."

"Do you like it?" he asked, pulling into a vacant space in the parking lot behind my building. I loved him more than anything, and knowing what I must do, I couldn't breathe, couldn't feel myself, couldn't look at him.

"Emma? What's wrong?" His hand shot to my shoulder. I trailed my fingers over the paper as if I could absorb the loving words.

"Baby, talk to me. What's wrong?" My heart. It was hurting badly. I pulled in a deep breath. It was time to set him free, to say goodbye.

"I can't do it anymore," I whispered.

"What? What are you talking about? Hey, look at me."

"I...I..." There wasn't enough air in the car. I felt like I was suffocating, so I popped the catch of the seat belt, grabbed my handbag, and opened the door, getting out. Wearing only a blue, long-sleeved shirt over an undershirt, and a pair of skinny jeans, a blast of cold hit my body, reaching my skin. I breathed in the earthy smell of rain and heard a door slam shut. Then Ryan was in front of me, his hands on each side of my cheeks. We were alone in the nearly empty parking lot, the street lamps casting soft light on us.

"Are you afraid that it's not really over? Baby, don't be. It is over. Trust me. I know them." I backed up from him.

"I...I can't...I can't do this anymore." My voice cracked.

His face crumpled with confusion. "Do what?"

"Us. I can't do us anymore."

He stared down at me for a few long seconds, like he didn't understand the words. "I don't...what? What are you saying? Are you..." He paused, mouth opening and closing, and then, "Are you br—breaking up with me?" He must have read the answer in my face, because his face became pale. We were silent. One second followed another, turning into a minute, then two. The wind grew stronger, yet I wasn't cold. I was numb. He shook his head. "No, no, no, it doesn't make any sense. You're just tired. You've been through a lot today. Get some sleep and—"

"No, Ryan, we're done." He ran his hands over his face and looked down at me.

"W-why? What happened?"

I watched his blue, blue eyes, which I'd forever remember, and took another deep breath. If I gave him the real reason, he'd probably deny seeing his mother and sister's killer in me, and I'd be so relieved, but after a week, maybe two, doubts about his denial would surface in my mind, and I'd never be able to shake the feeling that I was an incessant reminder of his painful past. He needed to move on with his life, to be with a girl who could help him heal. I wasn't that girl.

To make the break-up easy on him, I knew I'd have to hurt him so he'd hate me and forget about us. Praying I wouldn't break down and cry, I gathered all the strength I had in me and said with a steady voice, "It's too much for me. You and your sick world. I'm only nineteen. I don't need this drama in my life. And the song." I held the piece of paper up and let it flutter to the ground. "How can you write about the far, far future with me when I don't even know what I'm gonna do tomorrow? I like you, yes, but I'm sorry, I don't feel the same way about you. Goodbye, Ryan." I forced myself to walk around him. When I passed him, though, he caught my arm and pulled me back against his chest. His arms wrapped around me so tightly that I struggled to breathe.

"Please, don't go." His voice quivered with pain. He buried his fingers in my hair and pressed my head closer to his chest. The lump in my throat threatened to explode, but I fought it back. My eyes fell on the sheet of paper he'd written the love song on. It was sinking slowly in a puddle, near his car wheel. The ink under the water blurred, gradually turning into unreadable words. The burning feeling in my throat intensified as the lump of tears lodged there threatened to burst out of me in a sob.

"Ryan, let me go." I tried to pull away, but he wouldn't let me.

"You can ask me anything in the world, and I would do it, but not that. I can't." His grip became stronger. My rib cage was pressed until oxygen could barely get in. I felt a bit dizzy as I stared at the sinking words. When I thought it would disappear completely under the water, it stopped moving down. Five words at the top refused to sink, to be erased. They stayed proudly above the water, taunting me.

I will always love you.

It was then that I realized he'd never let me go, not unless I truly hurt him. I had to be cruel. *Ryan, I'm so sorry for what I'm about to say.* I pushed past the dizziness and said the only thing I knew would destroy us.

"Don't you get it? I. Don't. Love. You. I don't want you in my life anymore. Go find another girl who actually loves you." The words tore me apart, but I had to do it. I wasn't good for him. His grasp started to weaken, and when it loosened enough for me to get away from him, one teardrop touched my skin. It was warm. I pulled my head back to look at his face, and my heart lurched at the sight of Ryan's eyes brimming with tears, trickling down his face. He was blinking as if something had flown into his eyes, obscuring his vision. A clap of thunder pierced the sky. I stepped out of his arms. He just stood there, motionless, staring at me like I'd stabbed him in the heart.

I turned and walked away. A sharp wind whipped my hair into my face, howling. Tears gushed out of my eyes in wild torrents. In my room, I threw myself onto the bed and sobbed like a baby into my pillow as rain pelted the window. The tears kept pouring out until my chest couldn't endure the pain anymore. Finally, I ran out of tears. Exhausted, I lay on the bed, just listening to my breathing and the occasional noises from outside the door, trying to digest that Ryan—the love of my life—was not in it anymore.

Hours later, I was still staring at the window from my bed. The rain had eased to a drizzle and stopped altogether. Then my cell phone rang. I bolted up in bed and glanced at the wall clock. Two a.m. Could it be Ryan? I jumped out of the bed and rushed to my desk to open my bag and pull out my cell phone. The caller ID said Hannah. Hannah? Oh my God, something was wrong.

Before I could say a word, she said, "Come over here, *now*. It's Ryan. He's in bad shape and bleeding."

"Where is here? Are you at the party?" I panicked.

"Yeah, c—"

"Be there right away." I hung up and left.

Chapter 27

Too panicked to wait for a cab, I ran all the way to the Beta Kappa House. By the time I walked in, I was gasping for breath, chest heaving, heart pounding. The party was still going on and since it was a karaoke one, a guy was singing through the microphone *I Love Rock & Roll* by Joan Jett & the Blackhearts in the living room while people danced, flailing and gyrating their bodies. I pushed through the sea of partygoers, looking for Hannah. Someone grabbed my arm and turned me around. Hannah! Thank God.

"What's going on? Is he okay?" I shouted above the music. Instead of yelling back, she guided me through the crowd and up to the second floor. Down the hallway, Nate was pounding on one of the bedroom doors.

"Damon, come on, man, open up," he yelled.

"He got himself wasted," Hannah said as we hurried down the hall, "and after he finished singing, he just lost it, smashing the guitar onto the floor, splinters and pieces flying everywhere, and somewhere during all the mess, he managed to cut himself deep in the arm, maybe from a bottle of beer he broke too. He needs stitches, but he won't listen to any of us. He's been snapping at Nate, telling him to stop nagging him and closing himself in the room. He wants to be left alone. He isn't thinking clearly."

Nate's eyes went to me. "Emma, you're here, good. You've got to talk to him." Glancing down, I noticed drops of blood near his shoes. Alarmed, I hammered at the door.

"Ryan, it's Emma, open the door." I raised my voice and continued banging. The door swung open, and when I saw him, I sucked in air. He was in awful shape. Aside from his wounded face, his shirt was stained with beer, and the strong odor of alcohol and fresh blood emanated from him. The inside of his right forearm was cut deeply, bleeding on the carpet, and he was holding an open bottle of beer.

"You fucking called her?" Ryan's infuriated eyes bored into Nate's and then moved to me. "You can leave now. I'm fine," he said, spinning around and staggering back inside the room.

I walked in. "No, you're not. You need stitches."

He turned to me. "And why do you care? Huh? You dumped me, remember?" The bitterness in his voice knocked me back a step. Trying to reason with him in his current state was useless. I took off my jacket, tossed it to the floor, pulled my long-sleeved shirt off over my head, and ripped it into strips.

"It's just a damn scratch," he said.

"For Christ's sake, Ryan, it's a deep cut. If you don't want to go to the hospital now, then let me wrap it up." He turned, stepped to the bedside table, and thumped his bottle onto it. Beer sloshed out and splashed everywhere. He walked back to me and snatched the strips from me.

"You really think you can help me with this scrap of cloth?" He shook his head and scoffed. His gaze returned to mine. "YOU JUST BROKE MY HEART!" His roar was an enormous explosion, filling the room with emotional agony. A tear welled up in his eye, wetting his thick, black eyelash. Succumbing to gravity, the tear slowly rolled down his cheek. He sniffed and wadded up the piece of cloth in his hand. He threw it to the floor, and drops of blood splashed my white undershirt. "It or the stitches can't do a thing to heal me. Because this"—he raised his injured arm, crooking it at the elbow so that blood ran down his arm—"is nothing compared to what's going on in my heart right now."

"C'mon, bro, you've got to take care of that," Nate urged. Ryan sighed heavily. Bleary-eyed, he looked tired, sad, and so broken. I ached to fling myself at him, wind my hands around him tightly and tell him that I was sorry, that I loved him, that I lied, but I couldn't. I mustn't. I had to set him free.

"And the pathetic thing in all this is that I believed you when you looked me in the eye and told me you loved me and that you'd never leave," he said and teetered toward the door behind me.

"Finally, let's go," Nate said, and Hannah's hand was on my shoulder. I turned to her and saw that Nate and Ryan had left the room.

"He'll be okay. Nate's taking him to the hospital. Now, can you please tell me why the hell you broke up with him?"

I relayed what had happened with Tristan in the alley and explained why I ended it. A disapproving frown formed on her face. "Sweetie, I love you and all, but that's bull. He loves you, and that psycho, Tristan, really messed your mind up. Why did you even listen to him?"

"Because he's right."

"No, he wasn't. And I'm starting to think that the real problem here is that you're afraid."

"Afraid? Of wha—" I was interrupted by some drunk, frat guys wandering into the room while watching something on their cell phone.

"Dude, that was awesome. He totally smashed that guitar," one of them said, wobbling on his feet.

"You two—out." Hannah pushed them out of the bedroom and slammed the door behind them.

"Did they see Ryan's outburst?" I asked.

"It was more than just an outburst...he's really hurting, Em." She pulled her cell phone from her pocket and tapped the display. "He came in with his guitar, not saying a word to anyone—not even to Nate and me—and after he got drunk, he took the stage to sing. Then, well, you can see for yourself." She handed me her phone, and I watched a video of Ryan standing in front of a microphone where that guy had been singing, *I Love Rock & Roll*.

"It's not the song I intended to sing in the first place, but it's what I goddamn feel right now," Ryan said before his fingers moved across the strings of the guitar, releasing Bruno Mars' song *Grenade*. As he crooned the lines of the song, pain was evident in his bruised features. When he finished, it was like something inside him just snapped, and he destroyed the guitar in a crazy frenzy, and the video cut off. I worked at my lower lip with my teeth, feeling awful for the pain I'd caused him.

"Em, face it. You can't ask him what he sees when he looks into your eyes since you're afraid of his answer."

"No, I'm not, because I have no doubt he'd deny what Tristan claimed."

"And what about the look on his face when he denies it? Doesn't that scare you?"

I fell silent. Yes, it did. He would say one thing, but his expression would probably show another.

"Go to him and ask him!" She stabbed a finger in the direction of the door.

"Hannah, it won't change anything. He deserves a girl who won't remind him of the past all the time. His love for me was what made him stay with me, and I don't want that for him, or me. Swear you won't tell him anything about the Tristan thing."

"You're making a mistake you'll regret," she sighed, "but okay, he won't hear anything from me."

Later, back in my dorm, one question filled my head: Had I really made a mistake? Somehow, I couldn't get a reply.

Chapter 28

January snow covered the town in white. It was magnificent. Unfortunately, the freezing temperature prevented me from enjoying the outside and admiring the sights as I hurried to the Science building. Once inside, I clenched and unclenched my gloved fists to warm them up. It was the first day of winter semester, and the place was flooded with students bustling around me as I walked to my classroom. When I got there, I took a seat in the front row and glanced down at my cell phone to check the time. I was early, which was bad since I'd been avoiding moments of downtime. The past five weeks had been incredibly difficult for me. Whenever I hadn't had things to do, my mind meandered to memories of Ryan's eyes, smile, laugh, dimples, and everything else related to him.

After our break-up, I'd spent the winter break in Miami with my mom and her boyfriend, Tom. The first couple days of winter break, I'd practically locked myself in the guest room, crying. My mom had forced me to eat, so I wouldn't starve.

"A broken heart is never easy, but, honey, one day, the pain will go away," she'd said, trying to cheer me up. By the time Christmas Eve had arrived, I was able to force a smile on my face for Tom and his family. Though my mood was still gloomy. As one day had followed another, I'd busied myself with anything I could do in an attempt to keep my mind off Ryan. Hannah and I had spoken on the phone from time to time. She was with her family in Boston, where Justin and Kayla were as well, and she and Nate, being in New York for the break, kept in touch on a daily basis. Luckily, she knew not to bring up Ryan.

"Is this seat taken?" A male voice cut off my thoughts.

I looked in the voice's direction. "Justin? You're in Professor Horn's class, too?"

"Yeah." He slid into the desk next to me. "How was your break?" he asked.

"Fine," I lied. "Yours?" He detailed all the fun he'd had, and we continued with the small talk until Professor Horn rolled into the classroom. At the end of class, I waved Justin goodbye and walked down the hall. All of a sudden, someone slammed into me. Books were dropped and scattered across the floor.

"Oh my God, I'm so, so sorry. So, so sorry." A girl who'd just bumped into me kept apologizing as she bent down to pick up her books. I grinned, knowing too well how she must be feeling.

"It's okay, really." I knelt to help her gather the books.

"Thank you," she said when we stood up.

"No problem." I gave her the books back and a pair of black-framed glasses.

She began to mumble nervously, "Everybody always laughs at how clumsy I can be and—great, here I am rambling to a complete stranger about my..." She trailed off and wrinkled her noise as she squinted her eyes, looking over my shoulder. She put her glasses on and waved her free hand. "Hey, Ryan, Ryan, I'm over here." Ryan? I turned, and my heart tripped into double time. I hadn't seen him or heard from him in five weeks, and now he swaggered toward us. Being eminently gorgeous, he was clad in a black turtle-neck, blue jeans, and an open, black coat, all of it complemented perfectly by a stylish black, slouchy beanie and a blue scarf wrapping around his neck.

When he noticed me, the smile he'd directed at the beautiful, clumsy, blond girl vanished instantly. He paused, and the stare he gave me was so distant and cold that a chill rolled down my spine. I returned my gaze to the girl, ready to escape, but the sound of my name on his tongue fixed me in place. He was suddenly standing next to me—close. His cologne reached my nostrils, bringing back all the memories

I'd tried to bury. "You know her?" the blond girl asked, then sighed and answered her own question. "Of course you do."

He was looking down at me. "This is a surprise. I'm glad I ran into you, though. I've been meaning to get in touch with you about your stuff. I boxed them up, and you're welcome to come and get them." His voice was all business, matter-of-fact.

"Thanks, I'll ask Hannah to come over and get it. Is seven o'clock today okay?" I asked quickly, wanting this awkward moment to end as fast as possible. He nodded briskly, and I took off.

Had he moved on? Was he seeing her? I shook my head to push these thoughts out of my head. I was so not ready to face the answers, yet sooner or later, I'd have to. Nate was friends with him and the boyfriend of my friend. Eventually, our paths would cross again in the future, so if he got a new girlfriend, it was only a matter of time until I found out. The situation sucked because the thought of him with someone else was downright painful, but I wasn't entitled to be angry. After all, *I* had been the one who had ended it so he could find another love. Healthy love. My cell phone vibrated in my jeans as I was walking to my next class. I took it out and checked the display. It was Josh.

During winter break, we'd spoken on the phone several times, and I disclosed my past with Sadie when he recounted that they were a couple now, after he'd finally revealed his feelings to her and moved back to New York City to be with her. Of course, it hadn't been the first time he'd heard about my uncle. She told him the story too. However, in her story, her mother's boyfriend was the molester—not my uncle. It turned out that Sadie had been scared that her mother wouldn't believe her, so she fabricated everything about my uncle being a pedophile, hoping her mother would send her to live with her father. I didn't blame her. She'd been a scared child molested by her mother's boyfriend and had a mother who cared more about her lover than her own daughter. Shaking my head in disgust at the thought, I opened the text.

Josh: What are you up to tomorrow night? Sadie and I are in town, and she'd really like to meet with you. You two have a lot of catching up to do.

Me: I agree. Tomorrow night I'm free.

Josh: Great, I'll call you tomorrow.

Later that day, in my dorm room, thoughts of Ryan reminded me that I'd told him that Hannah would stop by to pick up my things at seven o'clock, and it was now seven-thirty. I called her three times, no answer. Recalling she was in yoga class and then she had reservations for some fancy restaurant, I closed my eyes and rubbed my face. "Wonderful—just wonderful." I growled sarcastically as I grabbed my coat, fluffy ear warmer, gloves, and headed for Ryan's apartment.

Snow dusted my face, and my breath emerging on white puffs of vapor clouds in the icy air while I, iced to the bone, stood in front of his intercom, staring at it like an idiot. At last, I gathered my nerves and pressed the button. I waited for a few seconds, but the door didn't buzz open, so I pushed on the button once more, and he buzzed me in. Was he busy? I wondered as I stepped into the warmth of the entry vestibule. I peeled off my gloves, pushing them into my coat pocket, and removed the ear warmer. My fingers and cold nose thawed gradually as I moved to the elevator.

When the door slid open, the beating of my heart grew faster. What if that blond girl was there? What if she kissed and hugged him like Ashley had used to do when I'd been there? How would I manage not to break down in front of them?

Reaching the top floor, I inhaled deeply and stepped into the white hallway, walking toward his apartment. His door was open, yet he wasn't in sight. I stepped inside. He was in the living room, his back to me, slipping on a long-sleeved shirt over a tank top clinging to his muscular torso.

"Ryan?" He spun to face me. Barefoot, he wore a pair of faded jeans slung low on his hips, and his hair was messy, like it always had been after waking up or...sex. My eyes moved to a blue sweater, the same one the blond girl had worn, thrown over the back of the sofa. She was here. A fierce stab of jealousy and hurt ripped through me.

"Your stuff is in the box on the dining table. Hannah couldn't make it?" His tone was warmer than when we'd talked in the Science building. I couldn't work out a single word. God, I needed to get out of there—fast. Tearing my eyes from the evidence of him moving on with his life, I shook my head and headed toward the dining table. I put my ear warmer into the small, open cardboard box as I fought the tears that were threatening to choke me.

"Emma." His voice was close, so close. I swiveled around and found myself facing his chest. I tilted my head back to look at him. His chin dipped down, and his thoughts were there for me to read: *You're clearly hurt by the girl in my apartment and mad at me because of it, which means you do love me, so I'm trying to understand something here.*

"Why the hell did you walk out on me?"

"Because you're better off without me." The words flew out of my mouth, and I couldn't take them back. Instead of excusing myself and leaving, I continued. "Without me in your life, you don't have a constant reminder of your past."

"What?" His face screwed up in bewilderment.

"Look at my eyes. They're the same as my uncle's." I turned back to the box and grabbed from it a spool of thread and a sewing needle, pricking the tip of my index finger and squeezing the drop of blood out. I faced him again.

"I can't change it." I held my bloody finger up to his face. "This blood is related to the person who killed your sister and mother. I had to push you away because Tristan was right; you're better off without me."

"Tristan?" His countenance twisted into a scowl. "That sneaky bastard!" Enraged, he dragged his fingers through his hair, then he turned and stepped away from me. "I can't believe how blind I was, not seeing this was all his doing, not figuring out that he manipulated you into breaking up with me."

He flipped around. His eyes moved to me, and his gaze fixed on my face. "How could you walk away without even talking to me about what bothered you?" His tone was chiding.

"Because it wouldn't have changed anything. The blood inside me, I can't alter it, or get rid of it. It'll always be in me."

"Ray?" A sleepy, feminine voice interrupted us. The blond girl who had slammed into me in the Science building, was standing at the entrance to the hallway, where the guest room was, wearing tight, cotton shorts, a black sweatshirt, and pink socks. She yawned as she rubbed her eyes. "I heard noises. Is everything okay?" She wasn't wearing her glasses, and she scrunched her face in an attempt to make me out.

"I gotta go." I grabbed the box and hurried to the door. As soon as I shut it, the tears battled their way free. My knees threatened to give out, but I willed myself to walk. Then I set my things onto the floor, and as I waited for the elevator, my gaze drifted in the direction of his apartment. An image of him pulling her into his arms and kissing her flashed through my mind. He'd moved on. I should be happy for him, so why did I want to scream? Why was I so angry and hurt? I jabbed at the elevator button.

After a moment, the door opened, and I stepped in and pressed the lobby button. Closing my eyes, I loudly drew in air, thinking about how all my things wer—my box! I'd forgotten to pick it up from the floor. My eyes popped open, and I gasped in surprise. Ryan? He was outside the elevator door, his foot preventing it from shutting. He snatched my crimson-stained finger and brought it to his mouth, sucking on it hard. My lips parted wide and stayed that way until he was done.

"Now your blood is inside me. And I wouldn't change it even if I could because, Emma, you are a part of me, and always will be." He pulled me out of the elevator and let the door slide closed. He gazed down at me. "The memories of your eyes, your touch, your smile, your smell, they're the only things that kept me going on. Without them, I would've fallen apart. Emma, whenever I look into your eyes, I see the person who saved me—not a reminder of their deaths and definitely not your uncle." His eyes held genuine sincerity; he truly didn't see my uncle in me.

Several beats of silence passed before I was able to speak again. "Ryan...I...I'm so sorry for everything I said to you when we broke up. I didn't mean it. I really believed I was doing the right thing."

"I know. That's Tristan's specialty." He cradled my cheek, and the corner of his mouth went up, softening the hardness in his face. "But in the future, to avoid the five weeks of pure hell I went through, let's make a pact. The next time you feel like dumping me because of what you think I feel—*talk* to me, and then you'll see that your fears are groundless because, baby, I love you more than anything, and God, I missed you like crazy." He cupped my cheek as his other hand tugged on my waist, pressing me to his body. His lips landed on my mouth, his tongue darting deep inside and entwining with mine. I slipped my hands around his back and held him tight.

"Ahem, um, Ray?" The scorching bliss I'd experienced in his arms shattered at the sound of the blond girl's voice. I ripped my lips from his and tried to pull away. He didn't let me. Anchoring me against him with his hand on my waist, he turned to look at her.

"What is it, Kim?"

"So you're back together? That's so awesome." Dressed in a puffy coat, jeans, and boots, she gave him a bright smile and pressed the elevator button. She looked at me. "I'm Kimberly. You probably recognize me as the girl who likes to ramble, but I'm also Ray's cousin." Cousin? His cousin? A wave of relief swept over me.

"And her babysitter," he added. He raised an eyebrow at me, his tone filled with amusement. Yes, he'd guessed what I'd been assuming about the two of them. "She transferred from NYU, and I promised my aunt I'd look after her, so she's staying here until I find her a nice apartment off campus."

The elevator doors opened, and she stepped inside.

"Yeah, well, you guys go back to your thing. I'm heading for the library. See you around, Emma." She grinned at me as the door slid closed.

Ryan took my chin and turned it so he had my full attention, and I was more than happy to give it to him.

"Emma Winstead, you are the only girl who holds my heart in her hands. There is no other for me, and never doubt it." I wrapped my hand around his neck, and my lips split into a wide, happy smile.

"I love you, Ryan Damon. So much." I got on my tiptoes and claimed his mouth, kissing him deeply.

Epilogue

Four and a half months later.

"Paris? You're going to freaking Paris? And in first class?" Hannah squealed in excitement, staring at the two airline tickets in her hand. "Ugh, I could kill you right now. I can't believe you're spending the summer in Paris, the city of love." Her hand flew to her chest, and a dreamy look came into her eyes.

I chuckled while I packed. "Yes, it's going to be romantic, just me and Ryan."

"Best birthday present ever," she declared. It *was* the best gift I'd ever gotten for my birthday. Yesterday Ryan had taken me to a nice Italian restaurant, and when dessert had been served, he'd put the tickets on the table, wrapped in a red bow.

Hannah placed them back on the nightstand and fell onto the king-sized bed next to my open suitcase, as I pulled five T-shirts and two pairs of jeans from Ryan's closet. I practically lived with him now, so I did the packing here and not in my dorm room. "Did you and Nate find an apartment for next year?" I asked her, stuffing clothes into the suitcase.

"We're still searching, but I'm not worried. We'll find something before the summer ends."

I smiled at her. "I'm sure you will." I was elated for them. When she'd told me Nate had gotten a job here, in one of his stepfather's companies, and had asked her to move in with him, I'd been thrilled. They were perfect together.

She glanced at the wall clock and surged up from the bed. "Crap, it's already eight. I'm gonna be late."

"Tell Kayla I said hi, and that I'm sorry I couldn't make it." Although I wanted to attend the get-together at Kayla's boyfriend's house, I couldn't. I had to finish packing, and then there was the flight.

"I will." She hugged me and spoke into my hair. "I'm gonna miss you. You know that, right?"

"I'm gonna miss you, too." I pulled her closer, and she drew her head back.

"Liar. You're gonna have so much fun on Champs-Élysées that you won't even remember I exist." She feigned insult and stepped out of my arms. I laughed and she headed for the door, turned to me, and threw me a warm smile. "Seriously, though, have fun, and you better send pictures."

"A lot of them." I spread my arms out wide. "Until you're sick of seeing Paris."

"Yeah, right. Like that will ever happen." She chuckled and right before she left the room, she tossed over her shoulder, "Au revoir."

My cell phone rang. I grabbed it from the bed and answered, "Hey, Mom."

"Honey, how are you doing? Are you packing?"

"Yes, just in the middle of it, actually."

"Oh, honey, I was so glad for the visit last week. It was a delight to meet Ryan again, and tell him that our home is always open to him."

"I will. He was glad to meet you and Tom as well."

"Okay, honey, I'll leave you to your packing. You take care of yourself out there and have a safe flight. I love you." Ryan walked into the bedroom, and my eyes moved to him.

"I love you too, Mom," I said, and we hung up. Reaching me, he took the cell phone from my hand and tossed it on the bed, pulling me into his arms and kissing me.

Then he looked down at me. "After we come back from France, you are officially moving in here. No more dorms."

A smile shimmered across my lips. Ryan had just graduated, but he was going to stay here. With me.

"No more dorms," I said, and my lips met his.

By eleven p.m., we were seated on the plane while we were waiting for takeoff. Ryan's fingers threaded through mine, and I stared out the small window, brooding over everything that had happened this year. If anyone had told me at the beginning of the year that I'd find out that there were dark secrets buried in my past, and that there was a nefarious group of people who called themselves the Elites and who had been taken down by the FBI after an undercover investigation, and that I'd find the love of my life, I would've told them that they needed to admit themselves to a mental hospital. I turned to look at Ryan, and I beamed.

"Baby, are you ready for Paris?" he asked, happiness on his face.

"Am I ever," I replied, and the plane started to move. After several minutes, its wheels rose off the ground, and we took off to the city of love.